Charlie Opera

Charlie Opera

A NOVEL OF CRIME

CHARLIE STELLA

CARROLL & GRAF PUBLISHERS
NEW YORK

CHARLIE OPERA

Carroll & Graf Publishers
An Imprint of Avalon Publishing Group Inc.
245 West 17th Street
New York, NY 10011

Copyright © 2003 by Charlie Stella

First Carroll & Graf edition 2003

Library of Congress Cataloging-in-Publication Data is available.

ISBN: 0-7867-1213-9

Designed by Simon M. Sullivan
Printed in the United States of America
Distributed by Publishers Group West

A few years ago Kent Carroll bought and edited my first book,
Eddie's World. *Having Kent to work with was a true blessing for a*
neophyte author. I owe him much. I will always owe him much.
Charlie Opera *is dedicated to Kent Carroll.*

This town needs an enema.

—The Joker (*Batman*)

Chapter 1

DONNA BELLA, A TWENTY-SIX-FOOT cabin cruiser, was anchored directly under the Marine Park Bridge in Jamaica Bay. An electronics technician had told the sixty-five-year-old underboss of the Vignieri crime family, Anthony Cuccia, that the bridge's metal would help to jam any electronic surveillance.

The old man wasn't taking chances. He let the boat's engine idle to cover his conversation with his nephew.

"You're flying to Vegas gonna solve this problem or make it worse?" he asked. "It's something you should consider."

It was a hot afternoon in mid-July. A stiff ocean breeze pulled at the umbrella shading the two men sitting on the back of the boat. The old man sucked on his twisted cigar, a DeNobli. He removed it to speak again.

"We got more important things to discuss than your personal vendetta with some mameluke broke your jaw," he said. "This Russian thing, for instance, it needs to come to fruition."

The nephew, Nicholas Cuccia, was forced to speak without moving his mouth from a broken jaw he had suffered the week before. He leaned forward and pointed at his chin.

"He's gotta answer for this," he whispered.

The old man frowned as he sipped club soda from a glass. He watched as a pair of jet skiers raced under the bridge about a hundred yards from *Donna Bella*. When the jet skiers were out of view, he turned to his nephew again.

"That's gotta mend, your jaw," he said. "What are you gonna do out there wired up like that? What's the point?"

The nephew closed his eyes in frustration.

"It's also a far reach, Las Vegas," the old man continued. "It isn't like the old days. There's protocol involved. Protocol takes time."

The nephew strained to speak. "I need a green light here," he said. "I want this guy whacked."

The old man stared into his nephew's eyes.

"There are rules," the nephew said. "Wiseguys don't get touched. What's it all about, we let a guy get away with this? Where does it stop? I had my jaw broken. I'm a skipper, for Christ sake."

The old man leaned back in his chair as a warm breeze brushed against his face. "You shoulda thought of that before you grabbed that broad's ass," he said. He was down to the end of his cigar. He tossed it over the side of the boat.

The nephew said, "I'm going out there because I want him to know it's me. I want him fucked up and then I want him dead. I want to be there when it happens."

"That's cowboy shit."

"Whatever. I want this guy to know it's coming."

The old man picked at a strand of tobacco stuck between his teeth. "That why you sent a couple guys from your crew out there?" he asked. "To stir up the shit? Make sure they leave a trail makes it easier for the law to come back to you?"

"They went out there to keep an eye on the guy. I gave them specific instructions."

The old man waved it off. "You want to whack a guy for breaking your face, you should probably wait it out."

"I'm not asking for permission here. It is what it is. The guy has to die."

The old man lit a fresh cigar and let the moment pass. He watched the jet skiers returning in race formation under the bridge.

"Last week we saw two broads racing topless on those things," he said. "They had their tops tied around their necks like scarves. They drove them things with their tits bouncing for whoever wanted to watch."

The nephew sipped club soda through a straw.

"You ever hear of getting your tit in a ringer?" the old man asked. "Like them broads, they get pulled over by the Coast Guard or something. Or they take a spill, maybe lose a tit, a couple guys drinking on a boat chase them down. Or worse maybe."

The nephew frowned.

"Because that's what this could be like," the old man said. "If the guy talked to people, filled out a police report you don't know about. If maybe his wife mentioned it to somebody. Which is why it's smarter to wait a few months. Maybe you change your mind by then, forget the whole thing. That would be even smarter, you forget it, this bullshit."

"The guy goes," the nephew repeated. "I'm reaching out. Either you help me or you don't."

The old man looked off toward Rockaway Island. "I have a guy out there in Vegas," he said. "Semiretired. A goodfella from here in New York. He used to do work for us, me and your father, ten, fifteen years ago. I know he takes on work from time to time."

The nephew wiped at drool forming at one corner of his mouth. "I'll pay him whatever he wants."

"We can't go through Vegas, though," the old man said. "Not through the people out there. It has to be a private contract. Strictly private. The guy running things out there, Jerry Lercasi, he don't meet with nobody. He has some accountant he sends in his place. They dress it up for the feds. You go out there for a sit-down with Lercasi, you gotta make like it's a real-estate investment or some shit. You gotta sign up for land development tours or golf club lunches. You drive around looking at new houses while you do business. Lercasi is very careful."

"So I don't go near Lercasi's people. That's not a problem."

"When I say you can't go through protocol, you understand what I'm saying here? My guy in Vegas can't be tied into Lercasi. My guy is strictly private. For everybody's sake."

The nephew nodded. "I understand."

The old man belched into a fist. "You know enough about this guy you want to whack? You know where he's staying and so on?"

"That's what Vin Lano and Joey Francone are out there for."

"And you're sure he's there?"

"Absolutely."

"You're gonna do this thing whether I help or not. It's better I help."

"I appreciate it."

"It's too bad that other kid got scooped up last year, Jimmy Mangino."

"Jimmy Bench-Press?"

"Whatever the fuck his name is, yeah. He was a machine, that kid. You pointed him and he went, got it done."

"He's not around. All I got is what I got. Francone and Lano. They know what to do."

The old man used a matchbook cover to remove tobacco from between his teeth. "About that other thing," he said. "What we're here to discuss in the first place."

The nephew reached into his front pants pocket to activate the wire he was wearing. "The Russian thing?" he asked.

"Yeah."

"Are they ready to go?"

"This week sometime," the old man said. "Few days. Week at the most."

"Just say when."

"It's still in Jersey, right?"

"At my guy's place."

"The new guy?"

"The one with the trucks, yeah. Rizzi."

"They won't take it from there, the Russians. They want security."

The nephew shrugged. "I can't do everything."

The old man spit loose tobacco from his mouth. He examined his cigar and tossed it over the side of the boat. "These fuckin' things," he complained. "They used to roll them tight. You open a box of six, you're lucky you can smoke three."

"You shouldn't smoke that crap. At least go to Cubans."

"Cubans are too expensive," the old man said. He fished another cigar from his pocket, examined it a few seconds, and placed it unlit to one side of his mouth. "I think it'll move this week," he said. "Can you do it from Vegas?"

"No problem. I'll have Rizzi fly out to Vegas to calm his nerves and you can take the truck. I can arrange it but you'll have to oversee it."

"I don't expect otherwise. Couple million dollars is a lot of money."

"Couple million in heroin is a telephone number."

"Besides, who else I'm gonna send with that kind of money while you're out there jerkin' off in Vegas?"

The nephew waved at a dragonfly. "So, this week?"

The old man removed the cigar from his mouth. "Couple, tree days," he said. "No more than a week. I want this over with already. I don't like sweating this out. The more that shit sits, the more nervous it makes me. It's one big headache, that stuff. These Russians have the money. Let's make the exchange and give them the headaches."

The nephew deactivated the wire. "And Charlie Pellecchia?" he asked.

The old man looked off toward the beach again. "Charlie who?"

The nephew smiled through the pain in his jaw.

"That was cute, your conversation on the boat," federal Drug Enforcement agent Marshall Thomas told Nicholas Cuccia.

They were seated side by side in the first-class section of an America West flight to Las Vegas. Thomas looked younger than his thirty-five years. He wore navy blue sweatpants and a light blue North Carolina sweatshirt. He was a broad man. His left shoulder bumped Cuccia as he leaned over to look out the window.

"You check the flight for wiseguys?" Cuccia whispered. "Or you trying to get me killed before your big heroin bust?"

"That's the second time today you used that word," Thomas said. "But that doesn't do me any good, you saying it. It's your uncle I need to hear discuss heroin. Not 'that other thing' or 'that Russian thing' or 'that stuff' or anything else. I need to hear him talk about heroin. You see what I'm saying?"

Cuccia opened the *Playboy* magazine he had bought at an airport newsstand. He flipped toward the middle of the magazine to the centerfold. He held the book up to let the picture drop open.

"Where do you suppose she lives?" he asked Thomas.

Thomas turned away from the nude picture. He looked up at the male flight attendant serving cocktails.

"Naked broads make you nervous?" Cuccia asked. He folded the centerfold back inside the magazine and turned it upside down on the folding tray. "There," he said. "Take deep breaths."

Thomas leaned into Cuccia again. "Like I said, I heard you talk about heroin. I didn't hear your uncle talk about it. I heard him talk about Russians."

"The old man is careful. If I pushed it, he would have known something. Relax. The closer he gets to the money, the more he'll talk."

"What about the rest of your conversation? You were on that boat for three hours. You brought back less than two minutes of dialogue."

Cuccia touched the edge of his chin. "Six fucking weeks I gotta have this thing in my mouth like this," he said. "He's got a guy debugs the boat every so often. I wasn't taking unnecessary risks. It's my ass, not yours."

Thomas opened the *New York Times* he had brought with him. He pointed to a headline in the Metro section. It read: MOB INDICT-MENTS IN BROOKLYN. "We're in a race against time," he said. "You're in a race against time."

Cuccia was still touching around his jaw with his fingertips. "There's nothing I can do until the man wants to move. So why not relax about it, already. Have yourself a drink."

The flight attendant leaned across Thomas to set a miniature bottle of Absolut vodka and a can of Canada Dry tonic water on a napkin.

"What's in Vegas?" Thomas asked after the flight attendant returned to the galley.

"Pussy," Cuccia said.

"How you gonna eat it with a broken jaw?"

"Who said I was gonna eat it?"

Thomas smirked. "I thought you guys were big on eating pussy. At least that's what I read in all the books you guys write after you make your deals."

"That's just to make the books sell," Cuccia said. "Me, I prefer going through the back door any day. Ask your wife, she'll tell you."

Thomas lost the smirk on his face. He leaned across his seat to whisper into Cuccia's ear. "Just don't get yourself in too much trouble while we're in Las Vegas, Nicky. Or your deal will go down the same shitter your mother flushed when you were born."

Cuccia forced a chuckle. "Tell me the truth," he said. "You stay up all night and work that one out? 'Down the same shitter your mother flushed.' You guys kill me."

Thomas sat back in his chair. He grabbed the headphones in the seat pocket in front of him and placed them on his head.

Cuccia continued forcing himself to laugh. "What a jerk-off," he said somewhere in the laugh.

Chapter 2

CECILIA BARTOLI NAILED UNA VOCE POCA FA as Charlie Pellecchia swayed back and forth. He watched from his hotel room as crowds of people waited for the Pirate Show in front of the Treasure Island Hotel-Casino across Las Vegas Boulevard. Charlie adjusted the volume on his headphones as the Rossini aria boomed into his ears. He felt the pure high of the violins as he closed his eyes.

A thick plastic hairbrush thrown from across the room smacked Charlie in the middle of his back. The sting of the hairbrush startled him. He dropped the portable CD player from his hands. The headphones remained attached to the unit and were pulled off his head.

Charlie turned to his wife as he reached behind him to rub at the red mark the hairbrush had left on his back.

"What the fuck?"

"I've been calling to you for five minutes!" Lisa Pellecchia yelled. "From the shower. In the bathroom. Five minutes!"

"I was listening to something," Charlie said. He was still trying to reach the painful spot on his back. "That hurt, damn it."

Lisa's face tightened. She looked about to burst with more rage. She shook her head instead and returned to the bathroom.

Charlie picked the CD player and headphones off the floor. He set them down on the small round table alongside the carton of cigarettes he had brought from New York. He turned to one side to look at his back in the mirror. He saw a red welt.

"Shit," he said.

He tried to reach the red mark on his back one more time. In the process, he noticed the roll of flab that had formed around his waist. He stood up straight again, turned to one side, and looked at his profile in the mirror.

He had gained weight. He guessed his weight was 230 pounds, maybe 240. At 5-foot-10, he figured he was at least 30 pounds overweight.

He struck a muscle pose. He was still well defined for his age. He had maintained a barrel chest and big arms. He flexed both his biceps in the mirror and quickly dropped his arms when he heard his wife in the bathroom. When he thought he was safe again, he looked into the mirror and whispered, "Figaro, Figaro . . . Figaro, Figaro, Figaro, Figaro, Figaro, Fi-ga-ro."

It was the second time since they'd come to Las Vegas that his wife had thrown something at Charlie. Earlier in the morning Lisa threw a pillow at him for whistling the overture to Mozart's *La Clemenza di Tito*. She was watching the *Today Show* on NBC, after her first cup of coffee. Charlie had just come back from a long walk and was listening to the Mozart opera through his headphones.

Lisa hated opera.

Charlie was starting to think maybe his wife hated him, too.

In the afternoon, he took his second long walk of the day. He walked north along Las Vegas Boulevard and noticed a busy construction site a few blocks off the Strip. He walked farther north past the Desert Inn, the Riviera, and the Sahara. He finally stopped walking when he reached the Stratosphere. He wondered how Las Vegas looked from the top of the Stratosphere.

Charlie had been a window cleaner for fifteen years in New York City before starting his own business in the same industry. He worked house rigs on fifty-story buildings. He had worked portable rigs on ten- and twelve-story buildings. He also had worked belts and ladders and an occasional boatswain chair. Heights were never a concern to him. He had always been fascinated with tall buildings.

He had recently sold the window cleaning business he started more than ten years ago. Charlie was retired now, but he wasn't sure what he would do with himself.

He wondered how the glass at the top of the Stratosphere was cleaned when he looked up at it from the street. In the lobby he wondered how many men it took to clean the transom glass.

On his way back to his hotel he stopped at the Mirage, where he bought a stuffed animal, a small white tiger, for his wife. He was feeling guilty about ignoring her earlier in the morning. Charlie hadn't turned up the volume on the opera intentionally, but he could understand why his wife thought he had. Lately they weren't getting along. Opera was one of many distractions Charlie used to escape their problems. He thought Lisa might be jealous of his distractions.

He hoped his wife would like the tiger. She had always liked receiving a surprise bouquet of flowers in the past. As he crossed Las Vegas Boulevard, a strange thought suddenly entered his mind.

Charlie wondered if his wife was having an affair.

"I almost killed him before," Lisa Pellecchia told her lover.

She cradled the telephone against her right shoulder as she lowered the volume on the television. She turned on the bed so she could hear the door if it opened.

"Stay calm," John Denton said on the other end of the line. "You know what you have to do. It'll be over soon enough."

Lisa shook her head as she leaned her back against the headboard.

"I feel terrible," she said. "I can't believe I hit him like that. I threw something else at him earlier. I can't do this anymore. I just can't."

"It will be all right. Just stay calm."

"I wish you were here."

"Me, too."

Lisa felt herself tearing. "I better hang up. He should be back any minute."

"Okay. I'll talk to you later."

Lisa kissed Denton through the telephone. "Good night," she said. "I love you."

"I love you, too," he said.

When she hung up, Lisa took several deep breaths. It was a method of controlling her emotions she had learned the year before in therapy. She tried to focus on what she needed to do as she controlled her breathing.

Her nerves had been on edge all day. She was anxious to end her marriage. She needed to confess the extramarital relationship she was having with the same man for the second time in two years.

As her breathing finally returned to normal, Lisa reached for a tissue. The door opened as she held the tissue up to her nose. When she looked up, Charlie was standing at the foot of the bed with a stuffed animal. It was a white tiger. Lisa burst out crying.

"The last time you told me," Charlie said. "That was fair. I think you should tell me now if there is something going on."

They were sitting alongside each other in the sports book area. Betting at the sports book had already ended for the day a few hours earlier. Charlie had refused to talk in their room. He had told his wife that he felt caged in upstairs. He looked around the expanse of the betting parlor as he waited for her response.

"There's nothing going on," Lisa lied. "There's nothing to tell."

Charlie sipped at his third gin and tonic. They had been sitting there for half an hour. Lisa had started with white wine. Now she was drinking Diet Coke.

"Well, then, what is it?" he asked. "Do you just hate me? Do you want to kill me?"

"Don't be ridiculous."

"Well?"

"Well what?"

"What gives with the brush this afternoon? You damn near took my head off, Lisa."

"I apologized for that."

"Jeez, well then, I guess I'm sorry for bringing it up."

"You know what I mean. I was wrong. I'm sorry. There, I said it again."

"What the hell brought it on? And what about the dam bursting when I walked in the room? I bought you a present, for Christ sakes."

Lisa turned away from him. "I don't know," she said. "I've been edgy. I think we have problems we can't solve right now." She looked around herself. "Not here, anyway. Not in Las Vegas."

"Oh, well, what the hell, then. Next time use a tire iron. We'll solve our problems in an emergency room."

"I'm through saying I'm sorry, Charlie."

"Right. Of course you are."

He was frustrated. It was obvious Lisa was holding something back. He knew he was drunk, but he wanted her to tell him the truth. He finished his third gin and tonic. He set the glass on a ledge alongside his chair and craned his neck to look for a waitress.

"I thought Las Vegas would be good for us," he said.

"So you could walk," Lisa said, with a touch of sarcasm in her voice. Charlie ignored her.

"Well?" she said.

"I thought we'd have things to occupy us," he said. "I like to walk. You used to like to walk. Now you like to shop. There's plenty of both to go around. I thought we wouldn't be on top of each other here. I made a mistake."

Lisa huffed.

He thought about the affair she had been involved in two years earlier. She had met another lawyer on the West Coast during a corporate case they were involved in together. They met secretly for more than three months before she finally confessed to Charlie.

"Have you talked to John lately?" he asked.

"Let's not go there, okay?"

He downed his drink. "I guess that's an answer."

"You're drunk," Lisa said. "I won't talk to you while you're drinking."

"Then I'll make it easier for you," Charlie said. He spotted a waitress near a row of slot machines to his right. He called to her.

"I'm not going to watch this all night," Lisa said. "You getting drunk." She stood up from her chair.

Charlie looked his wife up and down. She was still a beautiful woman. She had recently turned forty years old, but there was no way of guessing her age. At 5-foot-4, 108 pounds, she was both lean and muscular. A month ago she had changed her hair color from auburn back to her original color, brunette. She was wearing her hair short again, instead of the long cut Charlie preferred. In the tight black slacks she was wearing, Charlie saw Lisa for the knockout his wife truly was.

Of course she is having an affair, he was thinking.

"Waitress!" he yelled.

A chubby woman in a much too tight waitress outfit stopped to write his order.

"I think you've had enough," Lisa said.

Charlie lit a cigarette. "I think maybe we both have," he told his wife.

Chapter 3

EARLY THE NEXT MORNING, Charlie woke up in a ditch behind a construction site. A big man wearing a construction helmet was holding a towel spotted with blood.

"You all right?" the big man asked.

Charlie had trouble sitting up. His body was sore. His hands felt bruised.

"Where am I?"

"The Palermo," the big man said. He was waving somebody over to them. "Bring it over here!"

Charlie strained to see through the glare of the sun. Flashing lights made him dizzy.

"You're cut pretty bad there, mister," another man said. "Looks like you were mugged."

Charlie immediately checked for his wallet. The fingers of his right hand hurt from trying to jam them inside his front pants pocket.

"I think one of those fingers is broke," the big man said. "Maybe another one. Looks like you still have your wallet, though."

At Valley Hospital, Charlie learned the damage. He had a slight concussion. Two of the fingers on his left hand were severely bruised. His nose was fractured. Eight stitches were required to sew a cut along his hairline behind his right ear. He had a severely bruised rib on his right side and bruises to his chest, shoulders, and back. When he saw himself in the small mirror on the back of a door, Charlie saw that both his eyes had turned black and his upper lip was swollen. A small gauze bandage covered the stitches behind his right ear. The knuckles on both his hands also were bruised.

An emergency room doctor was asking him questions.

"Do you want to fill out a police report?"

Charlie shook his head. "No."

"Do you know who did this to you?"

"No."

"Is there someone here with you I should contact?"

"No."

"Are you sure?"

"Yes. There's no one."

"What about back home? Is there someone we should contact back in New York?"

Charlie shook his head again. "No," he said. "Thank you."

He was still trying to piece together what had happened the night before. He had spent a lot of time at one of the casino bars playing dollar slot poker while he drank gin and tonics. He remembered that he was pretty drunk. He had won a small jackpot.

Four aces, he remembered. He had hit a four-aces bonus poker machine for five hundred dollars.

He remembered making friends and singing with people at the bar. He remembered some guy and his girlfriend. They wore cowboy hats. They sang something country-western.

Charlie also had made friends with the barmaid, Samantha Nicole, or something like Nicole. She was a pretty redhead with freckles and a bright smile. He couldn't remember where the barmaid had said she was originally from, but she also had spoken with an accent.

He wasn't sure what time he had left the bar, but he knew it was pretty late. He had wanted to get some air before heading back upstairs to his room. He knew Lisa was still pissed at him for being drunk. He also remembered never going back to the room. He remembered drinking again instead.

When he finally left the casino bar, Charlie had walked across Las

Vegas Boulevard to watch the Pirate Show up close at the Treasure Island Hotel. He was standing in the middle of a huge crowd of spectators. A man had befriended him there, a short, bald man.

The two of them had stood there watching the show, making small talk. The short man was from Chicago, out to Las Vegas on business, he had said. He was with the construction company building the new hotel, the Palermo. Charlie told the short man how he had watched some of the cranes working through the night from his room at Harrah's.

"We have them working twenty-four hours a day out here," the short man had said. "Or they'd never be built in time. The money they spend on these things, it's important they can open their doors to pay for themselves."

Charlie had become fascinated with what the short man knew about the casino construction business. How many people it took to build one, how many dollars it cost for the electric, plumbing, carpets, glass, neon. Then Charlie told the short man about the window cleaning business he had recently sold. He was curious about how much money window cleaners were making in Las Vegas. He had asked how much a window cleaning contract for a place as big as the Palermo was worth.

The short man said he would find out and took Charlie to the Palermo model. It was closed, but the short man had keys with him. They did a walk-through together, the short man quoting facts about the costs of the room as he pointed at light fixtures and furniture. Charlie remembered shaking his head in amazement.

Then the short man walked Charlie out back behind the model. It was dark there. The last thing Charlie remembered was another man standing in front of him with a pipe. The man had said something Charlie couldn't remember. Then Charlie felt the air being knocked from his solar plexus. He felt kicks and punches. Everything went black.

It was nearly ten-thirty in the morning before he was released from the hospital. He took a taxi back to Harrah's, but Charlie didn't go straight up to his room. He walked again instead. He took the route past the construction site where he was assaulted the night before. Two uniformed guards stood watch at the front gates as construction trucks lined up to enter the site. The guards checked each driver for identification.

Charlie stopped at the Palermo model to look for the short man who had befriended him the night before. It bothered him that he was mugged but not robbed. It didn't make sense. He considered describing the short man to the people working at the Palermo model but decided against it.

He was getting too many looks from passersby to interrogate anyone. When he saw himself in the reflection of a mirror hanging outside the model bathroom, Charlie was reminded that his head and hands were bandaged.

When he finally returned to his hotel room, it was a little after one o'clock in the afternoon. Lisa was gone. He remembered denying there was anyone with him to the doctors at the hospital when he was asked if there was someone they should contact. He remembered denying there was anyone at all.

He wondered then if it had been wishful thinking on his part that there was no one to contact. He looked around the room and noticed something was strange. He crossed the room to the windows then turned around to look the room over again. The room had been tidied up by the housecleaning service, but something seemed out of order.

He lit a cigarette from a pack on the small table and immediately realized what was different. His wife wasn't just out someplace getting sun or shopping or working out. His wife was gone.

It was then that he spotted the note she had left him on his nightstand.

Chapter 4

"I CAN'T BELIEVE I'M sitting here," Vincent Lano said. He lit a Marlboro cigarette, coughed violently after inhaling, and rubbed his eyes to keep them from tearing.

"You think maybe it's time you quit?" Joey Francone asked. He was nearly half Lano's age at twenty-five. He was dressed in skintight black pants, a black T-shirt, and black shoes. His huge arms bulged under his tight shirt.

They were parked at the far end of a minimall lot. Lano had moved the rented Ford Taurus under the shade of a row of trees. It was 110 degrees in the afternoon sun.

"How long they been in there?" Lano asked.

Francone glanced at his gold Rolex. "A long time."

Lano stretched his neck. "Six fuckin' hours in a plane and now another six hours in a car," he said. "And then he's flyin' out here. For what?"

"He lost face in front of his crew," Francone said.

"Because he slapped some broad? Guess what? He should've kept his hands in his pockets."

Francone showed disgust at the comment. "First of all, the guy japped him, okay? Second, the guy broke his jaw. In front of people. He's gotta make it right."

Lano turned away from Francone to spit phlegm. "It's offensive is what it is," he said. "What it's become."

Francone craned his neck to see across the street. He glanced down at his watch. "Almost seven hours now," he said.

Across the street from the minimall was the motel the two men were watching. They were waiting for a woman to leave the motel. Then they would assault the woman and take one of her front teeth. It was what their boss wanted.

It was also a job that upset Lano. He had never hit a woman in his life. "I guess the joke's on me," he said as he took another drag on his cigarette and immediately coughed up more phlegm.

Lano was fifty-two years old and dying from throat cancer. He was diagnosed with the fatal disease shortly before he left New York, but Lano never shared the information. After thirty-four years in the rackets, the aging mobster didn't want anyone to know.

He was a made member of the Vignieri crime family of New York for more than twenty years. He had made his bones the old-fashioned way, killing his first man on orders by his twenty-first birthday. He had killed three more by his thirtieth birthday.

Now, so many years down the road, confronted by a death he couldn't avoid, Lano was having second thoughts about the life he had chosen.

Francone, the young wannabe seated next to him in the front of the rented Ford Taurus, waved at the secondhand cigarette smoke. Francone was a close friend of Nicholas Cuccia, another young punk, who had recently become Lano's new boss. Francone was a neat freak, nonsmoker, bodybuilder, with maybe five assaults, Lano guessed, to his entire mob résumé.

Maybe the kid had a hit under his belt. Lano doubted it.

Too many guys like Francone were next in line to become made men when the mob books opened again. It bothered Lano that punks like the one seated next to him would soon be his equal.

"Least you could do is take a walk with those things," Francone told Lano. "Gimme a break a few minutes. I'm suffocatin' over here."

Francone didn't like Lano or all of the bitching and moaning he did. He, too, had taken the long red-eye flight from New York to Las Vegas the night before last. He, too, had been sitting in the car all fucking day. To top it off, he was missing back-to-back workouts while the old bastard sitting next to him slowly killed the two of them with his never-ending chain-smoking.

"Fuckin' kids," Lano said. He let the driver's side window all the way down.

Francone shook his head. It was ninety-five degrees in the shade. He had two choices: he could choke to death on cigarette smoke, or he could sweat to death from the heat. He cracked the rear windows to let some more of the smoke escape.

"That guy really put this thing together," he told Lano.

Lano suppressed another coughing fit. "You make it sound like the Normandy invasion."

"The what?"

"Forget about it."

"He could've fucked it up," Francone said. "He got somebody to follow the broad. Who the hell knew she was gonna pull this? Imagine, this guy Pellecchia catches a beating from us and then his wife takes off with another guy?"

It was true. The guy who had arranged everything in Las Vegas, Allen Fein, told them how Charlie Pellecchia's wife had split on him in the middle of their vacation. One of Fein's people at Harrah's had actually seen the note the wife had left her husband.

"Poor bastard," Lano said.

Francone leered at Lano's sympathy. "You mean fuckin' loser."

Lano tossed one cigarette and lit another. Francone waved his hands wildly in frustration.

"I'm sorry," Lisa told John Denton. "I can't again. I feel like shit. I feel terrible."

She was feeling guilty about how she had left her husband the night before. Now she couldn't respond to her lover's touch.

They met at the airport immediately after Lisa had left a note for her husband. They had taken a room at a motel and made love as soon as they were alone. It had been passionate and exhausting. It had been what they both wanted and needed.

They planned to leave for California the next day, but now Lisa couldn't do it without speaking to her husband first. After leaving him a note, a phone message was out of the question. She wanted to meet Charlie someplace. She needed to talk to him face-to-face.

Denton tried to soothe her tension by rubbing her back. "I understand," he told her. "It's okay."

"When we're out of Vegas again," Lisa said as she reached back to hold Denton's hand.

"We can catch a flight to L.A. anytime," he said. "I can book one a few hours before we're ready to leave."

"I'm sorry," Lisa said.

Denton leaned Lisa back against his chest as he kissed her hair. "Don't think about it," he whispered. "Just relax."

She lay back slowly against her lover's chest. She closed her eyes as he kissed her hair again. She felt his hands gliding over her shoulders and down her arms. She felt his fingertips on her stomach. She felt his kiss on her neck as his hands reached for her breasts.

Lano was leaning against the door of the Ford Taurus as he smoked a cigarette outside the car. It was easier than listening to the piss-ant pretty boy complaining about it inside the car. He heard the passenger door open and slam shut, but he didn't turn around to acknowledge Francone.

"Maybe I should just knock on the door and get it over with," Francone said.

Lano took a drag on his cigarette, coughed a few times, and dropped the butt on the parking lot pavement. "You really gonna hit that broad?"

Francone scratched at his chin. It was one of many annoying mannerisms the pretty boy had that turned Lano's stomach. Francone scratched his chin as if he were about to perform brain surgery whenever he had to give something any thought. As if this situation required thought. The punk was about to assault a woman.

"Forget the tooth," Lano said. He pointed to an ice cream truck at the other end of the parking lot. "I say you get yourself an ice cream cone and we call it a day."

Francone finally stopped scratching his chin. He looked around himself and shrugged. "That's what he said to do. He was very specific. He said knock out a tooth. The boss wants to see a tooth."

Lano rubbed his temples. "You think maybe we should move the car first?" he asked sarcastically. "You know, just in case somebody notices you hit a broad, knock out her teeth, then stroll back to this car, get in, and drive away. You know, just so they can't write down the license number."

Francone responded with his own version of sarcasm. "Why don't you handle the security on this, okay? I'll take care of the broad. You go get yourself an ice cream. You make it back in time, maybe you can hold off the boyfriend. If it doesn't offend you, I mean."

Lano shook his head. "You ever think maybe you're saving your boss a big headache coming up with a better solution?"

Francone was stumped. "Better solution like what?" he asked.

"Like we find a fuckin' dentist give us a tooth and bring that to your boss," Lano said. He refused to acknowledge that Nicholas Cuccia was his boss, too.

Francone used both hands to wave the suggestion off. "Are you kidding me? Nicky said come back with a tooth from her mouth. Now he's flyin' out here to meet us and you wanna try and fugazy a tooth? What happens he wants to see the broad himself?"

Lano was rubbing his temples again. Where the fuck did they find assholes like this? He was almost glad he was dying so he wouldn't have to deal with them anymore.

"We're already under the radar on this," Lano said.

"Under the radar how?"

"You really think the old man, Tony Cuccia, you think he's behind this bullshit? He's been around too long to know better. Bustin' up a guy is one thing. Even though the guy didn't deserve it, he caught a beatin', big fuckin' deal. But a broad? You wanna crack some broad in the mouth for a tooth because she slapped you one in the face because you grabbed her ass in front of a hundred people?" Lano stopped to cough. "Bullshit," he added. "It's wrong. It's worse than wrong. It's stupid. This is the kind of thing makes us all look like shit."

• • •

Francone wanted to strangle the old bastard. Where the fuck did he come off talking about a skipper like that? This was what was ruining the mob, he thought, old-timers who were passed up for promotions and couldn't adjust. The old prick was talking subversive. If Lano had talked like that back in New York, they wouldn't have to wait for the cigarettes to kill him.

"So what are you tellin' me, Vinny? You're not gonna go through with this thing? Or you're gonna rat me out if we get caught?"

"Fuck you, sonny," Lano said. "I'm not hittin' no broad, and I won't even dignify your other remark. And, tell you the truth, you ever make another remark like that to me again, about ratting anybody, I'll shove one a my fists down your throat and pull out your clean fuckin' lungs for myself. You got that?"

Francone had to restrain himself. He thought better of the situation. They had a job to do. He could tell Nicholas Cuccia about Lano's subversive remarks the next day. Maybe the boss would give Francone the contract to whack Lano. After all the secondary smoke he had ingested today, Francone would whack Lano for the pleasure.

"Oh, you hear me or not?" Lano asked.

Francone forced a smile. "Yeah," he said. "I heard you."

She let Denton relax her into having sex with him. It was easy once she was calm again. It was as good as it had always been between them.

Denton rested peacefully beside Lisa as some of the guilt she was feeling seemed to fade. She lit a cigarette as she moved from the bed to a chair near the window. She pushed back the curtain and looked across the small parking lot. Except for a few cars, the lot was empty. She looked across the street into the minimall parking lot and saw an ice cream truck. She thought about having a milk shake.

There was a sudden knock on the motel door as she reached for her purse. She pushed back the curtain again and saw two men standing at the door. The younger one, although he stood in the shade, looked vaguely familiar. Lisa answered the second knock before it woke Denton.

Chapter 5

THE NOTE HIS WIFE left him was simple and to the point:

Charlie, I'm so sorry to do this to you. But I have to do this. I have to do it now. John is with me. I will call you tomorrow. None of this was planned. Please believe me.

And try to forgive me. I'll call you tomorrow to work something out.

Take care of yourself.

The note was signed: *Lisa*.

"It wasn't planned my ass," Charlie said aloud. "I should smack him in the back with that goddamned hairbrush."

He removed his wedding ring and picked up the telephone. He pressed the room service button, ordered a large pot of coffee, and made his way to the bathroom, where he found the Advil bottle. He dropped four capsules into his right hand, examined them a second, and tossed them into his mouth. He sipped water from a plastic cup to swallow the pills. He turned the shower on to let the steam build. He examined himself in the mirror before stepping under the hot water.

He had black eyes from his fractured nose. He frowned at the sight of himself. It would be another couple of days before the skin around his eyes turned green and yellow. It would be a full week at least before his skin bruises healed completely.

The bandage behind his right ear wasn't too bad. The contusions on both his hands had turned blue-black. The tape job on his bruised fingers annoyed Charlie. He removed the tape that restrained his fingers from bending. He had broken a finger in the past. He would live with the pain.

He examined his shape in the mirror for the second time in as many days. He knew he needed to work out more aerobically. His big upper body and skinny legs distorted his symmetry. The extra weight around his hips and waist didn't help either.

He wondered if that's what had finally triggered his wife's leaving him. Lisa was five years younger than Charlie. Her lover was a year younger than she was. Charlie couldn't help but wonder if it had always been just a matter of time for him and Lisa once she was intimate with John Denton two years earlier. The man his wife referred to in her good-bye note was an athletic attorney in near-perfect shape.

Was it his shape or his age?

As he walked the length of Las Vegas Boulevard to avoid the phone call Lisa had mentioned in her note, Charlie continued to wonder about his wife and her lover. If there were signs of his wife having an affair again, he had missed them a second time. Except for a few telephone hang-ups at the house, Charlie hadn't noticed anything peculiar.

They had grown distant the past few months. There were long periods of inactivity between their sexual relations. There were frequent gaps in their communication. They had stopped being friends to each other and had started doing things alone instead of together.

Charlie thought back to the night of the fight at the New York nightclub. It was a week before they had left for vacation. He had tried to buy tickets for an opera the same night Lisa was supposed to go dancing with a friend. When the opera was sold out, Charlie decided to join his wife instead. She became furious with him. It was as if she suddenly hated him.

The tension was thick between them at the nightclub, and they decided to leave early. As Lisa wove her way through a group of men around the bar, one of them grabbed her ass. She slapped the man in the face and was immediately slapped back. She landed on the floor at Charlie's feet, and he reacted without thinking. He ran behind the punch and knocked the man unconscious.

Now Charlie wondered if Lisa had made plans with her lover that night. He wondered if John Denton was there at the nightclub during the fight.

It seemed obvious to him now. Charlie had ruined his wife's plans by going dancing with her. It was why she was so angry with him.

Of course John Denton was there. He was the "friend" Lisa was supposed to have met.

When he finished his walk, Charlie realized there was something else bothering him about his fight at the New York nightclub, something about one of the men who had threatened him after the altercation. One of them had made his way up close to Charlie before the bouncers were able to pull him away. He had said something. Maybe it was a name. Charlie couldn't recall.

He let it go. He promised himself he wouldn't wonder about his wife again. She was history. His marriage was over. The sooner he accepted it, the better.

Chapter 6

HE NAPPED AT THE pool in the late afternoon. He skipped his second meal of the day when he felt hungry. When he was starving, Charlie picked at a fresh fruit salad from the poolside café.

When he returned to his room, it was nearly six o'clock. He immediately dressed himself as close to formal as his wardrobe would allow. He wore beige pants with a black polo shirt. He spent several minutes grooming in the bathroom. He had a problem combing his hair straight back with the bandage behind his right ear.

Charlie decided to finish the week-long vacation. He would take the drive to the Grand Canyon. He would visit Hoover Dam. He would even take the long drive through the desert his wife had wanted.

He would need the time to heal, anyway. Charlie was supposed to return to the hospital in three days to have the wound behind his ear checked. In the meantime, he would listen to his opera, read, and maybe catch some extra sun.

Lisa hadn't left a phone message so far. Maybe she had changed her mind about speaking to him. Maybe she was already in Los Angeles with her lover. Maybe she had returned home to remove her things from their house. Or maybe she was consulting with an attorney about a divorce.

He disguised his wounds as best he could and made his way down to the casino bar, where he was convinced he had made a total ass of himself the night before. He remembered that he was fairly drunk at the bar. He remembered singing an aria. He cringed at the thought of his singing voice.

Charlie also remembered the bartender, a redhead with freckles and a pretty smile. He remembered the way she wore her hair up and how she had spoken with an accent.

He adjusted his sunglasses in the reflection of a restaurant marquee as he made his way to the bar. He wondered how bad his bruises would look to the redhead.

"Devil's Lake, where?" he asked her.

She was wearing the standard casino uniform: black pants, white shirt with ruffles, and a checkered vest with a nametag. Her red hair was up again. It was held in place by a white barrette.

Her eyebrows furrowed when she saw him. "Charlie?" she asked.

"It gets even worse," he told her. He flipped his sunglasses down to expose his two black eyes.

"Ouch," she said.

"I was mugged. After I left here last night."

She was still looking him over. A customer called from the opposite end of the bar. "I'll be right back," she told him.

He watched her fluid movement behind the bar. He could tell she was experienced. She reached for bottles in the bar well without having to look at them. She poured drinks without having to measure.

Her body wasn't bad either. He guessed her to be 5-4, no more than 120 pounds. He put her age somewhere between 30 and 35 years old. When she was up close again, he noticed she had bright blue eyes.

Later, when the bar was less active, Samantha Cole answered his original question.

"North Dakota," she said.

Charlie was caught off guard. "Huh?"

She pointed to her nametag. Charlie read it aloud. "Samantha Cole, Devil's Lake, North Dakota."

"But you can call me Sam. We already did this last night, you know. You probably don't remember. You were pretty drunk."

"Let's do it again anyway." He extended his bruised right hand across the bar.

Samantha took his hand carefully and smiled.

"See? Now I remember." He was looking into her eyes then.

"What?"

"Why I came back down here tonight," he said. "Your pretty smile. I remembered your smile."

He was there the night before. He had left her a good tip and never caused her trouble. He had actually made her laugh a few times.

Tonight he was banged up from a mugging, he told her. She wasn't sure if he was telling the truth, but he wasn't making anything more of whatever had happened to him. He told her he was mugged. He showed her his black eyes and bandages. There were no excuses or macho story to go along with his bruises. He had remembered her and wanted to see her again.

Because she had a pretty smile.

Between serving drinks, wiping down the bar, and running tabs, Samantha enjoyed her brief conversations with Charlie. She watched him watching her as she worked behind the bar. Last night he was drinking gin and tonics. Tonight it was straight club soda. He had told her he was staying off the booze to regain his equilibrium.

"How long you here for?" she asked.

"Few more days," he said. "I feel kind of awkward going back home like this. I'm hoping some of the bruises will clear up."

She had noticed he was wearing a wedding ring the night before. Now he wasn't.

"I was a little worried I acted stupid last night," he said. "Being so drunk and all. Tell me I wasn't obnoxious."

"You were fine. You remember hitting the four aces?"

"Vaguely."

"Well, I do. You left me a fifty-dollar tip."

He thumbed over his shoulder toward the casino. "Better you than them."

Samantha was curious. "Did they get your money? The money you won from the four aces? When you were mugged, I mean."

"That's the crazy thing. No, they didn't. Nothing. They didn't take anything."

She pointed to his left hand. "Except your wedding ring," she said coyly. "Unless you're not wearing it tonight."

Charlie looked at the ring finger of his left hand. He smiled when he remembered why the ring was gone. "That's the other thing," he said. "My wife dumped me."

John Denton held a cold wet towel against the left side of Lisa's badly bruised mouth. She was barely awake. The painkillers permitted her to drift into sleep. She would need to go back into surgery again later. They would have to stay in Las Vegas another few days before she was healed enough to travel.

The oral surgeon had told them Lisa was lucky her jawbone wasn't broken. Although she lost one of her upper front teeth, the surgeon was pretty sure he could save the other three that had been pushed back. At least he was sure of saving one.

So far there were more than twenty stitches inside her mouth. She would need at least one false tooth. She might need an entire bridge. Her mouth would be sore for a few weeks. She would require return visits to a periodontist for several months.

Denton wasn't sure what had happened or why. He was awakened by a cracking sound he later assumed were Lisa's teeth breaking. There was a follow-up thud, he guessed, when she hit the floor. He saw two men in the doorway. One had pointed a gun at him. The other man was kneeling or squatting. He saw the man get up and put something in a handkerchief. He saw both men leave quickly. One of them slammed the door closed.

Denton had rushed off the bed to the floor where Lisa lay unconscious. Her mouth was bleeding badly. The floor was stained with a puddle of her blood. He turned the lights on. Her lips were one giant mass of swollen flesh.

He called 911 for an ambulance. Because of the nature of the emergency, the police responded to the call as well. They questioned him for a long time before Denton was released. He was forced to tell them the entire story: How he was the woman's lover. How the woman had left her husband during their vacation. How she had called him in California and asked him to come to Las Vegas.

None of it, he knew, sounded very plausible. He was an attorney himself. Denton knew how ridiculous a position he was in. He knew how bad he looked to the police.

"Yes, they knew each other a long time . . . more than two years . . . Yes, they had had a previous affair. . . . Yes, the husband had known about it. . . . Yes, he was married, too. . . . He had left his wife. . . . No, his wife didn't know who Lisa Pellecchia was . . . No, he didn't expect Lisa would ask him to come to Vegas. . . . Yes, he loved her. . . . Yes, she was leaving her husband for good. . . . Yes, Lisa left her husband a note . . . at the hotel they were staying . . . Harrah's . . . room 1719 . . . . Yes, he had met the husband before . . . in New York . . . on business. . . . Yes, he saw Mrs. Pellecchia during that trip. . . . Yes, the husband was confrontational. . . . No, but, well, yes, the husband had issued a threat . . . not exactly a threat . . . a kind of threat. . . . "

His Q&A with the police had gone on for more than an hour. In the end, the police seemed to think it was the husband who had assaulted Lisa. Denton didn't think so, but he couldn't be sure. Charlie Pellecchia had been dumped in a very abrupt way. Denton felt guilty about it, but only for Lisa. It made him sick to think he might be responsible for what had happened to her.

He didn't like providing the police with the story about how he and Charlie had first met, but Denton knew he could be liable as an attorney if he held anything back. He wasn't exactly on moral high ground, being where he was with another man's wife, but if it was Lisa's husband who had assaulted her, he wanted a full prosecution of the crime.

It wasn't starting off the way he had hoped. He was sick from what had happened to Lisa. He held her left hand as she lay asleep in the hospital bed. After a minute of watching her sleep, he leaned over to kiss her forehead.

Chapter 7

THEY DROVE TO THE resort town of Laughlin after taking care of Nicholas Cuccia's request for one of the woman's teeth. The plan was to spend some time in a few connected Laughlin spots for an alibi, should they need one. Lano was supposed to pay the balance of the fee they owed an emissary of a Las Vegas crew for setting up the Pellecchia couple. Then Lano and Francone were supposed to drive back to Las Vegas the following day to meet with their boss at the Bellagio.

It was a straightforward game plan except Lano had had enough of Cuccia, Francone, and his own mob life. What the aging gangster did instead was drop Francone off at the hotel where they were registered as guests for the night while he went to park the rented Lincoln Town Car. Instead of parking, however, Lano turned around and headed back for Las Vegas.

When his pager started to beep fewer than thirty minutes later, Lano turned it off. He made a decision about his own mob life: it was over. There were other decisions to make. Lano used the time it took to drive back to Las Vegas to consider them.

Charlie and Samantha managed to maintain a pleasant conversation while she worked the crowded casino bar. Samantha told him she was originally from North Dakota, divorced once herself, and attempting to finish off a psychology degree at the University of Las Vegas. She had been working at Harrah's for nearly three years. She was living in Las Vegas nearly ten years.

"I thought you had an accent," Charlie said when the bar was finally slow and they had a chance to talk. He slipped his Harrah's player's card into the slot to earn credits for playing the poker machine.

"It's midwestern," she told him. "I can't lose the 'oh' pronunciation. Like in 'boat' or 'coat' or 'throat.' I've tried, trust me. You want coins?"

Charlie stuck the end of a fifty-dollar bill in the money slot. "I'll use cash," he said. "Have you tried Brooklyn? To lose the accent."

"Maybe I should," she said. "I was once a real-to-life farm girl."

He tried to picture her in a denim outfit with suspenders and her hair tied up. He smiled thinking about it.

"What?"

"I was picturing you on a farm."

"Milking a cow?"

He shook his head. "Just looking pretty."

It wasn't a standard line, but Samantha knew where it was going. She had been propositioned a thousand times since working the bar station. For whatever reason, most men drinking at a casino bar assumed the women who worked there were desperate for dates. Sometimes it was flattering. Most times it was annoying.

Except Samantha was having fun with him again. She had had fun with him the night before.

"So tell me. What the hell was that you were singing last night?"

"Uh-oh," Charlie said. He started to blush.

"It was Italian, but we couldn't figure it out."

"'We'? This is getting uglier by the second."

She set a coaster for a new customer. When she looked back at Charlie, he was still blushing. His face was bright red.

"Well?" she said, waiting for him.

"Opera," he whispered.

"Is that what you call it?" She opened a fresh bottle of Heineken and set it on the coaster.

"Pretty bad, huh?"

"We thought it was opera, but I think you may be tone deaf."

Charlie toasted her with his club soda. "I've been called worse," he said. "To dinner."

Samantha was confused.

"Will you go with me?"

Samantha stuttered as she felt her own face blushing. "I-uh, I-uh, I can get fired for that."

Charlie was leaning forward, both elbows on the bar. "Make it lunch then," he said. "You owe me if I sang for you."

A customer sitting midbar held up a hand. Sam said, "I'll be right back."

She thought about it as she served a vodka tonic. He seemed interesting. He wasn't just another drunk hitting on a barmaid. She looked at him over her shoulder. He was watching her right back. She liked his confidence.

"What's lunch?" Samantha asked when she returned to his end of the bar.

"Setting the parameters?"

"It's a fair question."

"Whatever you say it is. And I promise not to sing."

Samantha smiled as a new customer waved to her. "Let me think about it," she said.

Francone slammed the telephone down as he shook his head at Allen Fein. "I don't know what the fuck he's doin'," Francone said. "He coughed up blood a few times, but he's always coughin' up blood. I figured he went to park the car."

Fein was middle-aged, short, and fat. He wore a baggy blue and black Sergio Tequini sweat suit. He looked up at Francone from the stool he was sitting on. "What makes you think he might have turned?"

Francone was still shaking his head. "Two fuckin' days I ain't been in a gym," he said. "You guys got a place here I can work out?"

Fein held up a finger. "Joey? What makes you think your friend may have flipped?"

Francone was examining his biceps then. "Huh? Oh, because of the way he was talkin'. It's been like that since Nicky was upped to skipper. Lano's pissed he was passed again. He was cryin' about Nicky the whole fuckin' trip. He was talkin' subversive about the thing we came out here to do. Especially the broad."

"Is it possible he just got sick and checked himself in at a hospital someplace?"

Francone was doing isometric wrist curls. "Who the fuck knows with that guy? He could be at the hospital, he could be at a fuckin' cigarette sale, or he could be talkin' with the Feds at an FBI office. He's got his own agenda lately, thinks who the fuck he is."

"I don't need this blowing up in my face," Fein said, clearly annoyed. "It was a simple accommodation. It shouldn't become a federal case."

"I agree," Francone said as he strained to curl an imaginary dumbbell. "I know Nicky had to reach out for this. And he appreciates it."

"Yeah, well, his appreciation won't do me any good should this thing turn up on the six-o'clock news tomorrow."

"Hey," Francone said. "Nobody wants that."

Fein took a deep breath. "Why don't you keep trying to locate your friend?"

Allen Fein had been fronting mob business in Las Vegas for more than three years. He was a certified public accountant as well as a licensed attorney in the state of Nevada. Recently he had stepped up his involvement to broker deals between mob crews visiting Las Vegas and others seeking to invest there.

He occasionally made deals his boss wasn't aware of. Arranging the surveillance of the Pellecchia couple in Las Vegas was one such deal. He had been contacted through channels. A New York crew was looking for help. Fein had arranged it without the proper authority. It was a dangerous backdoor move.

Setting up the husband at the Palermo construction site was a perk Fein received cash on the spot for. At the time, the five thousand dollars seemed like an easy score.

Now it looked like he would be forfeiting the remaining five thousand dollars. If Jerry Lercasi ever found out about the deal Fein had put together with the New York crew, the five thousand dollars would represent the cost of the accountant's life.

Dealing with the idiot bodybuilder from New York wasn't making the problem any easier. He was never impressed with the average intelligence of Las Vegas wiseguys, which was why he had become so confident getting more involved in the day-to-day operations of mob business. Talking with this musclehead, Fein was even less impressed with the pawns of the underworld.

Except his boss, Jerry Lercasi, wasn't just another wiseguy. Lercasi was the most powerful mobster in Las Vegas. He also was a ruthless killer.

Fein wanted nothing more than to spend some time with the two young girls he had requested through the escort service the Lercasi crew operated in Laughlin. He was told both girls were still in their teens. He was excited about their age.

Now, however, he was forced to deal with a moron in desperate need to lift weights.

He watched the bodybuilder slam the telephone receiver down one more time before deciding to contact a connection with the Las Vegas police. If the police couldn't find Vincent Lano, there was a good chance the New York mobster was on the run somewhere. If that was the case, he could deal with losing the five thousand dollars.

If Lano went to the feds, it would become a much bigger issue. There would be no place Fein could hide in Las Vegas.

If Lano went to the Feds, Fein was thinking, he would pack his bags and get the fuck out of the country.

Chapter 8

IT WOULD BE A simple hit. A guy flew out to Las Vegas for a summer vacation. Unless he was an inveterate gambler, he would go for the long walks, visit the theme parks, ride the moving walkway into the Caesar's Palace shopping mall, watch the Volcano, see the Pirate Show, and maybe have dinner at the top of the Stratosphere.

He might even use one of the escort services one or two times.

Or maybe he'd grab a hooker from one of the casino bars.

Also, sometime during his vacation, the guy would get killed.

Renato Freni watched Charlie Pellecchia drinking at the bar from a roulette table occupied by mostly Asian players. Freni wore a Boston Red Sox baseball cap and a navy blue flower print shirt with black shorts. He was a stocky man of average height. At fifty-nine years of age, his body was still thick from working out with weights. He was well tanned from several years of living in the desert.

He touched the muffler for the Baretta .9 he was carrying in the waist of his pants. The muffler was deep inside the pouch of the belt he wore around his waist.

He had been watching the man he would kill for little more than an hour. A contact inside the casino had provided Freni with Pellecchia's location from a casino player's identification card. He noticed that Pellecchia's head was bandaged behind one ear and that he wasn't drinking alcohol at the bar. He also noticed the conversation between his mark and the barmaid. The woman wrote something on a napkin before handing it to Pellecchia. It was after the exchange with the barmaid that Pellecchia finally left the bar.

Freni followed his mark through the casino from a safe distance. He stopped to read a pamphlet advertising a slot machine tournament when Pellecchia turned into the hallway where the elevators were located.

Freni used a phony room key to get past the security guard standing in front of the elevator bank. He waited less than a minute for an elevator door to open. He touched a floor button and smiled at a black couple riding in the car with him. When the elevator stopped two floors below Pellecchia's, Freni stepped out of the elevator. He nodded at the black couple as he got off.

"Good luck," they told him.

Charlie was feeling pretty good when he went back up to his room. He had managed to arrange a lunch date with his new friend, Samantha Cole. They were going to a water park where Samantha said she had bought a season pass for the tide pool. Charlie didn't have a clue what a tide pool was, but he looked forward to learning about it from Samantha the next day.

He had spent a long time at the bar with her. Although she was busy running back and forth serving customers, Samantha had helped Charlie forget why he was going upstairs to his room alone.

He managed to forget what his eyes looked like under the sunglasses until he saw his reflection on a marquee inside the elevator. Charlie flipped up his glasses in the reflection and squinted at what he saw.

"Joe Frazier, Joe Frazier," he said, imitating Muhammad Ali. "This may shock and amaze ya, but I'm gonna whoop Joe Frazier."

Freni walked around the elevator bank to the vending room to wait another minute before heading up to Pellecchia's floor. He wanted to give his mark enough time to get settled inside his room before knocking on the door.

Then he would either show Pellecchia the gun or shoot him from the hallway. He would go inside the room and make sure the man was dead. He would hide the body inside the bathroom in the event Pellecchia had called for room service. He would fish through the room for whatever cash his mark may have brought along. Then Freni would leave Las Vegas for a few days and maybe take in the other Nevada tourist attractions.

When Charlie walked off the elevator, a short, fat man with curly blond hair surprised him. The fat man held one hand up as an identification wallet dropped open.

"Police," the fat man said.

Charlie looked up as he saw another man appear directly behind the short man.

Freni turned his back to the ceiling camera and screwed the muffler onto the barrel of the .9 when he was alone in the elevator. He took the elevator up two flights to Pellecchia's floor and slipped the handgun into his front pants pocket. He kept his right hand on the gun inside his pocket as he stepped off the elevator. When he saw his mark talking with two men, Freni headed straight for the vending room. As he waited there, he overheard some of their conversation.

"Your wife was mugged."

"Where? When?"

"This afternoon."

"What happened? Is she—"

"She's in the hospital."

"Where were you this afternoon, sir?"

"Huh? What?"

"This afternoon, sir. Where were you?"

"Are you fucking serious?"

"Sir, why don't we talk inside your room."

"You think I mugged her?"

"Sir, can we talk someplace private?"

"Fuck, yeah, of course. My room's down the hall."

"If you don't mind."

Freni had heard enough. He waited until the voices were gone. He fished a few quarters from his pocket, bought himself a Diet Coke, and got out of there.

"What happened to your hand?" the fat detective asked.

They were inside his room. Charlie and the fat detective stood at the end of the bed. A tall, thin detective helped himself to a look at Charlie's belongings on the table across the room.

"It's worse than that," Charlie said. He removed his sunglasses. He turned around to show both detectives the bandage behind his right ear.

"Why didn't you report it?"

"I wasn't robbed. I didn't see the point. Some guys mugged me." He turned and saw the tall detective looking through his opera CDs on the table. "Excuse me. Can I help you?"

"You have any idea why?"

Charlie was still watching the tall detective. "Huh?"

"You have any idea why you were mugged?"

The tall detective stopped looking at the stuff on the table. "And not robbed?" he added.

Charlie shook his head. "No clue."

"Do you know who your wife is with?" the tall detective asked.

"She left me. You already know who she's with."

"She left you here?"

Charlie was getting annoyed. They were going through a routine. He wasn't in the mood. He had his own questions about his wife they hadn't really answered yet. "I'm here," he said. "She's gone. Yes, she left me here."

The fat detective became abrupt with his questions. "When was the last time you saw her?"

"One more time. Last night."

"What time?"

"About seven-thirty, eight o'clock."

"Did she leave you then or later?"

Charlie's eyebrows furrowed. "I don't know," he said, his voice angry. "Later, I guess. I went down to the bar."

"Did you argue?"

"We had a fight. I was drunk. I didn't hit my—"

The fat detective interrupted him. "Were you anywhere in the casino you could verify from the time you argued until the time you were mugged?"

Charlie took a deep breath. "Yes," he said. "Same place as tonight, in case you were watching. One of the bars downstairs. I played a poker machine there. I hit it. I'm sure I'm on the cameras they use."

"Your wife was mugged at a motel on the edge of the strip. She was there with a Mr. Denton. Mr. Denton said one of the men held a gun on him."

Charlie knew they had mentioned John Denton to get a reaction. He was too concerned about Lisa to give a shit.

"Is she all right?" he asked.

"They knocked out some of her teeth," the fat detective said. "Worse than what you got."

"The fuck could somebody hit a woman like that?" Charlie asked.

"That's what we'd like to know," the tall detective said. "Got any ideas?"

Charlie had had enough already. "No," he said. "Or I wouldn't be standing here wasting my time with you two clowns."

The detectives almost brought him in for calling them clowns. Charlie was eventually able to talk himself out of the situation. It wasn't that he didn't respect the police investigating Lisa's mugging, but they had asked him questions in an attempt to trap him. They seemed to have made up their minds about his role in his wife's mugging.

After he finished giving them a story without the details of what had happened in New York, Charlie called the hospital where his wife was admitted. He was told she was in surgery and wouldn't be able to speak without pain for a few days.

He felt a conflicting rage when he hung up with the hospital. He was furious at the thought of someone assaulting his wife. He was furious at himself for giving a shit. She had dumped him the day before. She had left him for a lover she was cheating with, a lover she had cheated with in the past. Why the fuck should he care what happened to her anymore?

He sat at the window in his hotel room and looked toward the construction site where he himself was mugged. He wondered what had actually happened to Lisa and whether her lover had tried to defend her. He wondered if both muggings had anything to do with what happened in the nightclub back in New York the week before.

Charlie wondered about a lot of things before he could finally fall asleep.

Chapter 9

Jerry Lercasi sat up in bed to smoke. He checked his watch for the time as he took a long drag on a fresh Marlboro. He scratched at the hairs on his muscular chest with his free hand.

He had just finished having sex with his girlfriend, a twenty-nine-year-old woman he'd been having an affair with the past two years. They had spent the night together in a private apartment above his twenty-four-hour gymnasium, Vive la Body. His girlfriend, Brenda, was a manager at the gym. When the big fights came to Las Vegas, she was one of the ring girls at the MGM Grand. It wasn't the really big time he had promised her two years earlier, but it was better than washing hair in the beauty parlor where he had first met her.

Now his girlfriend was coming out of the bathroom naked. She was a tall woman with a sleek body and long black hair. She had perfect breast implants and a naturally curvy figure.

Lercasi was smiling at her body as she walked across the huge bedroom. He focused on the stripe of neatly trimmed pubic hair. He frowned at the sight of the tissue he could see through her pubic hair.

"You gotta put that thing in there like that?"

"Unless I want it to leak," Brenda said, then mocked him. "Yes, I have to put that thing in there like that."

"What is it, like a plug?"

Brenda stood at the end of the bed. "Exactly. That's what it does. It stops it from running out."

Lercasi made a face. "You gotta describe it like that? It's disgusting."

Brenda rolled her eyes. "Then use a condom, Jerry."

Lercasi pointed at her crotch. "Cover yourself," he said.

Brenda grabbed the pair of navy leggings she wore to work at the gym. She sat on the edge of the bed and pulled the leggings on. When she arched her back to pull them up over her hips, Lercasi said, "You have such a beautiful fuckin' body."

"Except I disgust you."

He waited for her to roll off the bed. When she reached for a white athletic bra, he shook his head. "Not that," he said. "There's no plugs there."

Brenda half smiled. "Why don't you use a condom? If it bothers you so much."

"I hate them things."

"I hate it when your goo starts running out while I'm working downstairs."

Lercasi made another face. "You gotta talk like that?" he said.

Brenda put her hands on her hips. "You're the one with the problem."

Lercasi thought about it. It was true, he did have a problem with his women appearing anything but perfect. Except he didn't think it was too much to ask. He put them up, paid all their expenses, gave them phony jobs for play money, and provided them with the best connections in Las Vegas.

Right now, though, he knew he wasn't going to win this argument with Brenda this morning. He was fifty-six years old. The young women he kept around him had minds of their own, no matter how much he provided for them.

"I don't know," he said. "My first wife used to do that. It bothers me."

Brenda frowned as she put the athletic bra on. "I have to get downstairs. You want me to send that pervert up?"

"My accountant?" he asked. He knew the girls working in his gym hated Allen Fein. He liked to push their buttons about it.

"Why do you call him that, a pervert?" he asked.

"Because he is. He likes little girls. Everybody knows it. He doesn't even try to keep it secret. We also know he brings in private massage girls. That chink, for one. And we all know what he does with them in the massage rooms."

"What chink?"

"Chink or Vietnamese or Korean or whatever she is. She's giving him head in the massage rooms. My girls gag at the sight of him downstairs. He makes our skin crawl."

Lercasi feigned concern. "He ever make a move on you?"

"I don't wear a training bra. I'm not his type."

Lercasi tried to picture Allen Fein humping his girlfriend. The image was worse than the tissue plug she had used. "Send him up," he said.

"And if Nancy calls again?"

Nancy was Lercasi's second wife, a woman he saw as little as possible. "Tell her I'm busy."

"Sure," Brenda said as she stood up. "What do you care? I have to hear it."

Lercasi leaned over to crush out his cigarette in an ashtray on the night table. "Hey, Brenda," he said. "Don't break my balls this morning, all right?"

Brenda stopped at the door to turn around and give Lercasi the finger. He broke out laughing.

Twenty minutes later, Allen Fein sat on the couch in the private apartment above the gym while Lercasi combed his hair in front of the floor-to-ceiling mirror behind the bar. The accountant was fidgety on the couch. He examined a pair of crystal dice on a glass coffee table. He seemed nervous waiting for Lercasi's attention.

"How was Laughlin?" Lercasi asked.

"Huh?" Fein said. He dropped one of the crystal dice into his lap. "Oh, all right. I'm thinking of buying a condo there."

Lercasi stopped to look at his accountant in the mirror. "You pay those kids you fucked last night?"

"Of course."

Lercasi finished combing his hair. He turned to Fein as he struck a match to light a cigarette.

"I need a party tonight," he said, with the unlit cigarette dangling from his mouth. He lit the cigarette, took a long drag, and held the smoke inside his lungs a few seconds before letting it escape. "See what the mayor's doing," he added. "Or somebody on the City Council. Make it my party. Something public, where it'll be picked up on the news."

"Are you bringing your wife?" Fein asked. He set the two crystal dice back on the coffee table.

Lercasi opened his hands. "Am I bringing my wife? What kind of question is that? No, make it public, and I'll bring Brenda. Of course I'm bringing my wife."

"Should I know what it's about?"

"Somebody skimmed thirty-two six last month from one of Gilly's books. The somebody had a private line installed in one of his places a few months back for dime players. The tap come in last week. Thirty-two six in one month. Who knows how much the first five months before somebody figured it out."

The accountant swallowed hard. "I see."

"That's already taken care of," Lercasi said. He sat in a black leather recliner across from Fein. "Is it true you're getting head in my massage rooms downstairs?"

"No," Fein said defensively. "I don't need to get my head in the massage rooms."

"Brenda says you got some private noodle comes in to do you."

"Not true. Besides, Brenda hates my guts."

"Because I don't need that kind of shit blowing up in my face over here. Some broad using my place to give head. You should know better than that."

"You know what I like, Jerry. I don't need to get my joint copped in a gymnasium. I like to look, if anything. The worst she does is remove her top. And I don't know how Brenda would know unless she installed a camera."

Lercasi smirked. He liked humiliating his accountant. "Just so long as you know what you're doing," he said. "After all, you're my business manager, no?"

"Maybe you should tell Brenda about that," Fein said, acting offended then.

Lercasi thought about the tuft of tissue between his girlfriend's legs. "Brenda's got other things to worry about," he said. "Go make a party."

When Fein left Vive la Body, he ignored the contemptuous stare of Lercasi's girlfriend at the front desk. He was feeling lucky about having a built-in excuse for being in Laughlin the night before. He had avoided a potentially dangerous question-and-answer period with his boss. Had he not made arrangements to screw a couple of teenagers in the whorehouse in Laughlin, his boss might have looked into Fein's sudden trip to the mountains.

Now his boss had other business for Fein to take care of. One of the bookmakers operating under Lercasi's gambling business had skimmed money. Fein didn't know whether the cash amount his boss mentioned was real, nor did he care to know. The bottom line was he was expected to arrange an alibi dinner for his boss tonight.

Which meant the bookmaker who had skimmed the money was going to die. Probably at the same time the party was going on.

Fein knew some of the names of bookmakers and pornographers in Las Vegas, but he didn't study them. He figured he'd know within the next couple of days which one had robbed money from his boss. It would be all over the local news.

Chapter 10

NICHOLAS CUCCIA OPENED THE package that was delivered to his room and held the tooth that was inside up to the light for examination. It was bloodstained above where the root of the tooth was broken. He winced at the thought of the pain a woman might feel from a broken tooth. He touched his jaw with his free hand. There was no way losing her tooth was as painful as his broken jaw.

He had spent most of his morning annoyed. The six-hour flight from Kennedy with the DEA agent the night before was bad enough. When Cuccia first checked into his hotel, he noticed the woman doing his check-in staring at his mouth. Then when he looked at himself in the wall mirror behind the registration desk, he noticed he was drooling.

After watching the local Las Vegas news and glancing through the newspapers, Cuccia knew that Charlie Pellecchia was still alive. If the professional his uncle had contracted to kill Pellecchia did his job, the hit man was keeping it a big secret.

All he had so far was the souvenir from Lisa Pellecchia's mouth. Cuccia set the tooth on a night table and attempted to smile. He felt a sharp pain in his jaw. He slapped the tiny trophy off the night table and cursed under his breath.

He spent the rest of his morning observing the action around the pool with binoculars. When he was bored watching women take the sun, Cuccia used his cellular telephone to call his uncle back in Brooklyn.

"You call that guy?" he asked.

"Of course, sure," the old man said.

"Because there's nothing so far."

"Oh, one fuckin' day it's been."

"I'm just sayin'. Checkin', you know."

"Yeah, well, why don't you stay off the phone. Go get some trim or somethin'. Call one a them joints out there. It's legal in Nevada."

"Right," Cuccia said. "Maybe I will."

Which was exactly what he did. He called Pleasure Times escort service and spoke to a man with an effeminate voice. He told the man he wanted two women, one black, one white, for a possible threesome. He expected the women to do a lesbian routine with a double-headed dildo. He expected them to follow his directions.

Then he asked if Pleasure Times knew of anyone he might score some cocaine from. The man with the effeminate voice explained that Pleasure Times was a legitimate escort service, which could not procure drugs of any kind for its clients.

The disclaimer annoyed Cuccia. He told the dispatcher to "just mention the cocaine to one of the girls." Then he hung up and called the dispatcher a stupid fucking faggot cocksucker.

Later, he played the radio loud as he took a long, hot shower. He wondered how closely the DEA agent would watch him while he was in Las Vegas. He wondered if he would be able to set up his uncle with heroin charges before the mob indictments back in Brooklyn could affect the deal he had made with the government. He wondered if what the DEA had promised him was even possible anymore.

When he finished his shower, Cuccia thought he heard his telephone ringing. He stepped out of the shower and turned off the radio. He saw the message light blinking on the telephone and stepped out of the bathroom. Cuccia wiped his head with a towel as he listened to the messages.

On the first message, Joey Francone reported that Vincent Lano had disappeared the night before. Cuccia scowled as he waited for the second message.

It was Francone again, his voice somewhat more urgent this time. Lano had taken some money with him.

"Shit," Cuccia said. "What the fuck else can go wrong?"

He listened to the third message and learned what else could go wrong.

"I recognized him," Lisa said without moving much of her mouth. She was struggling to talk. The stitches inside her mouth were still too fresh to stretch. "He was one of the men in the nightclub."

John Denton frowned. "What do you want to do?"

"Nothing. If it is the mob, I'm not getting any more involved than I already am."

"They mugged Charlie, too."

"Shit. Is he all right?"

"Apparently. The police thought it might have been him who attacked you. That he sent somebody because of how you left him."

Lisa was shaking her head. "This is all my fault. Everything."

Denton took one of her hands. "You couldn't know what was going to happen. And they attacked you, too. Charlie can take care of himself."

Lisa was feeling her guilt. What else could happen to them? What else could happen to Charlie? It was all because she hadn't been able to tell him that she wanted out of their marriage.

"The doctors think you should stay here another couple of days," Denton said. "You may need more surgery."

Lisa couldn't think about herself then. She squeezed Denton's hand and closed her eyes tight.

The girls from Pleasure Times were named Kim and Daria, although Cuccia had no clue as to which one was Kim or which one was Daria. The white girl was a tall, tan natural blonde with a small chest and green eyes. The black girl was short and muscular. Her breasts were too big and round to be real. She had big lips, though. Cuccia loved a woman with big lips.

He had guaranteed their payment on his credit card over the telephone. He advanced them another two hundred dollars each before they changed in the bathroom. When they finally emerged from the bathroom, the white one was wearing a lace lingerie outfit with black garter belts and black high heels. The black girl was dressed in a leopard thong bikini and beige boots. Cuccia liked the look. He took a seat in a chair he positioned in front of the king-sized bed to watch the show.

He guessed the girls had worked together before. They moved through the lesbian routine without him once having to give them directions. There wasn't a word of discussion between them as they changed positions over and over. Except for his special request for the double-headed dildo routine, Cuccia thought the girls had read his mind.

The special request cost him an extra fifty dollars for each girl, but he was happy to pay it. He was as excited as the cocaine and booze permitted. When the girls finished their routine together, he had them kneel on all fours side by side on the edge of his bed. He went from one to the other, entering them from behind, until he could no longer restrain himself inside of Kim.

Or was it Daria?

The black girl left Cuccia a telephone number for her own personal cocaine connection in Las Vegas. He wrote it down on hotel stationery and slipped her an extra fifty.

When the girls from Pleasure Times were gone, Cuccia poured himself a tall glass of vodka and tonic. He sat back in the same chair he had watched the girls perform from earlier. He used the remote to turn the television set on. He switched channels until he found a local news station.

Earlier, the man hired to kill Charlie Pellecchia had left a message. He wanted to meet. There were complications, he had said. Something had gone wrong, something about a very close call with the police.

Cuccia had no idea what the close call with the police was about, except that it meant two things: Charlie Pellecchia was still alive, and it would cost more money to have him killed.

Cuccia was angry that he would have to renegotiate the price of a hit gone wrong. Because he wanted Pellecchia dead, he would be dealing from a very weak hand.

He waved his own thoughts off as he reached for his drink. He didn't care what it would cost. Charlie Pellecchia had to die.

Chapter 11

THE FIRST THING CHARLIE remembered when he woke up was what the guy who hit him with the pipe had said.

"Remember Decades?"

Charlie wondered if he had relived the incident in his sleep. He felt as if he had. He could see the man with the pipe. He could hear his voice.

The vague familiarity of that voice had bothered him since he was first questioned at the hospital. The man Charlie punched at the New York nightclub had been surrounded with friends. Two of them had tried to get at Charlie but were stopped by bouncers. A few dozen threats had followed. Then there was the one guy who had managed to get up close.

A young, cocky guy, he remembered.

The man with the pipe, he wondered?

"You got no idea who the fuck you just hit," the cocky guy had said back in the nightclub.

It was a voice full of arrogance and contempt. It was the same voice he had heard two nights ago.

"Remember Decades?"

Charlie licked at his swollen lip. The man with the pipe was the same man from the nightclub back in New York. He had been followed out to Las Vegas.

He thought about Lisa and what had happened to her. He wondered if she told the Las Vegas police what had happened back in New

York. He was about to call her when he remembered she was with her lover. He looked at the telephone. The message light was off.

"Fuck it," Charlie said.

He wondered whether his troubles were over. If it was the mob that had followed him to Las Vegas, was the beating they gave him the night before the end of it, or would there be more?

Might they go all the way and try to kill him?

Charlie decided it was over or he would be dead already.

He checked his eyes in the mirror to see if his bruises were starting to fade. There were two dark streaks of purple under each of his eyes. He put his sunglasses back on.

In a few hours he had a date with a woman he was anxious to spend some time with. He wasn't sure why, but Samantha Cole had intrigued him. He wasn't sure if it was because she seemed to try to listen to him while she worked a busy bar, or if it was because he was feeling rejected and lonely and Samantha had seemed interested.

Or maybe it was something more simple, like her smile. He definitely liked her smile.

He wondered if Wet 'n' Wild was the right place to spend some time with Samantha. His facial bruises were an ugly sight. He was also nervous about wearing a bathing suit. He was still ill at ease about the extra weight he had spotted in the mirror two days ago.

He put shorts on over the baggy bathing trunks his wife had packed for him. He picked a navy tank top to stay cool. He brought a loose-fitting shirt to cover the tank top.

The telephone rang, and Charlie sat on the bed to answer it.

"Hello?" he said. No one answered.

"Hello?" he repeated.

Whoever called wasn't talking.

"Right," he finally said, and hung up.

"Wear the one-piece!" Carol Curitan yelled to Samantha.

Carol was in the kitchen of Samantha's apartment. She was a

forty-five-year-old, beautiful, full-figured woman with thick blond hair and green eyes.

Samantha was checking herself out in the mirror behind her bedroom door. She turned sideways for a better view of her waist. She looked at herself up and down in the mirror.

"I feel better in this!" she yelled. She gave herself one more look in the mirror and opened the bedroom door.

Carol was in the hallway. She shook her head at Samantha when she saw her in the flower print bikini. "It's a first date, baby," she said.

Certain words or phrases highlighted Carol's Alabama accent. *Baby* was one such word. *Darlin'* was another.

"All he's seen you in so far is your work uniform," Carol continued. "Give him a dose, darlin'. Either the white one-piece or the coral bikini."

Samantha stopped to look at herself in the small hallway mirror near the kitchen. She liked the flower print of the bikini she was wearing. It was red and pink and aquamarine. She stood up on her toes to try to see her bottom, but the mirror was too high on the wall.

"This covers more of my rump," she said, slapping herself on one hip. "I don't want to show him everything day one."

"That's the point, baby," Carol said. "Even I know that, and I haven't tried to encourage anybody in fifteen years. You want them to want you."

Samantha was nervous about how she presented herself on a first date, although she kept reminding herself that it wasn't really a date. Charlie's wife had just dumped him, according to him. He would only be in Las Vegas a few more days. It's not like they would be seeing each other every Saturday night.

Which was why she wasn't so sure Wet 'n' Wild was the best meeting place for the lunch she had packed. She didn't want to send the wrong signals. She didn't want to show too much skin to a guy she might never see again.

She tugged down on her bikini bottom. "Nope," she said. "Not this fast. This'll have to do."

"Well, you're just scrumptious in that one, too, so there," Carol said. "My lord, how I wish I had your little body to dress up for myself."

Samantha chuckled. Carol combed her hair back to tie with a scrunchie. She had recently moved in with Samantha after fleeing from her husband across the country. They had known each other just over six months when Samantha started to regard Carol as family.

"Maybe I should take him back here and we can all go skinny-dipping," Samantha joked in her best mock-southern accent.

Carol cocked a hip. "Darlin', it's been so long for me, right now I'd pay just to watch you and your date skinny-dip."

Chapter 12

CUCCIA WENT DOWN TO the pool to catch some sun. He was to meet later in the afternoon with the man who was supposed to kill Charlie Pellecchia. It wasn't a conversation Cuccia was looking forward to but there was no avoiding it. Not if he wanted Pellecchia dead.

He applied suntan oil to his long, hairy legs. He scanned the pool for a blonde he had spotted through his binoculars earlier. She was a short, muscular woman with an orange one-piece thong. The skimpy bathing suit she was wearing displayed a perfect ass, Cuccia thought. She had golden-tanned skin with long, straight hair and big breasts he was sure were fake. She also wore a waterproof Rolex and earrings with emeralds as big as marbles, he remembered.

Cuccia also looked for the DEA agent as he scanned the pool area. He was sure the agent would show up to break his balls whenever it was most inconvenient. He was trying to stall the government's move against his uncle. In the event his deal with the government turned sour, Cuccia wanted to be sure that the man who broke his jaw was already dead.

Charlie Pellecchia had become an obsession for Cuccia. Nothing else mattered.

He used a cellular telephone to call the room at Harrah's. When Pellecchia answered the phone, Cuccia remained silent.

When he finally spotted the blonde he was looking for, Cuccia became unnerved about his recent injury. He was too self-conscious to talk to her through a wired jaw. He quickly turned his head when she looked his way.

• • •

Agent Thomas found the organized crime detective eating pizza at his desk. Thomas was there to try to find out why Nicholas Cuccia and two of his crew were in Las Vegas.

"You show me yours and I'll show you mine," Detective Albert Iandolli said as he folded a slice of pizza. He was a big man, 6-foot-4 at least, 230 pounds.

"It's not about Vegas," Thomas told the detective.

Iandolli stopped short of taking a bite of the pizza. "What's it about?"

"Two connected guys from New York staying at the Bellagio. Their boss came in last night, early this morning. I'm here about him."

Iandolli leaned forward to take a bite from the end of the pizza slice. He chewed while he held the pizza over a napkin on his desk. Oil from the end of the slice dripped into a reddish-gold stain on the napkin.

"And?" the detective asked after he swallowed.

"I was wondering if the two guys from New York are up to anything here in Vegas. If maybe they found themselves some trouble. Maybe you heard something here on your end."

"The other two guys? You just said you were here about their boss."

Here we go, Thomas thought. "Detective, I'm not here to break your balls. Please don't break mine."

Iandolli set the slice of pizza on the napkin. "You're being vague," he said. "How am I supposed to help you with the information you just gave me? Two connected guys from New York came out here. Two dozen connected guys from New York pro'bly came out here the last two nights. I can appreciate your need to keep things to yourself, being a federal agent and all, but the bottom line is, there's nothing much I can do for you, you keep talking in circles."

"What do you need from me?"

"Names, for starters. Then I need to know what I'm supposed to be looking for in the way of what the other two might be up to. What specific trouble they might be in. For instance, there's been a rash of johns getting rolled by hookers the last few weeks in Las Vegas. Guys take a broad up to their room, get drugged, wake up later, and find they're broke without gambling. That's one kind of trouble they might find for themselves. Then again, you'd need to speak with somebody from vice about that. You see what I'm saying? It's all very vague the way you described it."

Thomas gave the organized crime detective two names: Francone and Lano. He didn't mention Nicholas Cuccia. "I need to know if they met with Jerry Lercasi," he said.

"Now you're talking," Iandolli said. "He's my turf, Lercasi, but I can tell you right off something might save you a lot of time. Nobody meets with Jerry Lercasi. Nobody."

"And why is that?"

"It's his way. Lercasi doesn't meet with outsiders. Not here in Vegas. That's his protocol. Lercasi closed down the wiseguy tour business long before Hollywood made that *Casino* movie. Wiseguys come here from other cities, they're on their own. They may meet with intermediaries, but they never get to meet with Lercasi. Including his cousin, another wiseguy, lives in New York. Even that guy doesn't get an audience. Jerry Lercasi holes himself up most of the time. Doesn't peek outside of his gym unless he wants to pick up something to eat."

Thomas was doing his best not to explode. "What about the intermediaries? Could these two, Francone and Lano, have met with somebody around Lercasi?"

"Sure. I'll ask around." Iandolli was about to pick up the slice of pizza again when he looked up at Thomas with a smile. "Anything else?"

Thomas sarcastically smiled back at the detective. "You're right. I am wasting my time."

The semiretired hit man showed up wearing a pair of khaki shorts and a flower print shirt. Just like most of the tourists walking the Strip, Cuccia thought. He was a stocky but solid man. He had a thick neck and big shoulders. He seemed to have black hair with gray streaks. A Boston Red Sox baseball cap covered most of his head.

After they introduced themselves to each other, Cuccia walked

Renato Freni toward a concession stand without talking. Cuccia decided to take the hit man's lead. He glanced around the pool as they walked. The bright orange one-piece was easy to spot. She was sitting at the edge of the pool then, dangling her feet in the water.

"I missed a shoot-out with a pair of local cops, two detectives, by a few minutes last night," Freni said.

"What happened?"

"That's what I came here to find out. Why the fuck a pair of detectives are talking with a guy I'm supposed to whack out."

Cuccia shook his head.

"I saw the guy was banged up," Freni continued. "I saw his head was bandaged, but that's none of my fuckin' business. What is my business is I don't get jerked around. Why didn't your uncle mention the guy was hot?"

"It's not like that. The guy isn't hot. He's a nobody. It's got nothing to do with business."

Freni noticed Cuccia looking toward the blond woman. "Hey, I didn't come here to look at broads."

"Sorry."

"Let's walk around the pool once or twice and see whether or not we can still do business. First, I think I need an orange juice. This heat is giving me a headache."

Cuccia bought an orange juice for Freni and a Coke for himself. Freni immediately drank his juice. Cuccia sipped at his Coke through a straw as they continued to walk around the pool.

"You were that close, huh?" Cuccia asked.

"Two minutes. Maybe less. I come off the elevator and there he is with two detectives. They went down the hall into his room. I took off."

"Shit, I have no idea what that was about," Cuccia lied. "Maybe the guy got into it with somebody. Or he got mugged or something. Maybe his wife did it."

"That's the other thing," Freni said. "His wife took off. Then she was mugged."

"Huh?" Cuccia said. He acted surprised. "How do you know that?"

"That's my business. Except nobody bothered to mention the guy would have a wife with him when he came to Vegas. I was given a name and a hotel. I found out about the wife after my near-miss with the law. Which is the second fuck-up with this job. I don't intend to walk into a third."

"What are you saying? You think my uncle is fucking with you?"

Freni tossed the empty juice bottle into a trash pail. "I'm saying somebody is jerking off the wrong guy, my friend."

"I think maybe it's miscommunication," Cuccia said. "Trust me, nobody is out to jerk you off."

"Good. Then nobody will mind showing some good faith with this mess."

Cuccia let out a deep breath. "What is this, a fuckin' shake-down now?"

"Call it a miscommunication," Freni said. "You still want this guy dead, for whatever the fuck reason, give me a new number. Something I can live with."

Cuccia stopped walking again. He looked around the pool until he spotted the blonde. She was with a tall black man. He watched with disgust as the blonde applied sun tan oil to the black man's legs and arms.

"Thirty," he said.

"Forty," Freni said.

The blonde was bending over to kiss the black man. Cuccia nearly choked on his Coke when he saw the black man slip the blonde some tongue.

"Thirty-five," he managed to say.

Freni stepped in front of Cuccia. "Forty."

Cuccia frowned through his wired jaw. "All right."

"Say it. The number."

Cuccia hesitated a moment, then said, "Forty."

"Just so there's no more miscommunications," Freni said.

"Can you do it today? Now that I've been robbed, I should have some satisfaction here."

Freni made Cuccia wait for a reply. "Maybe," he finally said.

Cuccia wiped drool he could feel on his chin. He looked for the blonde, but she was gone. He searched the pool until he saw her head come up from under the water. Her wet hair hung straight down. It glistened in the sun. He wanted her.

"You don't have to say," Freni said. "I'm just curious."

Cuccia touched the corners of his mouth with his fingers. "What?"

"What it's about. Why you wanna kill this guy so bad."

Cuccia was caught off guard by the direct question. He pointed at his own chin. "Because he did this. He broke my fuckin' jaw."

Freni turned his head from side to side as he examined Cuccia's jaw. He squinted as he said, "You want me to whack a guy for that?"

Cuccia shook his head. "No," he said. "I want you to whack a guy for forty grand."

Chapter 13

CHARLIE WAS TOO SELF-CONSCIOUS for a day at the water park. The lines at the entrance gates were long and crawling with families and young children. He slipped the taxi driver a twenty-dollar bill to go ask the pretty lady with the picnic basket and cut-off jeans to come back to the taxi for a minute.

When Samantha leaned into the window of the taxi, Charlie said, "Would you hate me if I told you I was too uncomfortable to be around all these kids looking like this?" He pulled his sunglasses off for emphasis.

She smiled for him. "Can you take me to my car in the parking lot?" she asked. "We'll figure something out there."

She decided to take him back to her apartment instead of guessing where to have lunch together. She set a round white table on the small patio behind her apartment. She opened the table umbrella for shade while they ate.

They exchanged stories about themselves while they picked at a pasta salad. Samantha learned some more about his marital problems. She, in turn, confessed her own marital failure. When Samantha learned how Charlie's wife had left him, she was much more sympathetic to his situation.

"How could she do that?" she asked, then quickly apologized. "I'm sorry. Please, forgive me. I shouldn't have asked that."

Charlie seemed to take it in stride. "It's a legitimate question. How could she do that in the middle of a vacation? I don't know. To be fair, though, her note said it wasn't planned."

Samantha couldn't stop herself from rolling her eyes. "I'm sorry," she said again.

"I think Lisa wanted out for a long time," Charlie said. "This vacation must have been her breaking point."

Samantha steered the conversation away from his marriage. She told him about her roommate, Carol. She explained how they had met on the Internet and how Carol was a victim of abuse until she ran away from her husband six months earlier.

"So you took her in?"

"She's run from two places since she left Alabama. The first was New Orleans. Her husband found her there after a few months. Then she ran to Chicago. He almost got her there after another few months. Carol thinks he's determined to kill her."

"How long has she been with you?"

"A little less than a month. But she keeps one suitcase packed, she carries her laptop computer everywhere she goes, and she hides extra money for the day she says she knows she'll have to run off all over again."

"I assume the law can't do a thing."

"Not until she's dead. O.J. proved that."

"O.J. proved you could get away with it, too," Charlie said.

They had coffee in the kitchen. He liked the way she looked in the cut-off jeans and white T-shirt. When she let her hair down, he liked the way it curled in around her face.

"How far are you from your degree?" he asked.

"Thirty-four credits. But it may as well be ninety-four. Either I can't afford to take the classes I need, or they don't offer them, or I can't take the time off when they are offered."

"I was a two-year wonder before I dropped out to become a window cleaner and get married."

"High-up window cleaner?"

"Very high."

"And your kids were from your first wife?"

"Both."

"So, where does the opera come from?"

Charlie smiled. "My grandfather," he said. "He lived with us when I was young. Listened to opera all day. You hear something enough, you start to like it."

"Or you think you do," Samantha said.

"Touché," Charlie said.

Samantha mentioned how long it had been since her last relationship with a man and how she was trying to be extra careful with men since she was so close to erasing the final debts from her marriage to a compulsive gambler.

"So you don't trust men anymore to punish yourself," he said.

Samantha was taken off guard. "Huh?"

"That's what it sounds like. You're pissed at yourself for what happened with your deadbeat husband so now you don't take chances."

She looked at him with one eye closed. "Is this a trick question?"

Charlie smiled again.

"I had a boyfriend from where I work until six months ago," she said. "A partner."

"Like I had a wife."

"I guess. Only he didn't live here. But he wanted too much too soon."

"Marriage?"

"And kids."

"Ouch."

"Exactly. So we broke up. So it has been a while."

"For what it's worth," Charlie said, "it's been a while for me, too."

It was pretty late by the time they finished their coffee. He asked Samantha if it would be all right if they went out again before he returned to New York.

"Take off your glasses," she said.

"My eyes are black."

"I can tell a lot more about you if I can see your eyes."

He took the sunglasses off. She stared into his eyes a moment and giggled. "You look silly," she said. He put the sunglasses back on. Samantha took them off again. "No. It looks even sillier with them on."

"This part of a ritual? Humiliation before a simple yes or no?"

"I'm sorry. I can get used to your eyes like that. Well, not used to them, but, you know. I'd rather see your eyes."

"Well, will you go out with me again?"

"Of course. Whatever made you think I wouldn't?"

"I don't know," he said. "The glasses?"

Charlie stayed through dinner, and they learned a little bit more about each other.

Samantha loved dogs but was afraid to leave one alone while she worked. Charlie loved dogs, too, but he could never find the time to train one. Samantha loved to cook French cuisine. Charlie could cook a limited number of Italian dishes, hamburger, or steak. She loved to swim. He preferred walking. She had always wanted a house. He couldn't wait to sell his. She was a basketball fan. He watched football and boxing. They were both morning people, but Samantha required eight hours of sleep to Charlie's five. She loved country music. He was an opera aficionado.

"Ah, the hobby that drove your wife crazy," she said. "I don't know. You don't look that old."

She giggled into his arms. He was surprised. He held her loosely, barely touching her back with his fingertips. She smiled up at him and pecked him on the lips.

He was more surprised at the kiss. He held her until she stood up on her toes to kiss him again. The kiss was casual at first, their lips barely making contact. They held it for a few seconds before smiling at each other. Then they kissed again, and their mouths became involved. It was awkward for Charlie with his bruised upper lip. He held her tighter. She leaned into him. They kissed for a few minutes before they eventually backed off from each other.

They said good night when the taxi he had called finally arrived. She watched him leave from her doorway. She smiled when she saw he turned to look back at her from the taxi.

Chapter 14

DETECTIVE ABE GOLD SIPPED coffee from a styrofoam cup at the end of a hallway in Summerlin Hospital. At fifty-five years of age, the veteran detective found he couldn't make it for more than six hours without caffeine.

He was near the end of a double shift that had started when he was asked to respond to a motel mugging off the Las Vegas Strip. A couple had been assaulted in their room. The woman had been hurt.

Gold rubbed his temples. Random violence had become too common over the past few years. While Sin City's base population had blossomed from family-oriented promotional campaigns, a more transient populace had brought random and rampant crime. The woman at the motel appeared to be another victim.

When he learned that the woman had left her husband midvacation for a younger boyfriend she had had a previous affair with, and that the husband's name was showing up at another hospital as a mugging victim from the night before, Gold didn't know what to think.

The two detectives he sent to talk to the husband had come up empty. Charlie Pellecchia's story had checked out. Although they knew the husband wasn't telling them everything, there was nothing the detectives could do about it. Not without a formal complaint.

The married couple was from New York. They were supposed to be on vacation. Gold wondered if they were a pair of fruitcakes who had decided to take their marital frustrations to Las Vegas to see what the desert heat might stir up.

Then he wondered if they had arranged for each other to be assaulted.

Then Gold wondered what the hell the wife's boyfriend might have had to do with it.

He finished his cup of stale coffee as the young vice detective he was with ended a cellular telephone call.

Gold was a short, balding man. At 5-5, he had to look up at the young, baby-faced, 6-foot detective.

"You still married?" Gold asked.

The young detective, Donald Gentry, was the son of Gold's ex-partner. Since Gentry's father had died the year before, Gold had become his mentor.

"I have two more hours," Gentry replied.

Gold held up a short, stubby finger. "Better make it one, you wanna stay married."

Both men forced smiles. Gold wasn't looking forward to their conversation. Gentry suspected his wife was having an affair. Gold knew from experience, his own included, that once you suspected an affair, there usually was one.

"I found her diaphragm gel," Gentry told Gold. "I've been keeping an eye on it. One day it's there, in her night table drawer, the next day it's gone. I know she's not using it with me."

Gold was too familiar with the sinking feeling he knew was in the pit of Gentry's stomach. "I'm sorry," he said.

"At least she was taking it out of the house," Gentry added. "Until this afternoon. I called her from the courthouse. She didn't answer. I stopped by a few hours later. She wasn't home. But the bed was a mess, and the gel had been used. There was gunk all around the nose. I probably just missed them. In my own fucking house."

"You know who?" Gold asked cautiously. He was concerned that Gentry did know.

"No idea. That's why I came to you. To find out."

Gold took a deep breath. It had been a long, lousy day. It was about to get worse.

"Let's get some coffee," he heard himself say.

• • •

Nicholas Cuccia expected to see Vincent Lano and the missing five thousand dollars when he opened the door to his suite. Instead, he saw Joey Francone and a short, bald man he had never seen before.

"Who the fuck are you?" he asked the short man.

"He's Allen Fein," Francone said.

Fein extended his right hand to Cuccia.

Cuccia looked to Francone before taking Fein's hand. "He'da said Allen Funt, the *Candid Camera* guy, I might know him."

"He works for—" Francone started to say.

Fein interrupted. "I work for Jerry Lercasi. I'm the one who arranged things."

Cuccia clapped twice and opened his hands. "That's great. And what can I do for you?"

"There's a five-thousand-dollar bill outstanding," Fein said. "One of your men took off with it."

Cuccia turned to Francone. "You wanna tell me the rest, or do I have to hear this twice?"

It was a frustrating position. The DEA had followed the heroin from Florida up the eastern coastline to New Jersey. The heroin was trucked from the New Jersey docks to a warehouse in Jersey City operated by a known associate of Nicholas Cuccia. He had stumbled into the case the night Cuccia killed his partner in the heroin deal, a Russian gangster Agent Thomas had been keeping under surveillance at the time.

Thomas smuggled Cuccia from the Jersey City warehouse to a DEA safe house, where the Vignieri crime family captain was offered a deal that would save him from spending the rest of his life in jail.

Cuccia also was under surveillance by the FBI organized crime task force, as well as a New York City organized crime unit.

Deals were struck between the two federal agencies that permitted the DEA to run the show. Thomas was promoted and reassigned to Cuccia. Part of the deal required Cuccia to sting his uncle, the acting underboss of the Vignieri crime family, with the heroin bust. The hope of the federal organized crime task force was that Uncle Anthony Cuccia would be yet another underboss to turn on the head of a New York crime family. The DEA would take the credit for the operation up to the point of old man Cuccia's arrest for heroin trafficking.

An underlying hope had been that Nicholas Cuccia would remain unscathed from the drug bust; that somehow he could remain inside the Vignieri crime family as an ongoing informant. Thomas knew that it was a pipe dream to wish for the stars, but so far the nephew seemed to be buying the hard sell of the various federal law enforcement agencies.

Still, Thomas's direct future within the DEA depended on the government game plan attaining some measure of success, the least of which was keeping Nicholas Cuccia healthy enough to make the case against his uncle the underboss.

The fact that the federal organized crime task force was about to issue indictments against several key people in the Vignieri crime family complicated matters. None of the agencies was sharing significant information. It was a common problem during intensive long-term investigations. Sometimes years of manpower effort and millions of dollars were lost because of animosity between or among the various agencies investigating organized crime.

The pressure was on Thomas and the DEA to make the heroin bust before the organized crime indictments. But the central figure in the government's game plan was in Las Vegas with two of his crew for reasons totally unknown to Thomas.

He suspected it had something to do with the recent injury Cuccia suffered to his jaw. The mobster's jaw was broken a full ten days earlier. It was the only night Thomas had taken off in three weeks of surveillance. Cuccia had told Thomas that he fell riding a motorcycle. The agent knew the story was bullshit.

The New York City organized crime unit was the only law enforcement agency that knew what had happened the night Cuccia's jaw was broken. So far, they weren't sharing the information.

This was why Thomas was in Las Vegas this weekend instead of home with his wife. He hadn't spent back-to-back days with his wife in more than a month. Now he was making excuses for following a wiseguy across the country.

"But why?" his wife wanted to know.

"To keep an eye on him. Until this thing comes off, I'm his baby-sitter."

It was the truth. When he thought about it, Thomas was nothing more than a baby-sitter for a wiseguy.

"And what am I supposed to do in the meantime?" his wife asked. "I never see you anymore. When are you coming home?"

He had managed to get a room directly across the hall from Cuccia at the Bellagio Hotel. He had rigged a minicamera to the bottom of the door and connected it to the television. He was watching the television while his wife interrogated him.

"Hello?" his wife said. "Are you there? Marshall?"

"Yeah, yeah," Thomas told his wife. "I'm busy now. I gotta run."

He hung up the receiver without saying good-bye. He watched as a man he recognized as Joey Francone accompanied another man inside Cuccia's room. Thomas sat up in the bed to give the situation his undivided attention.

Chapter 15

DETECTIVE GOLD FOUND DETECTIVE Iandolli going through folders in a file cabinet along the back wall of a tiny office. Both men knew each other from working vice together eight years earlier. Both men were originally from New York.

Gold thought organized crime might know something about the assault at the Palermo construction site a few days earlier. Gold waited for Iandolli to shut the drawer of the file cabinet he was looking in before he spoke.

"A couple from New York," Gold said. "They come here on vacation, but they don't last three days. She splits with a former boyfriend. Leaves the husband a note while he's down playing the tables, getting drunk at one of the bars. He goes out later and gets drawn into the construction site at the Palermo, behind the model. He catches a beating from two guys."

Iandolli nodded.

"Then, the wife is with her boyfriend at some motel off the Strip. Two guys show up there the next day and assault her. Knock one of her teeth out." He held a finger up for emphasis. "They take a tooth with them. One tooth. One of them leans over and pulls it from her mouth after punching her."

"And the boyfriend?"

"One of the guys held a gun on him. They left after the other one took the tooth."

Iandolli squinted.

"Exactly," Gold said. "I got the call at the motel. I went there and listened to the boyfriend. I figured it was the husband followed them or something. Then I ran the name at the station and found out about the husband. Same last name pops up on a hospital report, how he got jumped the night before but didn't want to report it. I sent two of my guys to talk to the husband, but he didn't have anything to say. They tried to poke him a little, but the guy didn't bite."

"And the Palermo is Jerry Lercasi's turf."

"Public knowledge," Gold said through a yawn. "And there's a twenty-four-hour guard posted there. So how did this guy, the husband, wind up behind the model?"

"You look like shit," Iandolli said. "When's the last time you slept?"

"Two, three days ago. What do you think?"

"It's a good question. You don't get onto the Palermo construction site without a pass."

Gold popped Chiclets gum into his mouth. "I figure maybe they're running from somebody in New York. Which is why I came here to see you."

"The plot thickens."

"What do you mean?"

Iandolli held out an open hand. "Can I have one of those?" he asked.

Gold handed Iandolli the small red box of Chiclets.

"I had a federali here," Iandolli said after he popped two squares of the gum into his mouth. He chewed as he spoke. "He was dancing around a couple of guys in town from New York. Two guys flew up ahead of their boss."

"FBI?"

"DEA. Which is the same shit when it comes to the interference they run for each other. Anyway, he came asking about two guys with a New York crew. I called New York. There are two guys here. Three, you count their skipper. They're with the Vignieris. I don't know what the DEA wants with them, nor do I care. But I'll lay eight to one somebody caught a beating at the Palermo, our man in Vegas don't know about it."

"Jerry Lercasi."

"Which means somebody pulled an end run."

"This bookmaker they found, Benny Bensognio? The one in the news?"

"That was strictly skimming," Iandolli said. "These assaults were out-of-town shit, somebody working through one of Lercasi's diplomats. Allen Fein, for one, although I don't see that little pervert getting into the muscle end of the business."

"Maybe he wants to feel powerful."

"Maybe."

Gold leaned back in his chair. He didn't like it that a simple assault was quickly blossoming into an organized crime case. "And it could just be coincidence or some other crazy shit," he said. "Maybe the boyfriend had some friends take care of the husband, and the guy retaliated. A general cluster fuck or something."

"That's a stretch. Especially if the one guy is a lawyer."

"You're right, so's the wife a lawyer. What about somebody back East going it on their own?"

"If they're gonna do something like this, they'd send some of their own guys ahead of them, but they'd also ask permission. They'd need the help with logistics, like the Palermo, for one thing. They'd need somebody knows the turf. Then there's the protocol bullshit." Iandolli made a fist and pumped it a few times. "The respect for each other's turf."

"They don't trust our wiseguys to handle things?"

"Would you?"

Gold remembered the other reason he was there. "You know Jack Gentry's kid? He's working vice. Just promoted up to detective a few months back."

"I knew Jack Gentry," Iandolli said. "Died last year, didn't he?"

Gold nodded.

"What's up with his kid?"

"If you know anybody over at vice can keep an eye on him, I'd appreciate it. He just found out his wife's sleeping around."

"Oh, boy. How old is he?"

"Thirty-two. And he just picked up his shield. He's working vice, the latest ring of hookers rolling johns in the casinos."

Iandolli shook his head. "Talk about a cluster fuck," he said.

"Gentry knows she's out there," Gold continued. "He asked me to find out with whom."

"What do you do with something like that?"

"Pray the kid don't whack the boyfriend or his wife," Gold said. "Or himself."

"I'll talk to somebody," Iandolli said. "Sure."

Gold had gone to the organized crime unit detective because he wasn't sure of how to proceed with the investigation of the New York couple. Except for what had happened to the wife, the case had all the markings of a guy running from the mob. The victim was beat but not robbed. The victim was found on mob-protected turf. The victim wasn't cooperating with the police.

Except the guy was still alive and the woman was assaulted in a very particular way.

Gold had other casework to investigate. Getting help from the organized crime unit was a favor he would have to return someday, but at the time, he was too busy to do everything by himself. He had break-ins and robberies and other assaults to deal with.

Gold also had a young detective to worry about. Donald Gentry was going through something Gold was all too familiar with. Gold had gone through it himself, losing his wife to another man. He had gone through it twice.

When he left Iandolli, Gold headed for the insurance office where Jennifer Gentry worked. Gold's first guess was that Mrs. Gentry met her lover where most affairs seemed to start, at the workplace.

Although he hadn't slept in a long time, Gold was anxious to find the man who was sleeping with Mrs. Gentry before Mr. Gentry found him.

Chapter 16

WHEN HE WAS A teenager growing up in a mob family, Nicholas Cuccia listened carefully to the conversations among his father and his two uncles. All three brothers were captains in the Vignieri crime family and expected to one day rule the New York underworld.

As he matured, Cuccia also noticed how none of his uncles and father trusted each other. Conversations between any two always concerned the absent brother. It wasn't until his father died in prison while serving a life sentence for murder and racketeering that Nicholas understood the distrust among the three brothers. It was a philosophy of mob life he would forever embrace.

Assume the worst. Never trust anybody. Me first.

This was why he didn't trust his blood relations any more than he trusted the hired help. After putting up forty thousand dollars in cash for a hit on a civilian vacationing in Las Vegas, Cuccia was starting to wonder if maybe the last surviving brother, his uncle the underboss, had put a move on him. Maybe the government had made two sets of deals. Maybe the hit man who shook him down for an extra fifteen grand was whacking the money with Uncle Anthony instead of whacking Charlie Pellecchia.

Another day had passed without word of Pellecchia's death. Cuccia was starting to think if he wanted the guy dead, he would have to do it himself.

He went down to the pool when he spotted the blonde without her black boyfriend or husband or pimp or whatever the fuck he was. Cuccia was surprised to see the blonde swimming laps. He stood at one end of the pool, waiting for her to finish. When she finally stopped, some fifteen minutes later, Cuccia handed her a towel as she climbed out of the pool.

"That explains your shape," he told her.

She was wearing an aquamarine one-piece thong. He could hardly keep his eyes off of her body. She thanked him for the towel but ignored the compliment.

"You from around here?" he asked.

The blonde shook her head as she dried herself.

"Where you from? Because I think I may move there."

The blonde looked up at him and pointed. "You're drooling," she said. "What's wrong with your mouth?"

Cuccia could feel his facial expression change with his embarrassment. He wiped the drool from his mouth with the back of his hand. He looked the blonde up and down before saying: "I guess you just go for the dark meat, huh, honey?"

The blonde winked at him. "I just like them big," she said.

Cuccia stormed off, kicking empty lounge chairs on his way back inside the hotel.

Later, after he stopped at Joey Francone's room to vent, Cuccia's mouth was drooling all over again. This time it was from aggravation. When he saw the empty twin bed in Francone's room, he immediately remembered Vincent Lano.

"Jesus Christ," Cuccia said through his wired jaw. "What the hell is going on in this shit city?"

Francone combed his hair in front of a mirror. Except for royal blue silk bikini underwear, he was naked. "I think we can forget Lano," he said. "The guy either flipped or he's dead from cancer."

Cuccia sat on the edge of what should have been Lano's bed. The covers were untouched. "You see this motherfucker Pellecchia last night?"

Francone tightened his chest in the mirror. "Please. I sat in that fuckin' lobby all night. Security come over to me it musta been a dozen times. 'Can I help you, sir?' 'Anything wrong, sir?' Yeah, you can help me. Yeah, there's something wrong."

"So the answer is no, you didn't see him."

Francone shook his head in the mirror. He turned to one side and flexed his arm muscles.

"Oh, quit posing over here," Cuccia said. "You look to see he's still checked in?"

"I did that. He's still checked in. No answer when I call the room."

"This is bullshit. I think I got stung by the old man."

"Your uncle?"

"Between this bullshit and Lano taking off, yeah."

"You think your uncle—"

"Go put a fuckin' shirt and pants on," Cuccia said. "I don't get turned on lookin' at your hairy ass."

Francone went to the closet to pick a shirt. There were three polo shirts hanging inside; all were black. He grabbed one off a hanger.

"We could always get this fuck when he comes back to New York," Francone said. "It'd be a lot easier back home."

"Except I already paid for a hit out here," Cuccia said.

"At least we know it'll get done."

Cuccia nodded. It made him think one more time about taking care of Charlie Pellecchia himself.

Chapter 17

IT WAS NOON BEFORE Charlie woke up. The first thing he did was stand under the shower while listening to the opera *Tosca*. He sang in the shower. The crescendo of the "Te Deum" filled him with adrenaline. He pictured the villain of the opera, Scarpia, his hands shaking with ecstasy as he stands in the church singing his confession of lust. Charlie sang along with the villain.

"Tosca, me fei dimenticar, Iddio!"

Charlie's body tensed as a second rush of adrenaline surged through him from head to foot. He let the aria end before stepping out of the shower to dry off. When he heard someone giggling in the hallway, he turned the opera down.

As he was getting dressed, Charlie noticed he had a phone message. He dialed for the message and learned Samantha was pushing their date back to later in the day. He frowned when she didn't leave her phone number on the recording.

He examined his bruises again in the mirror. The black-and-blue discoloration in his face had started to change color. The edges of the bruises were yellow-green. It was ugly but a good sign. Charlie guessed he had another four days, maybe five, before the bruises would disappear completely.

If he had the chance to date Samantha again, he would extend his Las Vegas vacation an extra day or two.

He didn't like the idea of being run out of Dodge. If things were going well with Samantha, Charlie would hang around long enough for his bruises to heal and maybe make up for his lame kisses the night before.

"You kissed?" Carol asked Samantha. "That's a start, baby. And then what?"

They were sipping ice tea on the porch. Carol was up early after waiting tables through the night. Samantha was anxious about her second date in as many days.

"And then nothing," Samantha said. "It was awkward. His mouth is still swollen. I think it hurt him to kiss."

Carol moved her chair directly into the path of the sun. The umbrella in the middle of the table was closed. Samantha had to squint to see her.

"I can think of a way for him to forget his pain, baby," Carol said.

"I'm sure you can," Samantha said. She stood up to open the umbrella.

"Well, how was he? Swollen mouth and all."

"Gentle. But I think he was holding back. He's interesting. He has a lot of interesting hobbies."

"Any of 'em include sex?"

"I didn't ask. But if it helps, he has two sons, so he must not be a virgin."

"The man has potential."

"The man also has a wife, and I'm not totally sold on his story yet."

They were quiet for a while before Carol said, "I can feel Beau again. I hate to admit it to myself, but I just know he's around."

"What makes you say that?"

"I can feel him."

She had sensed her husband's presence at work the night before. When the diner was slow, after the rush, Carol had felt as if she was being watched from somewhere out on the street. She volunteered for counter work so she could avoid being seen through the diner windows.

Later, when the night manager asked if she could work a few extra hours because another waitress had called in sick, Carol was eager for the overtime. She would work until the sun came up, she had thought. At least then she could see who might be watching her.

She told Samantha about her premonitions the past few days. She started to tear when she mentioned she had packed her things again.

"Are you sure you don't want to try the police?" Samantha asked.

Carol used a tissue to wipe her nose. "Positive," she said. "It'll only make things worse. They won't do a thing until he does something to me. I'll be dead before they ever arrest him."

"Where will you go?"

"California, I guess. Or north. Maybe where you're from. I should be able to spot him coming up there, right, darlin'?"

She was trying to joke about it then, but the reality of the situation was unnerving.

Beau Curitan had tracked his wife down in New Orleans and again in Chicago. Both times Carol had narrowly escaped. With nowhere to turn, she accepted the offer of a friend she had met online, Samantha Cole, from Las Vegas.

"I wish he'd just die," Carol said.

Samantha moved her chair alongside Carol's lounger. She held one of her friend's hands.

"I have to run again, I know it," Carol said. "I don't know when he'll show up, but I can truly sense that man is near. He must have paid somebody to look for me. I guess he's going to run through every dime we ever had to find me."

"Do you want me to cancel my date? I hate to leave you like this today."

"No way, darlin'. Uh-uh. You go and you enjoy yourself today. You like that man, I can tell. And it sounds like he likes you."

They remained silent awhile. Carol wiped her eyes and sat up. She gave Samantha a quick hug.

"It does sound like he likes you," Carol said.

"Except he's married," Samantha said. "I can't just forget about that."

• • •

Beau Curitan circled the third telephone number on his list with a red flair pen. He had just paid two hundred dollars for the three telephone numbers narrowed down from hundreds more off the CompuServe Internet chat lines. Each of the three telephone numbers represented a possible location where his wife was hiding and were based on the billing addresses and connecting modem lines.

The trick was recognizing Carol's words in the Internet chat rooms, which wasn't very hard because Beau knew his wife too well for her to chat without being noticed. He could recognize her favorite sayings and slogans. In fact, there were times when Beau thought he could actually hear Carol speaking the words he would read online as she typed them.

A few weeks ago, he had recognized his wife's chat style from a screen name called LVBARTENDER35. Beau also recognized a similar style from the screen name RUN&HIDE. Once he gave the two CompuServe addresses, along with a couple of hundred dollars, to a technician, Beau was told the two addresses were from the same line. Then he paid another hundred dollars for the address of the telephone number.

Now Beau was closing in on his wife again. He already drove past the address twice during the day, but Beau hadn't seen his wife. He called both telephone numbers, but no one answered.

Until now, that is. A woman's voice he knew wasn't Carol answered. Beau listened to the woman's voice before hanging up.

He guzzled half a can of beer before letting go of a loud belch. He turned on the laptop computer he had bought back in Alabama after his wife first took off on him. He plugged the motel telephone line into his modem, then powered up the CompuServe program.

He kneeled back down to type in his password one key at a time.

HUNTER, he typed.

Chapter 18

AGENT THOMAS FOLLOWED THE short, bald man from the Bellagio to a gymnasium he assumed was the one the smart-ass organized crime detective had mentioned the day before. Vive la Body was located alongside a huge condominium development on Spring Mountain Road. A large parking lot blocked the gym from the boulevard.

Thomas managed to verify the owner of the gym as Jerry Lercasi, the head of the Las Vegas mob. The name he wasn't able to get was that of the short, bald man Thomas had followed to the gym, the same man who had visited Nicholas Cuccia at the Bellagio Hotel.

He assumed the short man was a liaison for the Las Vegas mob. Although he didn't expect very much help from FBI agents based in Las Vegas, Thomas expected he would learn enough to figure out what the hell Cuccia was doing there.

Half an hour later, after talking with an organized crime task force supervisor in New York, Thomas found out.

He managed to get over to Harrah's a few minutes after Charlie Pellecchia left the hotel. Thomas used his badge to find out where Pellecchia might have gone. When the girl at the reception desk tried the operator, they learned that Pellecchia had left a message for a Samantha Cole, should she call.

Pellecchia had gone to a music studio on Paradise Road. He was expecting to return to his hotel before five o'clock. Thomas jumped back inside the rental car and whipped around the small circular driveway at Harrah's. He had a general description and a faxed photo of Pellecchia to identify the man he had learned broke Nicholas Cuccia's jaw.

Thomas suspected that Nicholas Cuccia was in Las Vegas to kill Charlie Pellecchia.

He glanced at the fax of Pellecchia on the front passenger seat as he drove through the traffic on Sahara Avenue. When the light ahead turned yellow, Thomas cut across a grass divider to make the turn onto Las Vegas Boulevard.

It was well after noon when Pellecchia finally left Harrah's. Renato Freni was parked in the driveway for more than half an hour waiting for his mark to leave the hotel.

Freni was driving a stolen car with Nevada license tags as he followed Pellecchia's taxi to a downtown music studio. He parked at the curb across the street from the studio when Pellecchia stepped inside. Freni noted the time and laid his head against the headrest.

Charlie had been angry again when he left the hotel. Lisa still hadn't called him, and the Las Vegas police had left him feeling like a criminal.

He wasn't in the mood to lift weights or work out his frustrations aerobically anymore, and his fingers and body were too bruised to hit a heavy bag.

When he decided to vent his frustration on a set of drums instead, he found a music studio where he could rent a private room for twenty dollars an hour. He brought his Cream and Steely Dan CDs to the studio for music he could follow on his headphones.

When Charlie sat at the set of black Pearl drums, he instantly recognized the smell of the percussion wood. He felt the weight of the sticks he had bought at the front desk and noticed they were lighter than the Regal Tips, size 5-B drumsticks he used at home. It was awkward holding them with his bruised fingers. He turned the stick in his left hand upside down for better control and less pain. He took a roll around the tom-toms for a sound check. He winced when the back end of a stick caught his left pinky finger on the rebound.

Freni grew tired waiting in the stolen car. He checked his watch for the time. Twenty-five minutes had passed. His back was starting to ache. He needed to stretch his legs.

He felt the Baretta .9 inside the waist of his pants. He could just as easily walk inside the studio and take care of business as sit in a hot car all fucking day.

This was what he decided to do. He got out of the car and headed for the music studio across the street. He pulled down the baggy shirt he was wearing to cover his waist. He felt the gun through the shirt as he held the door open for a broad man wearing sunglasses.

Charlie was feeling Steely Dan's "Big Black Cow" as he played the twenty-inch ride cymbal above the hard beat. His head swayed with the rhythm as he carefully press-rolled on the snare. He bounced his sticks off the mounted tom-toms before he turned his beat on the high hat.

Charlie's head hung cocked to the left as he picked up the pace. He played the beat with a closed high hat until he heard someone yell. When he looked up, a broad man stood in the doorway of the private studio. Charlie hit the STOP button on the portable CD player and pulled the headphones away from his ears.

"They told me you were into opera," the broad man said.

"Who are they and who are you?" Charlie asked. He held both sticks up straight with one hand against his left leg.

"Agent Marshall Thomas," the broad man said. "DEA. Drug Enforcement Agency." He presented a badge to Charlie.

Charlie ignored the badge.

"It's not about drugs," the agent said.

Charlie removed the headphones from around his neck. "Is it about opera?"

"Not that either, no."

"You want to get to the point? I'm paying twenty dollars an hour for this room."

The door to the studio opened. A stocky man in a baggy shirt stood in the doorway. He looked from Charlie to the broad man and excused himself. "Sorry," he said.

Thomas stared at the stocky man until he was gone. When he turned back around, Charlie was setting his sticks on top of the base drum.

"A little more than a week ago you were involved in a fight in a New York nightclub," the agent said.

Charlie nodded.

"The man you hit is Nicholas Cuccia, a captain with the Vignieri crime family in New York. His uncle is the acting underboss."

"That explains a few things."

"Nicholas Cuccia obviously has a lot of clout. And very long arms."

"And big balls and no conscience," Charlie quickly added. "He attacked my wife and knocked a few of her teeth out."

"Yes, I know. And he probably had you assaulted, too."

"And he can't be touched because my wife won't press charges or testify. I'll assume you already know about me and my wife."

Thomas nodded. "I'm sorry," he said. "What about you? Now that you know who assaulted you."

"I assume I can't press charges, either. Not if I want to live."

"You could call it even," Thomas said.

"Except that big-shot gangster hit my wife."

"His men. Not him. But she left you anyway, right?"

Charlie glared at the agent then. "What do you want from me?"

"To warn you, first of all. To make you aware."

"What else?"

"To make a deal. I'm sure I can back Mr. Cuccia off. In fact, I know I can do that."

"Why don't I believe you?"

"Because you're skeptical?"

"That's not even close to cute."

Thomas held up his right hand. "I swear it. Nicky Cuccia won't bother you again."

"For what?" Charlie asked. "What is it you want?"

"To keep it between us."

Charlie narrowed his eyes at the agent. "You're protecting him?"

"What's the difference?"

Charlie gave it some thought.

"He won't go near you again," Thomas said.

"Like I have a choice," Charlie said.

Thomas pulled a card from his wallet.

"How do you know about the opera?" Charlie asked.

Thomas fidgeted as he walked the card over.

"Whenever you're ready," Charlie said.

"The New York City O.C. unit," Thomas said. "Organized crime. They saw your opera ticket purchases on your credit card."

Charlie shook his head. "I don't get it."

"You beat up a mobster, Mr. Pellecchia. An arrogant one. I think the New York police got a kick out of it. They put a name to it, not me. They're the ones calling you 'Charlie Opera.'"

"Great," Charlie said.

"You'll be a legend with the organized crime guys."

"Whether I want it or not."

"Whatever. Look, Mr. Pellecchia, the New York task force also knew that Nicholas Cuccia would make a move on you for breaking his jaw."

"And they didn't do a thing to stop it," Charlie said. "They allowed me and my wife to wiggle on a hook like bait. If you're trying to endear me to your cause, you're doing a lousy job."

"It's not like that."

"Where's he staying?" Charlie asked.

"You don't want to go there. Forget it."

"Let's put it this way," Charlie said. "I don't like to wiggle."

Chapter 19

THE LAST TIME CHARLIE saw John Denton was after his wife had confessed her affair two years earlier. His wife's admission back then had devastated him. It was an emotional upheaval Charlie wasn't prepared for.

His first reaction back then was to stalk Denton the following day. His wife's lover had been in New York on a business trip. Charlie found him leaving The Palm Too steak house. He approached the attorney while Denton attempted to hail a taxi on Second Avenue.

"You know who I am?" Charlie had asked.

Denton stuttered a few times before he could answer. "Yes," he finally said. "I know you. I know who you are."

"Good. You and Lisa decide what you want to do and do it. But I don't want it in my face. Keep it out of my house and off of my telephone. Understand?"

"Yes. Of course. Sure."

Charlie had wanted to hit his wife's lover, but he didn't. He pointed to a taxi on the next block instead. "Why don't you get yourself a cab before I shove you in front of one," he had said.

Ten minutes after his first encounter with Denton, Charlie felt stupid for what he had said. It had been a reaction of jealousy and anger he couldn't control.

Now he was about to meet with Denton a second time. He wasn't sure how he would react. He was nervous as he walked the length of the hospital hallway.

Before Charlie could think about it anymore, Denton was standing outside the room. Neither man offered the other a handshake.

"How is she?" Charlie asked.

"Bad. They knocked out a tooth. The dentist pulled another two. She'll need a bridge."

"Can I see her?"

"She's in recovery."

"Did she tell the police anything?"

"Nothing. She's afraid. She's very afraid. For you, too."

Charlie let an uncomfortable moment pass. "There was an agent came to see me today," he said.

"FBI?"

"DEA. Did he come here?"

"Not yet."

It was an awkward moment for both of them. Finally Denton said, "I'm sorry."

Charlie ignored the apology. "Tell her to give me a call when she can talk," he said.

"I'll give you three hundred," Vincent Lano told the gun dealer. He was pointing at a Smith & Wesson .380 on the display table.

The gun dealer, a fat, middle-aged man with a heavy beard, took a deep breath. "I can't give it to you with bullets for that price," he said.

"That's okay," Lano said. "I'm not done yet."

He added a Baretta .9 and a used .38 snub-nosed revolver. The snub-nose was the same type of weapon Lano had made his first hit with thirty-one years ago.

He had booked himself a room at a motel just outside of Las Vegas. He spent most of his first day in broken sleep and gazing out the window at the mountains. When he finally slept soundly, Lano had dreamed about his death.

He had the five thousand dollars he stole from Cuccia plus the fifteen hundred he had originally brought to Las Vegas. He guessed he had enough money to live in the desert at least another month.

Except now he was no longer sure he wanted to live another month.

When he saw the advertisement for a local gun show, Lano decided it was an omen. He would use some of the money to purchase a few weapons. Then he would spend another night at the motel on the edge of the desert. If his lungs permitted, he thought he might even get drunk.

When he was finished picking out his handguns, the gun dealer said, "Is there anything else I can interest you in?"

Lano looked up and down the rows of tables. The gun show was being held inside the tennis bubble of a local high school. He saw everything from assault weapons to swords on the tables. He saw military camouflage outfits, army boots, parachutes, and catalogs for missile launchers. He wondered what the hell anybody would do with a missile launcher.

He pointed at one on the cover of a military catalog. "Who buys those things?"

"Tell you the truth, I don't know," the gun dealer said. "Except we're supposed to report it when somebody asks for one."

Lano was curious. "Ever sell one?"

The gun dealer shook his head. "Not a missile launcher, no." He leaned across the table to whisper. "Grenades, yes. A few. A few mines, too. Claymores, I sold two of those. But never a missile launcher."

Lano smiled at the gun dealer. "Grenades?"

Francone joined Cuccia by the windows looking out over the pool. Both men leaned against the glass to better view the women lounging around the pool. Cuccia used binoculars.

"You believe the protocol?" he asked Francone. "They send me a fuckin' mouthpiece instead of one of our own."

"That guy, Fein, right? Yeah, I didn't like him either. He seemed like a real smart-ass, you know. Like he was better than me."

Cuccia followed a short woman in a pink thong bikini as she walked behind the far end of the pool with a drink in her hand. "All Fein wanted was his five grand," Cuccia said. "My uncle said the guy running things out here don't come out of his hole. Lives like a hermit to stay off the cameras. Pro'bly has guys like Fein to run his business errands."

"You do what you gotta do," Francone said.

Cuccia pulled the binoculars away from his face. "Speaking of which," he said. "This guy, Fein . . . he ever do what I just give him five grand to do? Except for that single fuckin' tooth, I don't have a clue why I paid him."

"Everything went fine. Except for Lano. The Pellecchia broad was where they told us she went. The guy broke your jaw they served up on a dish. Fein was the one brought the guy over to us at the construction site."

"So they did the right thing?"

"Vinnie took off with their money," Francone said. "It was wrong. Besides the other shit he said and did."

Cuccia rubbed at his crotch as he watched another woman in a tiny bikini giggling in the shallow end of the pool. Three men surrounded her. "Fuckin' waste, you ask me," he said, peering through the binoculars again. "Imagine having all this trim around and all you can do is lay low? Forget about it. I'll take my fuckin' chances. There's no way I ignore this, I'm a skipper out here."

Francone noticed the time. "What do we do about Lano?"

Cuccia was watching the short woman in the pink thong again. She was leaning forward. Her breasts were perfect balls of flesh beneath the thin pink top. He rubbed his crotch a second time.

"Jesus Christ," he said. "The talent parading around this place would make me crazy, I lived here." He turned to face Francone. "What about Lano?"

"The guy's a pain in the ass. We should whack him. We shoulda whacked him as soon as you got upped."

"What happened?" Cuccia asked again, annoyed he had to repeat the question.

"First of all, he wanted me to fugazy a tooth for you. He wanted me to go to a fuckin' dentist, you can believe it. He thought we were goin' too far goin' after the broad. Everything we did was goin' too far for Lano."

"He said that?"

"He said a lotta things, boss. A lotta things."

Cuccia held his best angry stare. He had practiced the stare in mirrors for years before being made.

"Subversive?" he asked.

Francone scratched his chin unconsciously before looking away. "All negative," he said. "Yeah, like I said back in New York. He ain't takin' to the changes."

"Don't beep him no more."

"What's the use? I stopped since last night. He's either gone or dead from those cigarettes he smokes all day and night."

"If he ain't dead, he will be. That's yours. Soon as we locate him, get our money back, you can take him out."

Francone grinned.

"I may have something else for you," Cuccia continued. He watched as a tall blond man joined the woman in the pink thong. "Tony Rizzi is coming out to join us. He thinks he's ready to make his bones. I think he's starting to pull back on his money. If I don't read where this cocksucker Pellecchia is found dead by tomorrow morning, maybe you take Rizzi and take care of everything before we leave."

Francone looked puzzled. "Rizzi?"

Cuccia frowned through the pain in his jaw. A large man blocked his view of the woman he was watching. "You set Rizzi up. You make him feel good about himself. Like he's in, you know. Bring him along, pump him up. Then you can whack Rizzi when we get back to New York. He's starting to hold back his cash anyway. What good is he without that? We're better off we get rid of him instead of squeeze him. We squeeze him, he might talk. He was a score. The score's over. We'll see what he brings out here with him. You bring him with you to get Pellecchia. Let him do it, you think he's got the balls, except I wouldn't count on it."

Cuccia wiped drool from the corners of his mouth. "Hey, you pull it off, this Pellecchia prick and Rizzi when we get back home, I'll bring it to my uncle. I'll see I can't get you made without waiting around the rest of your life."

A smile crossed Francone's face. Cuccia shot him a wink before he looked down at the pool again. The big man had moved. Cuccia could see the woman in the pink thong again.

"The things I could do with that," he said.

Francone scouted the men at the pool for muscle competition. He focused on one guy who was huge. "Steroid freak," he said.

"Huh?"

"The guy down there. He's juiced."

Cuccia furrowed his eyebrows. "Oh, Joey, you got nothin' better to look at down there?"

Chapter 20

JERRY LERCASI FIXED HIS grip on an Olympic bar as he lay on the bench under the weight. He sucked in air as he tightened his grip. He gasped loudly and pushed the bar off the rack. He steadied the weight before lowering it and blew out air as he pushed the bar from his chest. He did it again and again, in slow, measured repetitions, before reracking the bar.

"Morning, Hercules," Detective Albert Iandolli said.

Lercasi was wiping sweat from his forehead with a Vive la Body hand towel. He looked up from the bench to frown at the organized crime detective.

"The steroids do anything for your dick?" Iandolli asked.

Lercasi stood up from the bench. He was a few inches shorter than the detective. His body was well defined with muscle. He made a point of flexing his biceps as he wiped sweat from his neck with the hand towel.

Iandolli pointed at the Olympic bar. "How much is on there?"

"Three-fifteen," Lercasi said. His voice was rough. "You wanna give it a try?"

Iandolli shrugged. "What's the point, Jerr? You get all beefed up like that and somebody puts two behind your ear someday, like Benny Bensognio. You're as dead as a ninety-pound weakling would be, no?"

"You got a point," Lercasi said. "This a social call, or you want to join? We're running a special for city employees this month. A third off on a year."

Iandolli sat on the bench as Lercasi added weight to the bar. "Cute, Jerr. You're a funny guy. Except I have a situation came up the past few days I'm concerned about."

"My attorney already spoke to the police about Mr. Bensognio," Lercasi said. "I knew the man casually. I had no idea he was a bookmaker. I never placed a bet in my life. In fact, I was at a private dinner last night with two City Council members. If I'm not mistaken, some snoopy reporter was there and took pictures. I live in Las Vegas because of a respiratory condition. I have no idea why anyone would want to kill Mr. Bensognio. I sent flowers to his funeral out of respect for his wife and children. I'm sure this is a terrible time for them."

"He was probably skimming off your book operation," Iandolli said. "But Benny isn't why I'm here. Some guy and his wife were assaulted. They're from New York. Know anything about it?"

"Why would I know something about that?"

"I don't know. Except the guy was assaulted at the Palermo construction site. One of the workers there found him behind the model."

Lercasi stopped adding weight. "Are you serious?"

"As a heart attack. That's your turf, Jerr, the Palermo. And that's a big no-no, assaulting tourists on their vacation. Even if it is mob-related."

"What's mob-related? What the hell does that mean?"

"Right. Anyway, just so happens, a couple of the boys are in from New York the same day the unlucky couple were assaulted."

"Couple of the boys? I don't know any boys."

"You know, Jerr. That dumb-ass fraternity you're involved in that don't exist? The one where they rat on each other every time one of them gets busted? The one they made all those movies about?"

Lercasi continued adding weight to the Olympic bar.

"How much you got on there now?" Iandolli asked.

"Three-thirty."

"I wanna watch. You mind?"

Lercasi lay on the bench, took his grip, took a few deep breaths, and grunted as he lifted the bar from the rack. He brought the bar down to his chest slowly. He set the bar on his chest, held it a split second, then grunted as he pushed the bar up. He lifted the weight two more times before reracking the weights. When he sat back up on the bench, he was breathing hard.

"That really give you a woody?"

"You made your point," Lercasi said through gasps of breath.

"Good. Because if this Palermo thing comes back to you, my friend, you'll be lifting your weights inside the joint."

Lercasi wiped himself with the towel. "I don't know nothin' about it."

Iandolli mocked gasping for breath, as if he were about to lift the bar himself. "But I bet you'll ask around now, won't you," he said, squeezing the words from his lungs.

Lercasi picked up a ten-pound plate to add to one end of the bar.

Iandolli let out a long mock exhale of breath.

Charlie decided to tell Samantha what was going on. He told her about the fight in the New York nightclub and about his wife being mugged. Samantha flinched when Charlie described what had happened to Lisa.

"My God," she said.

"She's been in and out of surgery."

They were sitting at the kitchen table. Samantha was wearing white shorts and a navy blue blouse. Charlie wore gray Dockers and a maroon polo shirt. He had brought a navy sports jacket for dinner later. The roommate, Carol, was taking a shower.

"What does the DEA want?" Samantha asked.

"Who knows? Except I don't trust them. Not their motives. The guy I met was making a deal for the creep who assaulted Lisa." He lit a cigarette. "I wasn't sure if I should come here. I'm still not sure I should stay."

"Are you feeling guilty about your wife? Be honest."

He took one of Samantha's hands. "It's not about Lisa."

She tried to smile. "I like you, Charlie. But I don't want to get involved where I don't belong."

"It's not about Lisa."

Samantha nodded. "He said you were safe, the agent, right?"

"It seemed more important to him that I didn't go to the police," Charlie said. "He was much more concerned about his gangster than me."

Samantha took one of his cigarettes. "I haven't done this in five years," she said. She examined the cigarette a moment before sliding it back inside the pack. "Not even a filter?"

"And I didn't start smoking until I was thirty. How's that for stupid?"

"Pretty stupid. What are you going to do?"

"I'll stay away if that's what you want. It's why I'm telling you all this. You need to know. Obviously I don't want anything to come back here, to you."

"That's so unfair. No, I don't want you to do that. Why would they come after me? No, that's ridiculous."

"I was hoping you'd say that."

They held each other's hands. Samantha took a deep breath. She asked, "Did you get to see her?"

"She was in recovery."

"Are you going back to the hospital later?"

He could sense she was still concerned about how he felt about his wife. He shook his head.

"It was a little uncomfortable," he said. He told her about John Denton and the history of his wife's affair. Samantha seemed somewhat relieved.

"I'm not going back," he said.

Samantha took another deep breath. "I feel like the walls are closing in."

"I'm not pressuring you, Sam. I understand how you feel."

She reached for the cigarettes again. This time she lit one. She took a deep drag on the cigarette and coughed. "It's like breathing fire."

"You're cute when you cough."

She continued to cough. "I'll bet." She put the cigarette out in the ashtray. "Aren't you afraid to go home?" she asked. "To New York."

"I haven't thought about that. I guess I want to believe it's over.

They wanted me, they got me. What the DEA agent said. Not that I trust him any farther than I can throw him. But I'm not going to the police."

An uncomfortable pause followed. He wanted to hold her. He wanted to kiss her.

He asked her if he could have an ice water. He watched her move around the kitchen. Her leg muscles flexed as she stood up on her toes to reach for a glass. Charlie looked up her legs to the hem of her shorts.

She turned to him. "Get it all in?"

He felt himself blush under his bruises. "I didn't think it was that obvious."

"Well?"

He looked down at a bruise on the top of his right hand. "Sorry," he said.

"Don't be," Samantha said as she smiled.

He could fall in love with that smile.

When she brought him the glass, she sat on his lap and kissed him lightly on his lips. She removed his sunglasses and kissed him again, harder this time.

"Ouch," he said.

They made love as soon as Carol was gone. They had stood at the door and waved to Carol as she pulled away from the curb. Then Samantha closed the door as Charlie took her into his arms. Their kisses were passionate. They never made it to the bedroom.

They did it on the couch the first time. Samantha was vocal during their lovemaking. Charlie was more focused. They each wanted the other too much to engage in foreplay. When they were finished, they lay exhausted on the floor at the foot of the couch. Samantha cuddled against his chest.

"I wanted to do that since last night," she said.

"Me, too," he said.

"It was nice."

Charlie glanced down. He said, "We need more time before we can do it again."

Samantha poked him. "What do you mean 'we,' Kimosabe?"

It was slower and more deliberate in the bedroom. Samantha guided Charlie to where she wanted him. She pulled at his hair when she was close. She moaned loudly when she reached climax. Then she took over and brought Charlie back so they could both enjoy each other a third time.

They napped in Samantha's bed afterward. When they woke up, they were both hungry.

"How's the Chinese food in Las Vegas?" he asked.

"Fine," she said. "You want to order in?"

"That's what I was thinking. My treat."

"Big spender, huh?"

He kissed her on the forehead. "I have to check out tomorrow."

Samantha frowned. "You going home?"

"Unless you don't want me to."

"I don't want you to."

Chapter 21

Detective Gold approached Officer Michael Wilkes in the parking lot of the Denny's alongside the MGM Grand on Las Vegas Boulevard. Wilkes was out of uniform, on his way home after a ten-hour shift. Gold's shift had hardly ended from the day before. Except for a few cat-naps, the senior detective was living on caffeine one more time.

"Mike, we need to talk about something," Gold told the officer after sipping black coffee from a container.

Wilkes was about to open the door of his car. He turned around and leaned against it instead. He took Gold's right hand in his own to shake. "Sure, what's up?" Wilkes asked.

"Jennifer Gentry," Gold said, getting right to it.

Wilkes's face turned to stone. "Who?"

"Detective Gentry's wife. I know you're seeing her. I watched you embrace half a block from her office. I know what it's about, so let's skip the denial part of this."

Wilkes's face showed defeat. He licked his bottom lip as he shook his head. "It's one of those things," he said. "I don't know what to say."

"I'm not here to chastise you for falling in love or for getting a piece on the side," Gold said. "That's your business. And hers. But you gotta realize what you're playing with here before it explodes in your face. In all our faces. Gentry is a detective. He's a fellow cop. To go one further, not that it really makes a difference, but he's also my ex-partner's son. His marriage problems aren't my concern except for what could happen if it gets out of hand. I don't know how long you're involved with his wife, but he's aware of it. You should take this into consideration. He's aware his wife is cheating. He might not know who you are yet, but he knows there's somebody."

"You gonna tell him?" Wilkes asked.

Wilkes's concerns were justifiably selfish. Gold liked that. It was a good sign. Maybe it would deter some of what was going on. At least it might put a pause on the affair while the married couple separated or divorced.

"Not who you are, no. But I'm also going to talk to his wife now. Right from here. If she's gonna leave Gentry, she should do it already."

"She says she wants to."

"What about you and your wife?"

"We're split up already. Almost a year now."

Gold nodded. "Well, I just thought you should be aware of what's going on. And don't think you'll find friends inside the department this ever comes out the wrong way. There isn't a good way to handle this, but there sure is a wrong way. Use your head, whatever you do."

Half an hour later, Gold was at the home of Detective Donald Gentry, where he knew he would find the detective's wife alone. He rang the bell twice before she answered. Her face told him she already knew what he was there for.

"I'm sure Mike Wilkes called you," Gold said.

Jennifer Gentry didn't answer.

"I'm not here to threaten you," Gold said. "Your husband asked me to look into who's having an affair with his wife. He knows about it. You weren't careful with your diaphragm gel, for one thing."

Gold waited for a response. When there wasn't one, he said, "I won't bullshit you, Jennifer. My concern is for your husband. You know who his father was. I'm advising you to either separate or divorce or get some counseling or whatever. But do something now, before something worse than a divorce happens. I've seen it before with cops. It can get ugly."

"Am I supposed to be grateful about this?" she asked.

"No," Gold said. "You're supposed to smarten up."

It was the kind of thing he hated, getting involved in a marital crisis, but he saw it as the best possible chance to keep the situation from becoming violent.

"I'll talk to Donald," Jennifer Gentry said.

Gold nodded and she closed the door on him.

Officer Michael Wilkes told Allen Fein they would have to make different arrangements to meet in the future. They were standing at a pay telephone in a minimall on the Strip. Fein made believe he was talking into the receiver. Wilkes made believe he was waiting for the phone.

"There's another cop watching me," Wilkes said. "About a woman I'm seeing. Some other cop's wife. I have to lay low for a while."

Fein turned away from Wilkes. He spoke loudly into the receiver. "That's up to you, Officer," he said. "Maybe the cop's wife isn't worth it. In the meantime, do you have anything on the blotter?"

Wilkes was still thinking about Jennifer Gentry. He was in love with her. He didn't like it that Fein referred to her in so casual a manner.

"The name you gave me didn't show," he told Fein. "Not even at the Hertz in the airport."

"You checked with the organized crime unit?"

"I'm not in the organized crime unit. I asked a friend with O.C. He said he never heard of this Lano."

"You sure?"

"I couldn't go in and ask like it was my business. I asked my friend about the name you gave me. Lano. I told him there was a guy from New York looking to sell something. I said I got it from a kid I picked up driving a stolen car yesterday. My friend never heard of him."

Fein turned away from Wilkes. "What about that thing at the Palermo? There a police report or not?"

"Nothing."

"And you're sure about Lano?"

"The guy's name hasn't come up. How many times you want to hear me say it?"

Fein hung up. When he stepped away, Wilkes could see the familiar manila envelope. "That's yours," Fein said.

Wilkes looked around as he stepped up to the phone. He cradled the receiver against his neck as he tucked the envelope into his rear pants pocket. He fished change from his front pants pocket and dropped it in the coin slot. He dialed Jennifer Gentry's home number as he watched Fein drive away in a black BMW convertible.

"Jenn?" he asked when someone picked up. "It's me."

Whoever picked up wasn't answering.

Wilkes quickly hung up. He leaned into the phone until his head was touching the receiver. He closed his eyes tightly and felt a wave of panic rushing through his body.

Chapter 22

IT WAS NEARLY MIDNIGHT before Agent Thomas could talk to Cuccia in private. The New York gangster was standing at a roulette table watching the action among a group of Asians playing a fifty-dollar-minimum game. Thomas noticed that Cuccia was shuffling two black chips in his hands.

"Those fakes, or you just afraid to bet them?" Thomas asked.

Cuccia smirked when he saw it was the agent. "I was wondering what happened to you."

"What's up?"

"You'd know, you were doing your job," Cuccia said. He leaned over to watch a middle-aged Asian woman push five green chips onto the number fourteen.

Thomas watched the croupier spin the roulette wheel. "No more bets," the croupier announced.

"I never understood that," Thomas said. He pointed at the roulette wheel. "It's like a bazaar. Everything is a long shot."

"No guts, no glory," Cuccia said.

Thomas waited until the ball was bouncing on the wheel before he leaned into Cuccia again. "I found out why you're here."

Cuccia ignored the remark.

Thomas spotted drool in the corner of Cuccia's mouth. He dabbed at it with a napkin. "You're dribbling."

The gangster was startled. He stepped away from Thomas. "The fuck is wrong with you?"

"Who was the short guy with Francone this afternoon?"

"You tell me."

"An emissary to Jerry Lercasi?"

"Who's Jerry Lercasi?"

"Yeah, right."

"Double zero, green," the croupier announced as he set the marker on the number at the top of the board.

Both men watched the croupier take down the losing bets before paying the winners.

"I spoke to Charlie Pellecchia," Thomas said.

Cuccia's face tensed for a moment. "Who's Charlie Pellecchia?"

"Charlie Opera. The guy broke your face for grabbing his wife's ass."

"Charlie who?"

"It's what the organized crime unit nicknamed him. The guy cracked your jaw. Charlie Opera. O.C. was in the nightclub when you caught that beating."

Cuccia forced a smirk. "Ever hear of Pearl Harbor? The guy japped me."

Thomas took another glance around the casino. "I don't know. I just met the guy. He's a pretty big boy."

"You're needling me. What's the point?"

"Nothing can happen to Mr. Pellecchia. I want to make that clear."

"Please," Cuccia said. "Trust me, I've got better things to do." He pointed to his watch. "In ten minutes I have a date," he said. "You should give it a try. It's legal here in Nevada."

"I'm serious, fuckwad," Thomas said. "Or your deal gets flushed."

"Fuckwad?"

"You understand me?"

Cuccia forced himself to chuckle. "Flushed?" he said. "Like down the same shitter where I was born?"

Charlie couldn't sleep. He slipped on his pants and shirt and found his way back into the kitchen. He thought about calling his wife and her lover to see if the DEA agent had contacted them yet but decided to check for messages first.

When he called his room at Harrah's, he found he had several messages, all hang-ups. He replayed them and counted fifteen in total.

A few days had passed since the assaults on him and his wife. If the mob really wanted him, Charlie figured he didn't stand much of a chance, regardless of any promise the DEA agent had made.

He decided to find Nicholas Cuccia. He used a phone book and started with the most expensive hotels. When the operator at the Bellagio told him to hold for the connection, Charlie hung up.

This time Daria was wearing a white body suit with black high heels. She was racing from a line of cocaine she had just shared with Nicholas Cuccia. She told him that her usual partner, Kim, was recovering from a bachelor party at the Mirage the night before.

"How many guys?" he asked. He wiped a spill of drool from his chin.

"Ten," she said. "But there's always two or three more once you get there. The service knows it, but they let it slide. Especially when a girl is working solo."

His condition required an extra moment to process the information. When it registered, Cuccia was impressed. "Solo? She gonna do ten guys by herself?"

Daria took a large gulp of vodka from a highball glass. Her eyes required a moment to focus. "Not all the guys will want to do anything," she said as she shook her head. "Maybe half. Sometimes more. Hey, if it pays enough, why not? That's the business."

Cuccia sipped vodka from his own glass. "I guess so."

She laid out another line of cocaine on a small mirror. "What you do is a few of these. And you work fast. It's over before you know it."

He wiped vodka from his chin.

"Is your mouth okay, honey?" she asked.

Cuccia didn't hear her question. He was picturing the blonde, Kim, taking on a line of men at the bachelor party.

"You're smart to call the service," Daria said. "There's been a lot of rollings going on."

"Rolling? What, like joints?"

Daria giggled. "Like johns, silly. The girls cruising the casino bars. They put their johns to sleep and rip them off."

He touched one of her nipples through the sheer body suit.

"Mmmmm," Daria said. "You about ready, hon?"

The cocaine was numbing. "I don't know," he said. "I can't feel my dick."

Daria giggled again. "I can help you with that," she said as she reached down to fondle him. "You like that?"

His eyes were struggling to focus. "Like what?"

It was very early in the morning when Lano left his hotel room. He took a long glimpse of the sun rising over the mountains before heading for Valley Hospital, where he had located Lisa Pellecchia in room 2116.

He brought the weapons he had purchased at the gun show with him. Two of the guns remained in the car, along with the hand grenade. He had paid a total of twenty-six hundred dollars for the tiny arsenal. A Smith & Wesson .380 was well concealed in a tightly fitted ankle holster.

Lano felt a need to absolve himself for the assault of Lisa Pellecchia. It had been one more mistake in a life full of mistakes. Although the assault was something Lano never wanted any part of, he had allowed himself to go along with it. His conditions for taking part in the assault made him sick now. They were cheap.

"I'll stand guard, but I'm not touching that broad," he had told Joey Francone.

He could have stopped Francone. He should have stopped him.

The more he thought about the entire fiasco, the angrier Lano was with himself. He couldn't respect anybody who would hit a woman, much less the likes of Cuccia or Francone.

Going after the husband also had been wrong. The guy had defended his wife. Who could blame him?

If it had been Lano's wife, Cuccia would be dead.

Lano found his way down a short hallway to an elevator. He took the elevator up one flight. He followed a sign with room numbers the length of another hallway. He stood outside 2116 and immediately felt uncomfortable. A man he guessed was Lisa Pellecchia's boyfriend sat beside her bed. The man glanced up at Lano and quickly stood.

Lano held both his hands up. "I just want to talk," he said. "Just talk."

Chapter 23

THEY WERE BOTH SITTING up in bed having their coffee. It was still early in the morning. Samantha set her cup on the night table as she told Charlie more about herself and her family.

Both her parents were still alive. She had an older sister teaching high school back in North Dakota, but they didn't speak. She had tried to stay in touch with her family, but they were upset with her for leaving them.

"Sometimes it's hard for parents to let go," he told her.

"What about your sons?" she asked.

"I didn't raise them myself," he said. "They both lived with their mother. I came around once a week. I bought them lunch or baseball gloves or tickets to a rock concert. They were out of the house before I knew it. Before I was married to Lisa. Next thing I knew, they were both in and out of college and doing their own thing. Sometimes I feel guilty about it, not being there, but they're both good kids. They turned out fine."

She leaned against his shoulder. "Sometimes I miss my family," she said. "I don't think they care, though. Not really."

"I do."

It was a simple two-word statement, but it meant the world to her then. She hugged him.

"Tell me your favorite opera," she said.

"Huh?"

"Your favorite opera. What is it?"

"There are a lot. *Don Giovanni. Rigoletto. Tosca.* One of those three. *Le Nozze di Figaro.* I get chills from the Mozart overtures. Then there are the German operas. *Fidelio, Tristan, Der Rosenkavalier, The Flying Dutchman.* I could go on and on about this, you know. I warn you."

She laughed. "I can see."

"When you get to arias, though, that's another story," Charlie continued. "Then it's Puccini. 'Recondita armonia,' from *Tosca,* is probably my favorite favorite, but that's because I'm a romantic at heart. Then there's 'Nessum dorma,' from *Turandot,* 'Che gelida manina,' from *Bohème.* All Puccini. The 'Improviso' from *André Chénier* is a good one, too. And 'Una furtiva làgrima.'"

Samantha was smiling at him.

"What?" he asked.

"Are there any about a bartender who meets a guy who was just dumped by his wife?"

"The one where the mob's chasing him?"

"But the mob leaves him alone because of a DEA agent."

"I don't know about that DEA agent. He could turn out to be one of the bad guys."

Samantha rolled her eyes. "Work with me, Charlie. I was hoping for a happy ending."

Carol packed her laptop inside her shoulder bag. She brought an extra change of clothes for the suitcase she kept in the trunk of her car. She wasn't sure whether Beau had really found her yet, but she wasn't taking chances.

She would run if she needed to run. She could always start over in some other location. If she were just being paranoid about Beau, Carol would return to the apartment after work and continue to handle her situation one day at a time.

She also didn't want to upset her best friend. Things seemed to be going well for Samantha and her new boyfriend. Carol knew Charlie had slept over. She had felt in their way at the apartment and left for work early again.

If anything, Carol could pick up a few more hours of overtime. She knew that sooner or later the extra money would come in handy.

As she worked the breakfast rush, Carol wondered if she would ever see her friend Samantha again. If Beau showed at the diner, she would have to run from Las Vegas the way she had run from New Orleans and Chicago.

If Beau were more careful this time, Carol also knew she might die in Las Vegas.

He still had a few hours before he would have to check out of the hotel. His flight was scheduled to leave today, but Charlie already knew he was staying an extra few days. He recognized the signs for what they were. He was falling for Samantha.

He decided to take a room at another hotel for the sake of security. If the mob was still after him, he didn't want to lead them to Samantha. They had already gone after one woman in his life.

He took a long walk with Samantha through her neighborhood. He let her lead as he whistled a few overtures and arias from different operas to impress her. She joked about how they would soon be surrounded by all the dogs in Las Vegas.

They were walking for about twenty minutes when a black sports car raced up alongside them. The brakes squealed as it came to a stop. An Asian teenager leaned out of the window, made a gun out of his right hand, and pointed at Charlie.

"Bang-bang," he said. "You dead, white boy."

Chapter 24

ALLEN FEIN WAS CRAVING fast food as he convinced himself that everything was copacetic. It had become his routine whenever he engineered a small score behind Jerry Lercasi's back. The rush of victory was quickly followed by a few days of nervousness, during which he would live on fast food and stomach medication. It would take a week or two before he would dare look for the next freelance project.

He thought about making a present of his masseuse to Lercasi. Fein was sure that one or two sessions with his Asian masseuse were all his boss would need before she was hired. The idea of irritating Lercasi's girlfriend at the gym brought a smile to his face.

"Poor fucking Brenda," he said as he pulled into a McDonald's.

Renato Freni sat in a booth across from Jerry Lercasi in a Chinese restaurant in downtown Las Vegas. He told the mob boss about his situation with a bad contract from out of town. A tall, thin Asian woman in blue dungarees and a red T-shirt set a place mat. Freni nodded at her.

"Thanks, hon," he said. "Just get me a Diet Coke."

Lercasi was stirring noodles into his wonton soup. He blew at a spoonful of the hot soup before sucking it off the spoon. He waited until the Asian woman brought the Diet Coke for Freni before speaking.

"You're a lucky motherfucker," Lercasi said. He dipped at the hot mustard with a few dry noodles before popping them into his mouth.

Freni nodded. "Yeah, I know."

"You hungry?"

"No, thanks."

"You sure?"

"Thanks, really, no." Freni raised his Diet Coke to salute Lercasi. "I was to write a script, nobody'd ever believe it."

Lercasi shook his head. "I wouldn't. Two times in two days?"

"I'm either lucky or stupid."

"The real issue is your contract," Lercasi said. "And why it didn't come to my attention before today."

Freni took another swig of his Diet Coke. He wiped his mouth with a paper napkin. "No offense intended. But I won't deal with buffers. Not in my business."

Lercasi nodded as he sprinkled a few more fried noodles on his soup. "I can respect that," he said. "Still, you could've asked for a sit with me. You should've asked for a sit with me."

"This one came from pretty high up," Freni said. "I had to assume it was approved."

"Anthony Cuccia in New York," Lercasi said. "Except nobody in New York has juice out here. Not without me. And I have a cousin back there to remind them they forget the fact. I don't like it, New York or anybody else comes to my town and pulls shit without I know about it." He scooped up some of the soup-soaked noodles with his spoon.

"Still. I had to assume—"

Lercasi held up one hand as he rolled the hot noodles around his mouth before swallowing. "Please. Don't insult me. The old man went directly to you to avoid coming to me."

"We go back a long way, me and Anthony Cuccia," Freni said. "We came up together."

"I can respect that, too."

"Nothing happened. If that's any consolation."

"What the fuck is this, a game show? I could make noise if I want. I know my options."

Freni remained silent. Lercasi said, "You know what they did to the woman, right?"

"Hard to believe. Somebody knocked out a tooth?"

"Harder to explain," Lercasi said. He refocused his attention on a dish of shrimp toast. He cut one in half with his fork. "And much harder to ignore. Between the media and the law. I already had one visit from a local O.C. detective. You're talkin' about Feds around this Pellecchia. I expect I'll hear from them, too."

He forked a chunk of the shrimp toast and dipped it in hot mustard. "I was thinking if this Pellecchia guy was to get whacked by one of our city's many ethnic gangs, something real sloppy like a drive-by, maybe it would divert some of the attention away from us." He slid the shrimp toast off the fork into his mouth.

"Or maybe the guy don't get whacked at all," Freni said. "That's even less attention."

Lercasi sipped Diet 7UP from a can. "Not necessarily," he said. "If Pellecchia does turn up dead, it proves the New York crew went ahead without following protocol. I can tax that, too, I want. It'd be clout on my end. We remind the rest of the country that Vegas ain't the place to air your dirty laundry. Maybe the old man in New York loses his nephew in the process."

"Mingada," Freni muttered. "That sounds like a war."

Lercasi cut another shrimp toast in half. "You sure you're not hungry? The gooks in this joint can cook."

"I'm not hungry, thanks."

Lercasi spoke while he chewed on another chunk of shrimp toast. "I don't intend to invade New York," he said. "So unless they want to bring it out here, I'm not too concerned about a war."

"You want me to turn the contract around?"

"Something like that," Lercasi said. "Things have been getting sloppy out here lately. You read about that guy skimming the books, right? People are too comfortable. Like whoever the fuck arranged this bullshit thing with the New York crew in the first place. People get comfortable, they think they know what they're doing. They get lucky, they get more stupid, they cause more problems."

"Benny Bensognio?"

Lercasi slurped soup from his spoon. "Nickel-and-dimer," he said.

"A guy loyal for a long time, got comfortable, decided he could steal. It's human nature."

"Pellecchia is scheduled to check out today," Freni said. "If you're serious about a drive-by. You'd have to do it in the fuckin' airport unless he spends another day playin' drums."

Lercasi shook his head. "Playin' drums. People got nothin' better to do."

"I'll pick it up if you want. I already got paid."

"Some of these gangs, they'd do it in a church. Drive-by, walk-by, what's the difference? I already got some people on it. From what I understand, they already made a pass but there was some broad in the way."

"Anything else?" Freni asked.

Lercasi shook his head as he cut off the tail of a fried shrimp. He forked the shrimp into his mouth and used a napkin to wipe his lips. He used a pen to write two names on the napkin. "I got another Benny," he said. "And somebody else."

Freni nodded.

Lercasi pushed the napkin across the table. His thumb covered one of the names. Freni read the other name to himself.

"The other one?" Freni asked.

"This mameluke from New York," Lercasi said as he removed his thumb. "The one causing all these problems bringing his personal shit out here."

"I met with him already," Freni said. "He's got a wired jaw, what it's all about."

Lercasi scratched his head. "He's a real jerk-off, I know. But he's also your friend's nephew."

Freni shook his head. "Not a problem. I live out here now."

"Good," Lercasi said. "Because home-field advantage can make all the difference in the world."

Freni used a match to burn the napkin in an ashtray. He waited until the ashes were black before he emptied them onto the floor and scattered them with his right foot.

"Okay," Lercasi said. "It was good talking."

Chapter 25

WHEN CAROL FELT THE knots in her stomach again, she was sure her husband was close. She studied the faces of every patron who walked through the door. She scanned the parking lot and as much of the street as she could see from the front door. When the manager yelled at her for leaving her station, Carol told him she was sick and needed to leave early.

"Excuse me?" the manager said. "What the hell do you think this is, lady? Leave early and don't bother coming back."

"Okay," Carol said as she headed for the small locker room.

"Okay what?" the manager asked.

"I won't come back," Carol said.

Abe Gold glanced at the organized crime report Albert Iandolli had prepared for him. Iandolli was on his knees, patting down fresh soil for a flowerbed alongside his driveway. His wife and two kids were in the backyard, having lunch.

He motioned toward his yard. "If you're hungry, Angie just cooked some franks," he said.

Gold looked away from the report. "No, thanks. I grabbed something on the way over."

Gold admired the house from the driveway. Iandolli had just finished painting a few weeks earlier. It was a light blue ranch on a quarter acre of neatly groomed land. The driveway was paved. A white wood fence surrounded the lot. It was a house Gold had always pictured himself living in.

"The place looks good," Gold said.

Iandolli stood up from his knees. "Thanks," he said. He slapped dirt off his pants. "I'm too old for this."

Gold scanned a fax copy of a New York organized crime attachment. It provided details and comments about Nicholas Cuccia's criminal record. A list of bookmaking charges starting from when Cuccia was twenty-two years old made up the bulk of the sheet. There was a separate notation about a two-year jail sentence for loan-sharking when Cuccia was in his late twenties.

He was arrested, but not convicted, a total of fourteen more times. The arrests included assaults and bookmaking exclusively. A special notation suggested the year it was believed Cuccia became a made member of the Vignieri crime family, 1992.

The report also provided the following personal notation:

Cuccia is married with no children. He has two known steady girl-friends. He frequents known prostitutes and uses escort services. Kinky sex? His hangouts include Scores and Pure Plantinum, two expensive strip clubs in New York. Confirmed cocaine and alcohol use.

Gold wondered why the kinky sex notation was followed with a question mark.

The rest of the report was commentary concerning Cuccia's illegal businesses. He was alleged to operate a large bookmaking office in New York run by lower-level associates. His latest business ventures included Internet pornography and offshore gambling.

"Lano and Francone are the two guys came in ahead of Cuccia," Iandolli said. He washed his hands with a garden hose. "Two days ahead out of Newark. We can thank the DEA for their names. Otherwise we'd have fifteen names to pick from."

On the last page of the report, Gold saw a name circled. The notation read: *Anthony Rizzi coming to Vegas.*

"This Anthony Rizzi is coming in when?" Gold asked.

"This morning, later tonight, early tomorrow morning. America West out of Kennedy. An overnight. He changed the flight twice already."

"What's that about?"

"Anthony Rizzi. A guy with so much money he got bored and bought his way into the mob as an associate. It doesn't say it on there, but I spoke to an O.C. guy in New York. They think Rizzi's coming here to make his bones. Maybe to whack Lano or to be a part of whacking Lano." Iandolli chuckled. "The thing is, this Lano, the guy they think is getting whacked, was diagnosed with terminal throat cancer. His partners in crime don't know it, but O.C. does. His doctor gave him a few months."

Gold looked confused. "Maybe they wanna put him out of his misery."

Iandolli shook his head. "Lano's a mustache to these kids," he said. "They're purging the old mobsters for morons like this Rizzi character, clowns who have nothing better to do with million-dollar businesses besides trying to act like tough guys."

"So this Rizzi guy isn't a real mobster then."

"New York calls him 'The Crier,'" Iandolli said. "They fucked with him one night, sent one of their guys to test his balls, man to man. An undercover cop cut him off on a street outside one of his warehouses or some shit. Rizzi cried, he was so scared. Their guy pinned him against his Mercedes, and Rizzi sprouted tears like a fountain. They nicknamed him 'The Crier.' Imagine having a mob name like that?"

Gold was still confused. "So what makes them think they're sending this Rizzi here to whack this other guy?"

"They're bleeding Rizzi for his business. They get a sucker like this on the line and they make him feel like a gangster until he's dry. They let him play with the big boys until they don't need him anymore. Then they cut him loose or whack him. It happens here, too. Happens anywhere there's a mob and suckers with money and no life. They find these guys like Rizzi and clean them out. New York thinks Cuccia is setting Rizzi up. He comes out to Vegas to supposedly make his bones and they wind up killing two birds with one stone."

"Lano and Rizzi," Gold said.

"Sooner or later."

"This guy Rizzi is worth that much?"

"Ten million or so, what his business is worth," Iandolli said. "His wife dumped him for another woman. New York thinks he's trying to be a tough guy ever since. He's buying his button into the mob, and these guys are more than happy to sell it to him. Ten million to these guys is like owning Microsoft."

"That's an expensive button, ten million," Gold said.

"The money should be the least of his problems," Iandolli said. "Once they have that, they won't need him."

Anthony Rizzi checked in at the registration desk at Caesar's Palace a few minutes after noon. Now he was exhausted. He was having conflicting feelings the past few nights about his adopted lifestyle. Rizzi needed a drink.

He rubbed the sleep from his eyes as his bags were wheeled on a cart being pulled by a valet. He followed the valet through the casino to a long marble hallway with high-priced stores on either side. He noticed the number of Asian women in the walkways and wondered if he might lure one into his bed before he left Las Vegas.

He left several messages with the front desk at the Bellagio for both Nicholas Cuccia and Joey Francone. He spent the next ten minutes dressing. He spent the following twenty minutes combing his hair. It lay in a perfect left-to-right swirl, covering the large bald spot on the top of his head.

He was a short, fat man with very light skin, puffy cheeks, and dark blue eyes. His mother was German-Irish. His father was Dutch-Italian. He had concocted a long, involved story about his last name. Mostly, he denied his mother's side of the family and his father's Dutch mother.

After painstakingly grooming himself, Rizzi spent the next hour on the Cleopatra Barge with a tall Asian prostitute who called herself Niko. He had spotted her and another prostitute, a tall blonde in a red-sequin dress, earlier. Both women had propositioned him as a team, but Rizzi told the blonde he could only handle one at a time today and that he was kind of looking forward to an Asian broad because it had always been a fantasy of his to "eat a noodle."

The prostitutes had both giggled while they huddled a few seconds before breaking up. The blonde left Rizzi to negotiate with his fantasy date.

"Let's just say I'm a businessman," he told the prostitute when she asked what he did for a living.

"What kind of business?" Niko asked. She had a slight Asian accent. She was swirling a plastic straw in her white wine spritzer. She licked at the straw just before Rizzi answered her question.

"Little of this and a little of that," he told her.

"You sound very mysterious to me," she said. She sipped her spritzer carefully. She set the glass back down on the napkin as she sat back in her chair.

The cleavage showing from her low-cut blouse caught Rizzi's eye. "You're a very beautiful woman," he told her.

"Sank you. Also very espensive."

"I'll bet," he said as he took a sip of Absolut.

He figured Niko was worth five hundred for the night, but he'd go as high as seven-fifty.

"You ever stay here before?" he asked.

"Overnight? Yes, of course."

"Do you have a change of clothes?"

"No, silly. That would be your present to me."

"That depends on where you buy them."

"Gift store," she said. "Sweatshirt, T-shirt. I have underwear in my purse."

Rizzi gave a quick glance at the purse on her lap. "In your purse, huh?" he asked. "What else you got in there?"

"Condoms," Niko said. "Lipstick. Advil. K-Y Jelly. Tums. I have sensitive tummy."

"Ah, so you swallow."

The prostitute suppressed a giggle. "If you are generous," she said. "Yes, I do that."

Chapter 26

THE GUY AT THE hospital told John Denton he could go to the police or to the woman's husband or he could forget the whole thing. The guy had given him the information. It was up to Denton to decide what to do next. The guy had said his name was Vincent Lano. He was the same man who had held the gun on Denton at the motel. He had told Denton that he was ashamed of what he had participated in. He apologized for what had happened to Lisa.

Denton had frowned at the man. His apology wouldn't change anything.

Now he was struggling with the information he possessed. Lisa deserved to know what was going on. So did her husband. So did the Las Vegas police.

Denton couldn't talk to Lisa in the condition she was in. He didn't want to talk to her husband, and he was afraid to talk to the police. The fact that he was an attorney and was legally bound to report a crime made the problem all the more daunting.

Because the mob was involved, Denton avoided calling the police. He decided to talk with Charlie first.

He called Harrah's and was disappointed when nobody picked up. He left a message on voice mail:

Charlie, this is John. I'm at Valley Hospital with Lisa. A man came here today with information about what happened to you and Lisa. He gave me the names of the people responsible. I'll wait for your call. I'm not sure if I should call the police. I don't know if calling the police will make it more dangerous for Lisa. Please get back to me as soon as possible.

He added the bit about it possibly being more dangerous for Lisa if he called the police to protect himself.

Then he felt guilty for worrying about his own problems while Lisa lay in a hospital bed on painkillers with a mouth full of stitches.

Then John Denton thought better of everything and called the police anyway. He asked to speak to a Detective Abe Gold.

Gina Iandolli suddenly appeared at the far end of the driveway. She stood at the gate of the fence blocking off the yard. She was a short, thin woman with long, dark hair. She wore a light blue housedress and white sneakers.

"You guys want something to eat?" she yelled. "I'm about to turn the grill off."

Gold waved to Gina from the driveway. "I have to run. Thanks anyway."

Gina waved back and disappeared behind the house.

Gold pointed toward the yard. "You're a lucky man," he told Iandolli.

"I know," Iandolli said.

Gold folded the report and started to stuff it inside his jacket pocket. "It's all right I hold on to these?"

"I don't know how much it'll help. In the meantime, I stopped by to rouse Jerry Lercasi."

"You think there's a chance Lercasi okayed this thing at the Palermo?"

"No way. That was an end run, if it had anything to do with his crew at all."

"Think you'll ever know for sure?"

Iandolli nodded. "Sure," he said. "If another Benny Bensognio turns up the next few weeks, we'll know. Lercasi has a nasty habit of killing people who fuck with him."

"You ask around about Gentry? The kid I told you about with the marital problems?"

"Yeah. And it ain't good."

Gold's face tightened. "This gonna hurt?"

"I'll know more in about half an hour, you want to stick around. Otherwise, I suggest you find your way to this apartment they gave me." He pulled his wallet from his front pocket and sifted through the papers stuffed inside for an address. He showed Gold. "Park down the street from this address and wait for me."

"What's it about?"

"Her boyfriend," Iandolli said. "The one Mrs. Gentry is playing around with, Officer Wilkes. The kid is dirty."

Gold slumped where he stood. "I already spoke to him."

Iandolli put a hand on Gold's shoulder. "Internal Affairs knows all about the affair," he said. "Gentry's wife was picking up envelopes."

Gold cursed through his clenched teeth.

Joey Francone managed to find a hooker who was cruising the casino. She was a tall blonde he guessed was in her late twenties. She wore a tight-fitting, red-sequin dress.

She was playing the dollar slots, a dollar at a time, when he first met her. She smiled at him when he stopped to look her over. She said hello to Francone, then smirked as soon as he asked her if she was a "whoah."

Francone negotiated with her outside the hotel entrance. They both faced the giant pond with the high-tech fountains. Beyond the fountains and the pond, the traffic on Las Vegas Boulevard was heavy.

"You know what a strap is?" Francone asked.

The hooker held her cigarette out for him to light. He frowned as he fished his front pants pocket for a book of matches. Francone hated smoking. Carrying matches was a prerequisite to hanging around wiseguys. Wannabes waiting to move up had to light their cigarettes.

He held the match to the end of the hooker's cigarette and waited again for an answer as she took her time inhaling.

"Do you know what a strap is?" he repeated.

"A strap-on. Sure. For a dildo, right?"

"I have no fucking idea. You think this shit is for me?"

The hooker's eyebrows rose. "Who's it for, then?"

"A friend."

"A friend?"

"A friend, yeah. A friend."

The hooker wet her lips before taking a long drag on her cigarette. "Well, tell your friend it'll cost him five hundred an hour without the strap-on act. The dildo-up-the-ass routine will cost him more."

Francone laughed as he held both hands up. "Oh, oh, oh," he said. "I just need you to buy the fucking thing, not jam it up his ass. Besides, I think he's the type would wanna do the jammin', honey, not the other way around."

The hooker smirked at Francone before looking him off. "You really think that, huh?"

"Forget about it," Francone said, somewhat less sure of himself then. "What do you want to buy the thing? Just to buy it."

The hooker sucked hard on her cigarette. "Two hundred," she said. "Plus the cost, about another fifty. At least another fifty. Maybe more. You don't want something that might break. Not on your friend."

Francone waved his hands. "Are you fuckin' nuts? You want two hundred bucks to walk into a store and buy something with my fuckin' money?"

"Two hundred," she said. "Or your friend can try sitting on his own dick."

"It ain't for him to sit on!" Francone nearly yelled.

The hooker took another drag on her cigarette. "Then what's it for, hon?"

Francone scratched at his chin. "Just give me a price," he said after a while.

"Two hundred," she repeated. "The time it will take me to go get it, I could make a lot more than two hundred bucks, honey. We're talking about at least an hour of my time, and I already told you what that'll cost. I'm not cheap."

Francone counted ten twenty-dollar bills from his money clip. "Fuckin' robbery," he said. "You're a thief is what you are."

The hooker took the money and pointed to the cab stand line. "We'll need one of those, sport. Unless you trust me to meet you back here."

"Let's go," Francone said as he placed a hand on her back to guide her. "I trust you about as far as I can throw you."

The hooker winked at him. "You're a smart one, all right."

Chapter 27

CUCCIA SPOTTED THE BLONDE with the perfect ass and the nasty attitude through his binoculars. She was lying on her stomach on a lounge near the Jacuzzis. The tall black man sat up beside her. Cuccia could see the black man pouring lotion into one of his hands.

Cuccia had just taken a long, hot shower. He was wearing a complimentary terry-cloth hotel robe. He leaned against the windows and focused on the crack of the blonde's ass through the binoculars. The thin white strap of her thong disappeared in the crevice. It excited Cuccia. He reached inside his robe to masturbate.

When he finished, Cuccia washed himself off again in the shower. He had some time before Francone would return with a hooker. Cuccia was anxious to see what Francone would bring him. He was hoping for a blonde.

There were two women Charlie guessed were prostitutes sitting in a car in the lot behind a strip joint on Hacienda Boulevard. The one behind the wheel was a tall redhead. The one in the passenger seat was short and wearing a dark wig. He approached the car with his hands held up above his shoulders.

"I'm not a cop," he said.

"Who asked?" the woman in the passenger seat said.

Charlie stopped a few feet from the car and let his hands down. "Can I ask you ladies a question?"

"Fifty for half an hour," the short woman said.

"Thirty for straight head but you have fifteen minutes," the redhead added.

"Unless you want us both," the short one said. "One-twenty for half an hour."

"I'm looking for a gun," Charlie said. "Like I said, I'm not a cop."

The driver leaned across her friend and winked at Charlie. "Looks like you been beat up by a few," she said.

"They weren't cops."

"How do you know we aren't?" the short one asked.

Charlie shook his head. "I don't know that. How can you prove you're not?"

The short one opened the door and turned to face Charlie. She spread her legs and raised the short skirt she was wearing. Charlie saw her bare crotch and turned his head.

"You're not cops," he said.

"Whatcha need?" the redhead asked.

"Anything," Charlie said. "A revolver if you know where I can get one. I'll take anything, though."

The redhead waved him around the car. He walked around the front and she opened her purse for him.

"It's a twenty-two but it works," she told him. "But it's not a revolver. I can probably get you one, but it'll take a few hours."

"How much for that one?" Charlie asked.

The redhead shrugged. "Two hundred?"

Charlie nodded. "Deal," he said. He peeled off four fifties.

"Hey," the short woman said. "Don't I get anything for the flash?"

Charlie peeled off a ten-dollar bill and handed it to the redhead. "For her efforts," he said. "*Brava, bravi.*"

"Huh?" the redhead said.

Charlie hopped a cab back to the Strip, where he examined the Taurus P-22 he had just purchased. The small handgun had a pop-up barrel for loading. He slipped the weapon inside the waist of his pants and had the taxi drop him a few blocks from Harrah's. He stopped at a souvenir store to see if he might find something less dangerous than a handgun.

He ruled out the silly-looking souvenir knives and found a foot-long baseball bat with "Las Vegas Slugger" engraved on the barrel instead. He used a fresh twenty-dollar bill for the bat and a Las Vegas T-shirt that read: "Lost Wages, Nevada."

He took his time walking back to Harrah's. He had more than an hour before the late checkout time he knew his wife had already arranged for them. As he crossed the lobby toward the hall for the elevators, he noticed an Asian kid watching him from behind a column adjacent to the casino floor.

Charlie felt his heart beating faster as he watched the kid in the reflection from a pane of restaurant glass. He draped the T-shirt he had bought over the small baseball bat and headed for the elevators. He saw the kid pick up a house telephone in the glass reflection when he stopped to present his room key to the security guard in front of the elevator bank.

He rode the elevator wondering why they would approach him in such a public place. They had missed a perfect opportunity in a much more remote area near Samantha's house earlier. He touched the .22 through his shirt but was hesitant to take it out. What if someone saw it? What if he had to use it?

He was glad he had bought the baseball bat. He gripped the thin end with his right hand as the elevator approached his floor.

He decided he would look for a housecleaning person once he was off the elevator. He would make believe he had lost his key and ask to call security to let him in. He didn't think they would wait inside his room, but there was no point in taking unnecessary risks.

When the elevator stopped and the doors opened, he saw a tall, skinny kid standing across the hall. The kid's back was turned to Charlie, except why would anybody wait for an elevator with his back to one that had just arrived?

Charlie saw the kid was Asian about the same time he saw the knife. It missed his chin by inches when the kid swung. Charlie stepped to his right and tossed the T-shirt straight up. The Asian flinched, and Charlie was able to nail him on the forehead with the bat. The sound was distinct and loud. His eyes stared blankly as he backpedaled out of control.

Charlie saw blood on the Asian's forehead as he followed through with a second swing, this one aimed at the side of the head. It was another hard blow but not nearly as flush as the first one. The Asian toppled over and crashed into a closed elevator door. Charlie looked around himself, wiped the blood from the bat on the T-shirt, and got out of there.

Beau Curitan sipped Diet 7UP from a can as he hunkered over the laptop on the small table in his motel room on Las Vegas Boulevard. He wiped sweat from his forehead with the back of his left hand as he adjusted his mouse on the small pad to the right of the laptop.

"Daddy's almost home again, honey," he said to himself. "And I got something sweet for you."

He smirked at the screen name he was about to start a private chat with through the CompuServe Internet program.

He typed with one finger, slowly, as he stared at the keyboard.

"You can run butt you can't hyde," Beau typed.

He grabbed the can of Diet 7UP while he waited for the reply. His eyebrows furrowed as he spit the last of the soda from his mouth in an effort to cough and yell "fuck" at the same time.

"Asshole!" he yelled. "I'll give you asshole!"

Beau typed furiously then, without any regard for which keys he was striking in the heat of the moment.

"I ring yure fuckin neck you cont bihgh twat!" he typed. He said the words he meant to type aloud to himself. Then he read ONTHERUN's response as it appeared on his screen.

"Fuck off, Beau," the words read.

Beau slapped the laptop off the bed. He wondered if it would ever work again or if he had just cost himself another few hundred dollars.

Carol trembled with fear at her response to her husband's Internet threat. She hoped her husband had punched the screen or kicked out the plug in anger. She hoped maybe her husband was in the bathtub and managed to pull the laptop into the water with him.

That was a better image, Carol thought as she nervously packed her laptop.

She had taken a room in a motel on her way out of Las Vegas when she realized Beau had probably traced her to the phone lines in Samantha's apartment. The thought of harm coming to her best friend because of her ex-husband forced Carol to engage him one more time, at least for Samantha's sake.

She was heading west. She needed Beau to follow her.

Chapter 28

THE HOOKER WAS HOLDING her hand out for another hundred dollars for a blow job. Joey Francone wanted to slap her in the face, but he wasn't in New York. She could make problems for him in Las Vegas.

Besides, he still had to deliver her to his boss. The blow job was just a bonus Francone figured he might pick up cheap, except she wasn't cheap at all.

"What the hell," he told her. He peeled off another five twenties from his money clip. "You might as well while you're here."

The hooker set her bag on the night table beside the bed. "Can I get a drink first?" she asked.

"Can I take it off the top?" he asked.

"Nope," she said.

"I didn't think so. What'll you have?"

"Vodka tonic. Sprite on the side, please."

"Right," Francone said. He picked up the phone to order the drinks from room service as the hooker excused herself into the bathroom.

He was doing the math in his head, wondering where the cost for the strap-on dildo he was no longer sure his boss was going to use on some broad was going to end. The hooker had told him stories about men who had asked for sex toys like strap-on dildos and how they almost always wanted the girls to use the paraphernalia on the men themselves. It made Francone a bit sick to think that of his boss, but the hooker seemed to know what she was talking about.

Actually, she wasn't so bad once you got past her sarcasm. She had told him she was originally from Kansas, but Francone didn't believe her. At least he was skeptical. After a while, once she seemed to settle down with him, the hooker did reveal an innocent side of herself. She could have been raised on a farm somewhere. Her father or brother or uncle could have raped her. She could have turned to prostitution for any number of reasons.

She opened the bathroom door as Francone rubbed his chin from thinking. She had removed her sequin dress. She wore white garter belts with a matching white lace bra.

Francone swallowed hard from how sexy she looked. "Holy shit," escaped from his mouth.

The hooker shifted her weight onto one leg. She turned to the side and asked Francone if he liked her lingerie.

Francone swallowed hard a second time. "Ah, yeah," he said. "Who the fuck wouldn't?"

She licked her lips as she smiled. Francone hardly noticed. He seemed stunned by her beauty. He wondered for the second time since he had met her if hookers could change into normal broads. He wondered if there were any you could ever change enough to take home and maybe settle down with.

Charlie stopped in his room to grab his suitcase and as much as he could pack in a few minutes after beating the Asian kid unconscious outside the elevators. He figured he had at least a few minutes before someone discovered the unsuccessful assassin. He guessed he had another five to ten minutes after that before somebody might try his room.

He packed quickly. He tossed whatever clothes were hanging in the closet into the suitcase. He grabbed his cigarettes and airline tickets from the table. He packed the baseball bat in with his clothes. He ignored the toiletries except for his bottle of Pavarotti cologne. He stood at the end of the bed to give the room a once-over look when he noticed the message light blinking on the telephone.

There were three more messages on his voice mail. Charlie played them back. The first two were hang-ups. The last message was from his wife's boyfriend, John Denton.

Denton's voice was telling Charlie that he had been visited by one of the men who had assaulted Lisa. The man had given Denton the names of the men responsible for the assault. Denton wanted to talk to Charlie. Denton wasn't sure if he was going to the police.

Charlie remembered that the DEA agent had given him a card. He took it out of his wallet but could only stare at it. The agent was the same clown who had told Charlie that he was safe.

He heard a commotion in the hallway and pressed his ear against the door. He could hear the sound of a radio. Then he heard someone talking into the radio.

"We need an ambulance," he heard someone say. "Someone was mugged outside the elevators. I think he's unconscious. He's bleeding pretty bad."

Charlie figured it was safe to leave the hotel again. He went back to the telephone to call Samantha first. As he reached for the phone, it began to ring.

Lano reached Francone at the room they were supposed to be sharing at the Bellagio. He tried to whisper into the telephone, faking an occasional cough when it wasn't a real one.

"Where the fuck you been?" Francone asked in his best angry voice.

"The hospital," Lano said through a hoarse whisper. "I was spitting up blood soon as I left you. I couldn't breathe. I came to the hospital. They kept me here for tests."

"And you couldn't return our beeps?"

"No," Lano said. "They put me through the emergency room. They took all my stuff to give me tests. I was naked, for Christ sakes."

"I hope you still got that five grand."

"Yeah, I got it. I put it away in the car before I went in the hospital. They put me to sleep with these fuckin' drugs. I'm at the hospital now. I'm gettin' released in a few minutes."

"It's those fuckin' cigarettes. They finally caught up with you."

"I know. You were right. I think I got cancer. They want to do a biopsy tomorrow. They got a big spot on my lungs on the X-ray thing. Like a softball, the doctor said."

"You throw away your cigarettes yet?"

"I will now. I have to."

"Yeah, right," Francone said with a laugh. "In the meantime, get your ass back over here. Nicky's fuckin' crazy we didn't know where you were."

"I'll be there as soon as they release me," Lano said. He waited for Francone to hang up. Lano held the receiver to his ear until the line was dead. He held down the receiver for a new dial tone, then said, "And then I'll shoot you right in the fuckin' face."

"Sorry for the interruption," Francone told the hooker.

"I usually don't spend so much time with a client," the hooker said. She was stroking Francone's chest hairs while he talked on the telephone. They lay beside each other on the bed.

Francone pushed the hooker back gently so he could turn toward her. "With that face you could charge me a million," he said.

"You're nice," she said. "Most of my clients aren't so nice. Most of them I don't even talk to."

"Don't consider me a client," Francone said. "Take the money, but don't consider me a client. I sure don't consider you a whoah."

Chapter 29

LANO HAD CALLED FRANCONE from a pay phone on the Strip. He had baited the punk for a reaction that might hint at what Cuccia's plans were, but the muscle-bound wannabe seemed preoccupied. Francone's only real concern was about the five thousand dollars Lano had run off with.

Now Lano craved another hit of nicotine. He was anxious to get to Cuccia and Francone before they got to him.

Lano headed south on the Strip. He was thinking about Francone. He would take care of the pretty boy first. Maybe shoot him in the chin Francone was always scratching when he made believe he could think.

Then he would find their skipper, Nicholas Cuccia. Lano planned on shooting the young boss in the mouth. Hopefully, when he jammed the gun in Cuccia's mouth, he would rebreak the bone Charlie Pellecchia had fractured in the New York nightclub.

Lisa Pellecchia awoke in the late afternoon after having undergone a third oral surgery. She felt dehydrated and exhausted.

She was hooked up to several intravenous tubes. She assumed that that was how she would be fed until her mouth healed. Lisa was aware of what had happened to her, but she wasn't clear about the damage inside her mouth.

She knew she was missing at least one upper front tooth. She could feel the gap with her tongue if she dared press it against her teeth. When she did brave the pain, the gap felt bigger than one tooth.

So far it had been like a nightmare. She wondered if Charlie was safe or in danger or alive or dead. The man who had punched Lisa was one of the men in the nightclub back in New York. She had recognized him just before her brain could process the information in time for her to defend herself at the motel.

She felt the stitches inside her mouth with her tongue again. She could still taste the blood. She wondered if John was with her at the hospital, if he was resting somewhere in the lobby, or if he was with the police. Lisa was too drugged to move anything except her eyes and tongue. She wished she could move her arm to the remote control to call for a nurse. When she turned her head to find the remote, a streak of pain raced through her head.

She closed her eyes and lay motionless.

Agent Thomas couldn't make his wife understand the demands of his job. She was fed up with him not being home. She was tired of sleeping alone. She was sick from worrying.

Thomas told his wife things would get better as soon as he finished with the case he was working.

"Another few days," he told her. "No more than a week."

They had been married a little more than three years. When she hung up on him, Thomas wasn't sure if they would make it to their fourth year.

So far the indictments back in Brooklyn were falling around Anthony Cuccia. Two captains directly under the sixty-five-year-old underboss were charged with federal racketeering violations. Thomas didn't know the specifics of the indictments except for the leverage that RICO statutes carried.

Ten years was a long time. Mobsters were trading information for a lot less than ten years. It was added pressure for Thomas. If either of the two captains indicted were to cut a deal of their own with the organized crime task force, his potential drug case against Anthony

Cuccia could fall apart. The last three weeks of his surveillance would have been for nothing.

Thomas wished his wife could understand his situation better. It was bad enough trying to baby-sit a wiseguy in Las Vegas. Now he had to sweat out indictments against two mob captains facing a minimum of ten years each. The least his wife could do was show some compassion for his situation instead of breaking his balls.

His eyes were growing tired from watching the television screen when his cell phone rang. He was expecting updates from his supervisor back in New York, but it also could be his wife calling back to haunt him some more. He thought about not answering the phone.

When he heard Charlie Pellecchia yelling at him, Thomas was caught completely off guard.

Chapter 30

CHARLIE USED A PAY phone near a men's room in the casino to call Agent Thomas of the DEA. When the agent picked up on the second ring, Charlie said, "It's Charlie Pellecchia. Your boy just took another shot at me. I was lucky. The punk they sent is on his way to the hospital. I just wanted to thank you for all—"

"Wait a minute! Wait a minute!" the DEA agent yelled. "Talk to me. I just observed—"

"Fuck you!" Charlie yelled. He hung up the receiver and juked his way through the lobby crowd. When he reached the driveway, he could see the flashing lights of an ambulance.

When he stood on the line for a taxi, Charlie spotted John Denton heading his way. Charlie clenched his teeth in anticipation of a confrontation.

"We need to talk," Denton said. "I know this is weird, but we need to talk."

Charlie searched the crowd behind him for the Asian kid he had spotted on the house telephone in the lobby earlier.

"Charlie?" Denton persisted. "We need to talk."

Charlie pushed his wife's lover to move up in the taxi line.

"I'm not asking you to come along," he told Denton.

"Come along where? I came to you when the police didn't show up at the hospital. I already called them."

"You gave them the names?"

"No. I just called the detective I spoke with originally. I left a message for him to call me back. He didn't call, so I came here. I didn't know if you got my message or not."

Charlie shoved his way past Denton as he sat inside a taxi. When Denton followed him, Charlie said, "I'm going there right now. I'm going to see this guy who's trying to kill me."

"That's crazy," Denton said. "This is the mob we're dealing with. I'm a lawyer. I can lose my license if I don't report this. I can't hold back information."

Charlie told the driver to take them to the Bellagio.

"It's insane," Denton continued. "I already called that detective. I'm just waiting for him to get back to me. I'm not even sure Lisa will want to go along with it, pressing charges. It's the mob, damn it! You can't fight them."

"You're right," Charlie said. "You are a lawyer."

"That's a cheap shot."

Charlie glared at Denton.

"Suppose this guy today is setting you up?" Denton asked.

"What guy?"

"The guy who came to the hospital. The one I called you about. Suppose he just wanted to find you. Maybe he already has. Maybe they're following us right now."

"Somebody already followed me. That's what that ambulance was about back there. I was lucky. I'm not giving them a third chance."

"Which is why you should go to the police with this."

"I don't have time to explain it now," Charlie said. "Nicholas Cuccia, right? That's one of the names."

"And a Joey Francone."

"And a Joey Francone. Fine. Nicky and Joey, welcome to my world."

"What about Lisa?" Denton asked.

Charlie glared at his wife's lover one more time.

"I feel like a nap," Francone said. He was down to his royal blue bikini

underwear and muscle T-shirt. He sat back against the pillows propped up against the headboard.

The hooker handed him a refill of his drink, a Stolichnaya screwdriver. "Have another sip," she said. "It'll help you relax. Then I can finish relaxing you."

"I'll bet you can," Francone said before sipping the drink.

The hooker stroked his thigh near his crotch. He was stuck in a semierect stage but was too drugged to notice. The hooker sipped at her Sprite through a straw. Her lips formed a smile around the straw.

He had told her as much about his work as he could fit in a twenty-minute conversation. He was waiting to become a made man, he had told her. He was waiting for the mob books to open again back in New York. He was so close he could taste it.

The hooker wasn't sure what mob books were. She had heard about made men and wiseguys and other gangsters, but she had also heard or read about how gangsters testified against each other once they were arrested. She had watched that special on *Dateline* or *20/20*, or maybe it was on CNN, about one boss testifying against another boss. Or maybe it was the assistant to the boss testifying against the boss. It didn't matter. It made her dizzy then and it made her dizzy now to think about it. Who cared about the mob or mob books? She had another sucker about to fall asleep right in front of her.

"So, are you really a gangster?" she asked as she watched him slide slowly toward unconsciousness.

"Yesssss," he said as he started to slur his words. "But you shouldn't be thcared. I ike you. I rearry rike yourrr."

"I like you, too," she said.

"You erra been to Rcw Rork?"

"Sure," the hooker said. "Lots of times."

Francone's eyes closed before he could register her answer.

Chapter 31

CHARLIE WALKED STRAIGHT TO the registration desk in the Bellagio Hotel-Casino to reserve a room. He handed a clerk there his credit card and driver's license. He asked for a smoking room high up, if one was available.

"You really think this is a good idea?" Denton asked as they waited for the room keys.

"Yes," Charlie said. "This gets us upstairs."

The desk clerk handed Charlie a small folder with keys and a min-imap of the Bellagio. Charlie signed a card authorizing payment by room number and waited for his credit card to be returned.

"This is crazy," Denton said.

"I know," Charlie said. "And sometimes crazy is a good thing."

Minh Quan took the call while he was playing a pinball machine in the basement of the restaurant. He listened intently as one of the men he had sent with his brother to kill Charlie Pellecchia explained how Nguyen was beaten unconscious and was on his way to the hospital.

Quan turned away from the pinball machine as he wiped sweat from his forehead. He checked his watch and spoke in French, the language he sometimes used to confuse surveillance.

"*Suis-le mais ne fais rien,*" Quan said. "*Moi-même, je tuerai ce Blanc foutant. J'y vais.*"

He told the caller to follow Pellecchia but to leave him alone. Quan would kill the fucking white man himself. He was on his way.

First he had a sit-down with Jerry Lercasi. A meeting with the Italian big shot meant there was money to be made. Quan would stay in touch with his men and avenge his brother's injury after doing business.

She had been drinking Sprite, but the comedian in the silk bikini underwear never noticed.

The hooker managed to find just less than seven hundred dollars in the room, not nearly as much as she had hoped for. She did have a Rolex, a money clip with diamond-studded initials, a couple of designer leather belts, the strap, and the dildo. She kept the hand-written receipt with the inflated price. She figured she might get fifty bucks for the unused items.

Francone lay on his back snoring on one of the twin-size beds. The hooker tied his hands with his belt. Then she tied his feet back to his hands with one leg of his pants.

She left him in the silk royal blue bikini underwear. She had laughed out loud at the sight of the underwear earlier and covered up by saying drinking made her giggly.

She was just finishing making herself up in the bathroom when she thought she heard him move on the bed. She frowned at the thought. She had given him enough codeine to knock out a horse. She put her lipstick in her bag and hurried out of the bathroom. She stopped with a gasp when she saw an older man across the room pointing a gun at her.

Lano's eyebrows rose about as far up into his forehead as was possible once he was inside his room at the Bellagio. There was the young punk snoring in his sissy silk underwear, hands tied to his feet with a belt and a pair of pants. Lano smiled at the sight until he heard somebody in the bathroom across the suite. He stepped to the side and pulled the .380 from his ankle holster. He pointed the gun at the bathroom until a woman dressed like a hooker stepped through the doorway.

"Huhhhh!" the woman gasped.

Lano took the scene in again, looking from the punk to the hooker, and then back at Francone again.

"You rolled him?" he asked as he lowered the gun.

The hooker put both her hands up for emphasis. "I don't know what happened to him, mister. He got all funny on me and then he passed out."

"But he tied himself up before he passed out, right?"

Charlie's room at the Bellagio was two floors above Nicholas Cuccia's suite. Before he stepped inside the elevator, Charlie sent Denton to a hotel store for some changes of clothes. He gave him two hundred-dollar bills and a list of items to buy: T-shirts, sweat pants, and two hats. Denton wanted an explanation, but Charlie waved him off as he stepped inside the elevator.

He was feeling rage he hadn't felt in a long time. He needed to control his anger before it got the best of him.

He had boxed in the New York City Golden Gloves when he was seventeen. After six easy victories in the heavyweight novice division, Charlie made it to the semifinals, where a much faster Hispanic kid defeated him on points. Charlie knocked the Hispanic kid down in the third round, but it was the only solid punch he had landed, a vicious left hook. Three one-minute rounds had just not been enough time for Charlie to stalk his prey.

Knocking the Asian kid unconscious had been instinct. Charlie saw the knife. He saw the kid swing. He reacted.

Breaking the wiseguy's jaw in the nightclub was a similar reflexive action. He saw the gangster grab his wife. He saw the smack, and he reacted.

Going after the gangster now was no longer instinct. Charlie had decided to take the offensive. He knew who and where his enemy was. He would stalk Nicholas Cuccia, but he wouldn't take his time about it.

• • •

Samantha was desperate to find out where Charlie had gone. She watched the story on the local news about a mugging at Harrah's Hotel. She knew Charlie had gone there to check out. He told her he would call if anything were wrong.

She picked up the phone receiver at least three times before slamming it back down from fear of making things worse than they already were. When she couldn't stand the suspense any longer, Samantha called his room at Harrah's and was told that Mr. Pellecchia had already checked out.

She was full of anxiety when the doorbell rang. She ran to the door, expecting to see him. Somehow, as she opened the door, Samantha knew it was careless not looking through the peephole first.

Before she could finish asking who the man standing there was, a fist caved in her solar plexus.

Instead of getting everything Charlie told him to buy, Denton bought whichever items he could find in one store and headed back to the elevators as fast as possible. When he didn't find Charlie inside the room, Denton had a good idea where he had gone.

He could call Detective Gold one more time, or he could call hotel security and ask for help. He also could get the hell out of there before he regretted it for the rest of his life.

Except then he would have to face Lisa again. He would look and feel as helpless as he had felt back in the hotel room the night she was assaulted.

Denton wondered what the hell prison would be like as he stepped inside another elevator.

Chapter 32

AGENT THOMAS CALLED CUCCIA immediately after Charlie Pellecchia called. He let the phone ring a long time before giving up. Thomas wanted to pound on the door across the hall, but it was too dangerous. No matter how frustrating the situation had become, he couldn't compromise Cuccia.

Pellecchia had sounded as if he might go to the police after all. Thomas couldn't blame him, except local criminal charges against Cuccia could create a boondoggle of paperwork between the DEA and the Las Vegas police department. It would take time Thomas didn't have.

He had assured Pellecchia of his safety. He had insisted that Cuccia's vendetta was over. Now he knew how foolish his claim had been. As long as the mobster had something the government needed, it was Cuccia who called the shots. As long as the heroin sat in a New Jersey warehouse, Cuccia could pretty much do whatever he wanted.

Thomas had to find out what the hell was going on before it was too late. He had come to Las Vegas to make sure nothing went wrong. So far, nothing was going right.

He knew Pellecchia was staying at Harrah's. He could be there in fifteen minutes if he ran. He might make it in less time if he grabbed a car.

Nicholas Cuccia sipped at a vanilla milk shake through a straw as he watched the end of a pay-per-view action movie. He was forced to drink most of his meals since his jaw had been fractured. He was lucky he liked milk shakes.

The phone rang again, and Cuccia had to adjust the volume on the television to hear what was going on in the movie. He turned the ringer on the phone off and propped a few pillows against the headboard to rest against.

He was anxious to catch a nap before Francone returned with a hooker. He watched as a black woman in a tight black skirt danced on the television screen. It reminded him that he would need to call the black broad from the escort service if he wanted to score more cocaine for later.

He was just finishing the milk shake when there was a knock at the door. He set the large glass down on a tray as he pushed himself off the bed. He glanced back at the television as he headed for the door. Another knock startled him.

"Fuckin' hold it!" he yelled.

He wiped his hands on a towel as he reached for the door.

"Maintenance," a deep voice said as Cuccia started to open the door.

"Who?" Cuccia asked as the door slammed into him.

Cuccia was knocked to the floor. The back of his head slammed against the legs of a marble cocktail table as the pain ricocheted through his jaw.

When Cuccia was able to focus again, a big man stood over him. As the man removed his sunglasses, Cuccia's eyes opened wide as he recognized the intruder. It was the guy from the nightclub in New York. The guy who should've been dead already. It was Charlie Pellecchia.

Cuccia clenched his teeth and immediately winced from the pain.

"Stand up, tough guy," Pellecchia said. "Unless you want to take this beating laying on the floor."

Cuccia was in agony from his jaw. He held both his hands up from where he lay. He pointed to his jaw with his right hand as he shook his head.

Pellecchia looked around himself before stepping toward Cuccia. "What's that?" he asked. "You have a toothache? Which one is it?"

Cuccia's eyes opened wide with terror as he realized what Pellecchia was about to do. He tried to block the kick with both hands, but he wasn't going to make it.

He heard his jaw crack for the second time in less than two weeks. He felt a sharp pain as he experienced immediate dizziness. He felt his eyes rolling as the numbness took over.

"Look, mister, I know how this looks," the hooker said. "But he was into some strange shit." She pointed at the plastic bag on the bed. "Look in there. He made me get one of those."

Lano moved closer to the bed. He opened the bag with the barrel of the .380. His eyes squinted at the strap he saw inside the bag.

"The hell is it?" he asked. "A belt?"

"Look more," she said.

Lano turned the bag upside down. Both the strap and the dildo spilled onto the bed. He looked from the items on the bed to Francone to the hooker and back. He laughed until he turned red from coughing.

"You all right?" the hooker asked.

"This is fuckin' priceless," he said through the rough coughing spell.

"You sure you're all right? That's some bad cough."

"Tell me about it."

"You should have it checked."

Lano nodded. "I did."

The hooker took a small step forward. "Can I go now?"

"You take anything of mine?"

"Just what was on him, I swear it."

"You get his watch? It's okay if you do. I want you to have it. That and that stupid fuckin' money clip he carries."

The hooker smiled. "I have them both."

He remembered the envelope he was carrying inside his jacket pocket. He fished it out and tossed it to the hooker. "There's a couple grand in there," he said. "It's yours now. Don't spend it all in one place."

The hooker felt the envelope with both hands and dropped it inside her bag. "Thanks," she said. "Thanks a lot."

Lano motioned toward the door with his gun. "And be careful," he said. "They're not all as stupid as this one."

Chapter 33

GOLD'S LOWER BACK WAS sore from sitting in the car. He was waiting for Iandolli and thinking about Donald Gentry. Knowing the young detective's wife was embroiled in an Internal Affairs investigation was frightening. Gentry's marital problems had gone from bad to worse.

Gold was exhausted. He cracked the front window to light a cigarette. He jumped when the front passenger door suddenly opened.

"Get some sleep?" Iandolli asked. He was holding two containers of coffee. He handed one to Gold.

"Catnaps," Gold said. He rubbed his eyes with his free hand. "Technically, I'm off the next two days."

Iandolli set his coffee on the dashboard. "Internal Affairs has them on tape," he said. "Gentry's wife picked up a few envelopes for Wilkes. Then she took it a step farther and deposited them in a safe-deposit box. Both their names on it."

"Jesus Christ."

"Exactly. So they'll definitely drag her in when they pick up Wilkes. I don't know they'll charge her with anything, but they'll definitely use her to lean on Wilkes."

Gold was staring out the windshield. "When's this happen?"

"Nobody's saying."

"Of course not."

Iandolli touched Gold's right arm. "There's something else," he said. "Wilkes is on tape with Allen Fein. Fein is Lercasi's front man in and about town. His legit man."

Gold was confused. "You said Wilkes is dirty. So?"

Iandolli frowned. "Guess who else is on the same tape?"

"Al, I'm not in the mood for *Jeopardy* right now."

"You," Iandolli said. "Twice. My guys taped it. Organized crime. You approached Wilkes yesterday, right?"

Gold was nodding defiantly. "To warn him about Donald Gentry, yeah."

"Then you approached Jennifer Gentry. Internal Affairs didn't know what it was about. Neither did my guys. You understand what I'm saying? It looked dirty, Abe. Like maybe you and Wilkes and Fein—"

"Don't tell me this," Gold said. "Please don't tell me this."

Iandolli waited.

"What, there's more?" Gold asked. "Of course the fuck there is. What else?"

Iandolli took an extra moment. "You can't warn Gentry," he said. "I'm sorry, Abe."

"Bullshit."

"You can't."

"Bullshit."

"Abe?"

"Why the fuck not?"

Iandolli needed a distraction. He reached for his coffee cooling off on the dashboard. "Because Internal Affairs and my guys know that you know about Wilkes."

Gold shook his head. "Come again? How the fuck do they know that?"

"Because I had to tell them," Iandolli said. "I had no choice. It's why I mentioned it in the first place, about you being on tape with Wilkes and Jennifer Gentry. Internal Affairs and my guys wanted to know why. I had no choice, Abe. I had to tell them."

"About me, yeah. I can understand that. But why tell them about Gentry's old lady? You told them that?"

"They already knew about the affair. From surveillance on Wilkes. They knew she was seeing Wilkes. They knew about the safe-deposit box."

"Fuck me," Gold said.

"I had no choice," Iandolli continued. "Or they wanted to know what you were doing with Wilkes."

"And you," Gold said. "And what I was doing with you?"

"Right," Iandolli said without looking at Gold. "So I covered both our asses."

Gold opened his window all the way and tossed his coffee into the street in disgust.

"You're here watching for Jennifer Gentry," Iandolli said. "You're doing another cop a favor. I'm here watching for Allen Fein. I'm doing my job. It's how I'm selling this thing right now."

Gold closed his eyes.

"You okay?" Iandolli asked.

"No," Gold said. "I'm not. Not at all."

Chapter 34

IT WAS A WHILE before Joey Francone awoke from his drug-induce
sleep. When he did, Vincent Lano was the first person he saw. Fran
cone's pupils dilated from the light. His mind was groggy. His speech
was slurred.

"Ah-ohhh," he said, still not aware he was tied. "What the faaaa?"

"Smile," Lano said.

"What?" Francone said as he struggled to move his arms. He
looked around himself a few more times before he realized he was
tied. The flash from the camera blinded him.

"What the fuck?" he said as his eyes struggled to refocus.

Lano laid the dildo across the wannabe's neck for the next picture.
Francone struggled to see what it was. Another flash from the camera
blinded him a second time.

"What the fuck arrrr ou doin'?"

"Takin' pictures," Lano said. He had gone down to the lobby to
buy a disposable camera a few minutes after the hooker had left. As
soon as Lano saw the strap and dildo, his plans changed. Instead of
killing Francone, he decided to take pictures.

He grabbed the dildo by its base and moved it to Francone's mouth.
"Open up," he said.

The wannabe moved his head to one side. Lano grabbed him by the
hair and yanked back until Francone's mouth opened. Lano jammed
the dildo into his mouth. The thick rubber shaft split a corner of the
wannabe's lip. Francone immediately gagged. Lano held the dildo in

lace with one hand as he took a picture of it with the other. Then he pulled the dildo out as Francone coughed his way out of choking.

"Now," Lano said, "you wanna position yourself for the next shot, or should I?"

Agent Thomas commandeered a taxi with his badge outside the hotel lobby. He had ordered the driver to run red lights and get him to Harrah's as fast as possible. They made the drive in just under ten minutes.

Thomas went straight to the security desk inside the casino and flashed his badge a second time. Hotel security was summoned by radio. Ten minutes later, Thomas was inside the room the Pellecchia couple had reserved for their six-night vacation.

The head of hotel security filled Thomas in on the assault that had occurred outside the elevator banks on the same floor earlier. A hotel guest found an Asian teenager sprawled unconscious on the rug. The rug was still stained with blood. Nobody knew what had happened. Security assumed the Asian kid had tried to rob somebody off the elevator. When the kid was finally conscious, the security guard told Thomas, he wasn't talking.

Thomas couldn't find anything inside Pellecchia's hotel room. He called the hotel operator to ask if there was any way to listen to phone messages a guest might have erased.

"Sorry, sir, no," the operator told him.

Thomas needed to find Cuccia. He needed to get him out of Las Vegas before local law enforcement arrested the New York mobster. The heroin case seemed long lost. Now it was a matter of jurisdiction. If Cuccia managed to kill Pellecchia in Las Vegas, he also might manage to get arrested for the homicide.

Thomas's race against time had become a sprint.

John Denton had to knock on the door to suite 24-B several times before Charlie opened it. When he was inside the suite, Denton saw a man lying on the floor, unconscious. His mouth was bloody and swollen.

"He didn't see you yet," Charlie told Denton. "So maybe you want to get the hell out of here before he wakes up and does."

"Is he dead?"

"No. He's out, though. But I don't know for how long."

"What else do you intend to do?"

"Knock one of his teeth out," Charlie said. "At least one."

Chapter 35

Detective Donald Gentry stared at the green-and-white tiles he had installed in his kitchen the year before. They were expensive tiles. His wife had picked them out shortly after they moved into the house.

Gentry had thought he was building a future with his wife the day he started work on the kitchen. It had been their first project in the new home. They were planning on many more home improvements before they would have children.

Sometime during the past year, however, things had started to change. Gentry had put in longer hours since his promotion to detective. Jennifer also had started to work longer hours. When she began working weekends, their time together became sparse. The couple drifted apart.

Sometime during their unspoken problems, Jennifer fell in love with another man.

At first, Gentry had thought that if he ignored his wife's betrayal, she might come to her senses or grow bored with whomever she was seeing. He loved his wife enough to forgive her. At least he was willing to try.

When her affair didn't stop, Gentry found he could no longer live with it in his face. When he suspected his wife of using their own home, he decided to end their marriage.

Except it wasn't as easy to follow through with what he knew was the right thing to do. He became caught up in the sordid details of his wife's affair. He wanted to know who her lover was. He wanted to know what they were doing.

He had bought a minicamera from a spy shop. So far, he was unable to watch what the hidden camera had already recorded. It was a denial he was terrified to confront.

When she was late returning home, Gentry decided to finally view the tape. Thirty seconds into the recording, he gagged at the sight of his wife kissing another man he immediately recognized. He ran into the bathroom and was sick. His stomach muscles wrenched as he heaved until he was dry. He moaned from crying, but there were no tears.

When he returned, a few minutes later, his wife was naked on the screen. So was the cop between her knees.

Allen Fein had made two stops on his way home. After eating a Big Mac, fries, and hot apple pie at McDonald's, he stopped at Kentucky Fried Chicken and ordered a small bucket of spicy chicken and French fries. He ate the food in his BMW in the parking lot and later stopped at a Dairy Queen for a chocolate milk shake. He ordered a super-size Coke for the drive home and was sure to stop for a bottle of Pepto-Bismol.

Now he was sitting in pain on his toilet. The super-size Coke cup rested on the marble edge of the bathroom sink. The cup was half empty.

Fein rocked back and forth on the toilet seat as he proposed deals with God to alleviate the stomach pains he was suffering.

"I swear it," Fein said between gasps of breath. "I'll never eat this crap again. Please, God. Please. I swear it."

He broke into a cold sweat. The pains in his stomach were relentless. He wiped at his forehead with the back of a hand as he groaned on the toilet seat.

He thought he heard a noise outside the bathroom. He had been in a rush to use the toilet and had left the door open. He leaned forward on the toilet seat, but a stomach pain set him to rocking again.

"Oh, God," Fein chanted, "please let me go. Please."

He heard a second noise outside the bathroom. He guessed it was his cat jumping from the landing above the stairway down the hall.

As his bowels finally started to move, Fein heard yet another noise outside the bathroom. He called to his cat as he wiped sweat from his forehead with the back of his right wrist. He let out a long sigh of relief and started to smile when he looked in the direction of a shadow crossing the doorway. Fein was startled when he saw a stocky man standing there holding a gun.

"Jesus Christ," Renato Freni said after shooting Allen Fein off the toilet seat.

He held his breath as he stepped closer and fired another round into the accountant's head.

When he was sure Fein was dead, Freni stepped around the body and made his way back out of the condo. He had completed half of a new contract with Jerry Lercasi. Freni wasn't thrilled about killing Fein for free, but it was the price he had to pay for taking on the Pellecchia contract without going through Lercasi first.

The thing about doing a hit for a guy like Lercasi was you didn't get a chance to make mistakes. It was more like the old days. You had one chance. You didn't fuck it up.

This was a serious consideration for Freni as he headed back toward the Strip. Killing an accountant was one thing. Killing a wiseguy was an entire other matter.

Chapter 36

THE FLASH FROM THE camera caused Francone to blink. He felt a searing pain in his lower back as his eyes refocused. When he could see clearly again, Lano was standing there.

Francone realized the pain was from his rectum. He tugged against the restraints on his arms and legs, but it hurt to move. He looked down at himself as Lano started to laugh. Francone's mouth was cotton dry. He couldn't speak.

"There's about eight inches of a twelve-inch dildo up your ass," Lano said. "You better be careful you don't turn over and jam it into your stomach."

Francone was trying to wet his lips. "The fuck are you doing?" he asked.

"Ruining your life," Lano said.

"We'll kill you for this. You know that, right?"

Lano winked at Francone as he spoke though a coughing fit. "In case you don't get it yet, pally, I'm not too concerned."

Francone tried to move his right leg, but the pain in his rectum sent a spasm up his back. "Fuck!" he yelled.

A knock at the door stopped Lano from laughing again. He did his best to suppress another coughing fit as he stepped back to block the door. A second, louder knock followed.

"Who is it?" Lano asked through a cough.

"The guy from the hospital," a voice said.

Lano checked the peephole in the door for police. If they were out there, they had moved out of his view.

"Who else is there?"

"The husband," the voice said.

"Shit," Lano whispered to himself. He knew there was a chance the husband would get involved. He wasn't sure about the boyfriend, but the husband was the one who had broken Cuccia's jaw in the first place.

He opened the door a crack and stepped away fast. He held his gun up for whoever else might be there. "Go easy," he said. "I've got something in my hand."

Charlie touched his gun and immediately thought better of it. His life wasn't in imminent danger yet. He could turn around and leave right now.

He had intended on using the same move he used upstairs with Cuccia. As soon as the door opened a crack, he would force his way into the room, shoulder first. But now the guy on the other side of the door was telling Charlie he had a gun, too.

Charlie pushed the door open instead of rushing through it. An older man dressed in black stood with a gun at the foot of one of two beds. The man's shape looked somewhat familiar.

Charlie definitely recognized the other man. A flesh-colored tube was jammed inside his rectum.

"You must be Charlie Pellecchia," the man with the gun said. "I'm Vincent Lano."

Charlie waited for Denton to close the door behind them. He nodded at the man holding the gun. "You're also one of the scumbags who did this to me," he said as he pointed at his facial bruises.

Lano didn't flinch. "I'm sorry about that," he said. "Really. I followed orders. I was wrong."

"And what about my wife?"

"I didn't touch her," Lano said. He pointed the gun at the ridiculous sight on the bed. "That was this clown. On orders from the guy upstairs." Lano motioned at Denton with his gun. "I gave him the names. Suite 24-B, in case you haven't made it up there yet."

"We just came from there," Charlie said.

Lano motioned at Denton again. "I went to this guy to give him the information," he said. "It don't make me innocent, but I didn't lay a finger on her. I had no intention of doing that. That isn't me."

Charlie looked to Denton. Denton was staring down at the man on the bed.

"Can he get hurt like that?" Denton asked.

Before Lano could answer, Charlie grabbed the base of the flesh-colored tube and pushed it from side to side and down. The man on the bed gasped loudly. His eyes and mouth remained wide open from pain. Blood trickled outside his rectum around the tube.

Denton moved between Charlie and the bed. "Enough," he said.

"What are you gonna do?" Charlie asked Lano. "Shoot me now?"

"Not if I don't have to."

"What if I want to break your nose?"

"I'd think this would stop you."

Denton was terrified that Charlie would take his personal vendetta to another level. He had already assaulted one mobster. Now there was another one holding a gun. Denton tried to stay between them. He knew he was the voice of reason in the room. He also knew his vote counted the least. Charlie was running on rage. Denton wasn't quite sure what was motivating the man with the gun.

"Look," Denton said to Charlie. "We're in deep enough shit already. And I know I don't wanna get shot."

Charlie pointed behind Denton at the bed. "That piece of shit broke your girlfriend's teeth."

Denton looked to Lano. Lano said, "He's right, he did."

Denton clenched his teeth at the man on the bed. He looked at the dildo but couldn't bring himself to touch it.

"Not that," he said.

"Then what?" Lano asked.

Denton walked around Charlie to the dresser. He opened a few drawers and found a white T-shirt. He wrapped his right hand with it and walked back to the bed. He aimed a straight right lead down at the man's mouth as hard as he could throw it. The man on the bed took the punch flush on the right side of his face. Blood splattered from a split lip.

"There," Denton said. "Now can we go?"

Charlie shook his head. "I'll give you one more try before I take out a few of his teeth with my foot. Or you can break his nose. They fractured mine, and I intend to break his."

"This is crazy already!" Denton yelled.

"If you guys'll hear me out, I think I have a better idea," Lano said.

"Really?" Denton asked.

"What's that?" Charlie asked.

Lano smiled.

Chapter 37

GOLD COULDN'T HANDLE SITTING around thinking about what might happen to Donald Gentry when the Las Vegas police finally arrested the young detective's wife.

"Let's go do something," he told Iandolli. "You don't want me to go to Gentry with this, give me something to occupy my mind."

"You wanna go talk with the guys from New York? Cuccia, Francone, and Lano."

Gold started the car. "About the Pellecchia assaults?" he asked. "I don't really give a fuck about this Pellecchia couple. I have a hard time giving a shit about people who don't cooperate. I'm not so sure they're so innocent in all this anyway."

"So we don't ask about the Pellecchia couple. We talk about something else."

Gold pulled away from the curb. "Can we break their balls?"

"Why not?" Iandolli said. "It's one of the few perks goes with this job. We break their balls and then watch them turn colors."

"Remind me of our motivation here."

"My wife'll tell you I'm just evil sometimes," Iandolli said. "You, I think, have other motives."

"Gentry."

"You have to let the steam out somewhere."

Gold was approaching an intersection. "Where they staying?"

"Bellagio."

Gold spotted the lights of the Strip off to his right. He turned right at the intersection. "Fine," he said. "Let's go break balls."

Jennifer Gentry was startled at the sight of her husband with the tequila bottle. She avoided direct eye contact.

"Your boyfriend protect himself, or you just give him a blow job?" Donald Gentry asked his wife.

He was sitting at the kitchen table. Half the bottle of tequila was gone. Jennifer was wearing black leggings and a white sweatshirt. She had just come home from wherever she had spent the past few hours after work. Her look, or maybe it was where she might have been, somehow turned him on.

"You look good in those tight pants like that," he said. "He run his hands up there, or just slide those pants off nice and slow?"

"Don't do this," Jennifer said. Her voice was trembling.

Gentry saw another man undress his wife in the video running in his head. He couldn't stop his mind from replaying the haunting images. "Nice and slow, right? And while he was down there, he buried his face, right?"

Jennifer tried to remain calm. "Please don't do this," she said.

"Do what? I'm not doing anything. You're the one doing, babe."

"Please, Donald."

"What's his name? The guy you're doing. Tell me. I wanna hear you say it."

Jennifer folded her arms across her chest as she tried for strength. "What's the point, Donald?"

"I want to know," he said, maintaining a calm voice. "I have a right to know. Since he's been in my house, fucking my wife on my bed. I think I have a right to know."

Jennifer's arms immediately uncrossed as she shook her head. "We never," she said. "Not here."

"Bullshit!" Donald yelled. His wife jumped from the volume of his voice. "Yesterday. I just missed you. I came home but you must've just left. Your gunk, the sperm gel, was out of the cap. Unless you put it on before you go see him. I know you don't use it for me. You haven't for a couple months now."

Jennifer avoided her husband's eyes again. "And the bed was messed up," he added. "And something else."

She waited in silence with her eyes closed. "What?" she finally asked.

Gentry smirked at his wife.

"What?" she repeated.

"I got it on film."

Chapter 38

WHEN SHE WOKE UP, SAMANTHA was on her back, and her hands were restrained. A gag had been stuffed in her mouth.

A flabby, pale-skinned man stood over her in the living room. He had a short buzz haircut and a thick Confederate flag belt buckle. One hand held on to the buckle. He held a can of Budweiser in his other hand.

"I'm Beau Curitan," he told Samantha. "You know, Carol's husband."

Then the man leered as he stepped on Samantha's left thigh.

His field supervisor had been blunt. "If you even think this case is going down the shitter, then cuff the son of a bitch and bring his ass back here right now," the supervisor had told Agent Thomas.

That was ten minutes ago. Now Thomas was standing at a house telephone in the lobby of the Bellagio. He had been ringing Nicholas Cuccia's room for the past fifteen minutes. He had called Joey Francone's room as well. Then Thomas asked hotel security to check on his good friend in suite 24-B, just to make sure he was all right. They had an important business appointment to make.

Thomas was impatient waiting for security to get back to him. He scanned the constant flowing crowds in front of him for the New York mobster he was there to baby-sit. There were too many people to pick out any one person. At least he couldn't find Cuccia amid the sea of gamblers and tourists.

When he could spot the head of security finally heading his way, Thomas was still hopeful.

"There's nobody in suite twenty-four-B, sir," the head of security said. "But one of my men did say there was blood on the rug."

Thomas could feel his strength being sapped. "What do you mean, blood?"

"One of my men said that's what he saw after he went inside the suite. Blood. Some drops leading to the bathroom and to the door."

Thomas flashed his badge for the third time the same day. "Let me up there," he said in a defeated monotone.

Donald Gentry looked his wife up and down. The image of her breasts bouncing in the video while her lover took her from behind was suddenly clear to him again.

"You just fuck him again now?" he asked.

"No," she said.

He was picturing things he hadn't even seen on the video. His thoughts raced out of control with jealousy and rage. "You just run over to his place for a quickie? You fuck him in his kitchen? In the car? Or did you just get on your knees and suck him off?"

"Please, Donald. Don't do this."

"I saw the tape, Jen," Gentry said. He closed his eyes tight and growled from somewhere deep inside. "I already saw you on your knees!" he cried. "I already saw it!"

She put her hands together as she pleaded with him. "Please don't."

Gentry drank from the tequila bottle again. He wiped his mouth on his shoulder and said, "Maybe I should sell the tape to a local porn store. Or make copies and lend them out at bachelor parties. What do you think?"

Her face tightened as she flushed red with anger. "I want that tape!" she yelled. There were no more tears behind her voice.

"Is he still married?" Gentry yelled back. "Does Wilkes have a wife, too? Are you ruining her marriage, too?"

"You don't know what you're doing!" she yelled. "I have to have that tape!"

"I know exactly what I'm doing!"

"Give me the fucking tape, you pathetic bastard!"

Gentry suddenly smiled at his wife. All he could hear were the words "you pathetic bastard."

An emotional weight was suddenly lifted. He no longer saw his wife standing in front of him. There was an image of a blond woman in a white sweatshirt and black leggings. It was as if she were a ghost. It was as if he were watching himself and his wife from another ceiling camera.

He pulled the Glock .9 from his ankle strap and focused on the white sweatshirt. Spots of blood filled the sweatshirt as his wife was hurled backward into the hallway.

He closed his eyes and could see his wife's breasts being pierced in slow motion by the bullets he had just fired.

Then he saw the barrel of the gun inside his mouth. He felt a burn from the edge of the barrel. He heard himself curse from the burn. He tilted the gun down as he felt himself pull the trigger. He felt a lancing, burning sensation through his throat as he fell off the chair he was sitting on. He gagged and choked as he spit up blood. He felt himself kneeling in the kitchen as he spit up more blood.

He was straining to scream, but there was no sound. He looked down and saw the puddle of blood forming at his knees. The realization that he was still alive filled Donald Gentry with terror. He turned to his left and saw his wife dead in the hallway. He tried to scream again, but there was still no sound.

Chapter 39

FRENI SPOTTED THE FLASHING lights in the driveway as he drove up to the Bellagio. He saw a pair of ambulances and at least three police cars parked directly in front of the lobby. A group of hotel security guards stood outside and blocked off a set of doors from public access.

He drove through the driveway and pulled into a gas station on the Strip. He parked in front of the air hoses and used a cellular telephone to call the Vive la Body gymnasium. He gave the receptionist at the gym the number for his phone and waited for a return call. Three minutes later, his cell phone rang.

"One down, one to go," Freni said. "But there's a lot of activity around number two."

"I'm busy now, but we can meet for a bite," Lercasi said.

"No problem," Freni said.

"How's Chinese again?"

"Chinese is fine."

"Okay, I'll call you back."

Both men hung up without saying good-bye. Freni lit a cigarette and glanced at his watch. He figured he'd stay close in case things changed. Jerry Lercasi would be a lot more generous if both ends of the contract were serviced.

Lercasi had traded favor for favor with a few of the ethnic gangs of Las Vegas in the past. Usually for the strong-arm work he could no longer entrust to his own crew. Usually for the work the mob officially considered against the rules.

Now he had a conversation with the head of a Vietnamese gang in Las Vegas, a skinny gook with slicked-back hair and a diamond-studded Rolex wrapped around his skinny right bicep.

Minh Quan was born in Tonkin Province in Vietnam. He had entered the United States illegally when he was fifteen, and before he was twenty he had used relatives who were legalized citizens to open a Chinese-Vietnamese take-out restaurant. It served as a front for the extortion and drug dealing of his Black Dragons street gang. Quan was the eldest of the gang. At twenty-eight, he had already killed three men. Two were rival street gang members. The third was a contract hit on a Russian gambler.

The conversation was expensive, but twenty thousand dollars was well worth Lercasi's peace of mind. Erasing the links between himself and the disappearance of his accountant and business manager, Allen Fein, was textbook damage control.

The botched job the Vietnamese crew had pulled at Harrah's with Charlie Pellecchia would work for Lercasi now. He had instructed Minh Quan to make the hit on Pellecchia look as close to a mugging as possible.

Lercasi knew the organized crime units would continue to suspect the New York crew. His own reputation as a deliberate and ruthless killer would protect Lercasi from the series of botched jobs over the past week. Whacking a few key people would further distance him.

Allen Fein's killer had become a key player in the mix of events.

Lercasi warned the Vietnamese gang leader about the man he would be killing. "He's a professional," he told Minh. "He'll know it's coming if your people are sloppy. He might pick one or two off, so you better work in teams."

"No worrey," the skinny gook told Lercasi. "Everything taken care of."

"I'm just warning you," Lercasi said. "For your own good. Don't bother sending kids again. That was a civilian who put one of your guys in the hospital today. This guy is a pro."

"No worrey," Minh repeated.

Chapter 40

BEAU CURITAN REMOVED THE gag from the woman's mouth. He used an extension cord to tie her hands. He tied her feet with a belt he found in her bedroom closet.

She was unconscious from the chloroform he had forced her to breathe. She lay motionless on the floor, her hands tied together on her stomach just above her waist.

Beau went through the wallet he found in her purse. He learned her name was Samantha Cole and that she was born on December 3, 1967. Beau counted forward by tens from 1967 to figure out her age.

Samantha Cole was attractive but too skinny, Beau thought. Beau liked full-sized women like his wife, Carol.

He opened Samantha Cole's blouse to peek at her chest. Her bra blocked his view. He looked around himself before he reached inside the blouse to try to feel her breasts. He leaned in close to her skin as he pushed the top of the bra down off her right breast.

Beau jumped back when she suddenly moaned. He lost his balance as he fell into the couch.

"Shit," he said when he landed on the gun tucked inside the waist of his pants. He removed the gun and set it on the television.

He went back through her wallet and found sixty-five dollars. He removed the money and set it alongside where he sat on the couch. He also found a credit card.

He went to the refrigerator for a beer when he heard the telephone ring. He went to the kitchen, where it sat in a cradle. It was one of the portable kinds he used to hate to watch his wife parade around their house with.

The phone continued to ring while Beau stared at it. He was afraid to answer. He had broken in, assaulted a woman, tied her, and peeked inside her clothes. If he were caught now, he would never get to his wife.

Beau ignored the telephone. He would have to wait it out, at least until Samantha Cole woke up. She had refused to tell him anything earlier, but that was before he put her to sleep. This time when she woke up, he would show her how easy it would be to take advantage of a sleeping woman.

Beau turned on the television and sat on the couch when he found a wrestling show.

Lano had taken two more sets of pictures for Charlie and Denton. He spilled the two disposable cameras from a plastic bag onto the roof of a parked car. The three men were in the parking garage behind the Bellagio. They had just come from Francone's room, where they had deposited and posed Cuccia with his younger protégé gangster, Joey Francone.

Lano handed the cameras to Charlie.

"I already got my own set," he said. "I knew they'd be priceless someday."

"Why the extra two?" Denton asked.

Charlie tossed one of the cameras to Denton. "One for each of us."

Lano nodded. "For souvenirs."

When Samantha was twelve, she had played spin the bottle with her best friend and two boys from one of their classes. Samantha and her best friend had liked the taller of the two boys. Each had wanted the bottle to point at him rather than at the shorter boy.

They played the kissing game in her friend's basement a while before it graduated from a simple public kiss to going into the

walk-in closet for two minutes. Samantha was the first to win at th
more private game. She and the boy of her preference stepped inside
the closet. When the door closed behind them, the boy immediately
stood behind Samantha and groped at her flat chest. It was an awkward feeling for her. She stopped it by turning to face the boy. When
she went to kiss him, he backed away.

"Turn around," he had told her. "I want to feel your tits."

Samantha had called him a jerk and stepped out of the closet a full
minute and a half short of their allotted time. She remembered
walking past her best friend to head up the stairs.

"What's wrong?" her friend had asked.

"I'm going home," Samantha had told her.

She never played a kissing game again. When she reflected on her
experience later in life, Samantha knew it was just a dumb kid game
she had been engaged in, but the idea of being groped like a piece of
meat had angered her ever since.

Now she could feel fingers under her blouse. Beau Curitan thought
she was still unconscious, and he was groping her. She didn't dare
open her eyes. She knew he was dangerous. She also knew her only
chance was to surprise him somehow.

The stale smell of beer off his wet breath was sickening. Samantha
wanted to scream. She forced herself to remain still and hoped Beau
would climb on top of her just enough so she could nail him with a
knee. It was no good where he was then, leaning over her from one
side. She needed for him to be directly in front of her. She needed for
him to be on top of her.

Chapter 41

HALF A MILE FROM the Bellagio, Anthony Rizzi sipped an Absolut on the rocks laden with Valium and codeine. It was his second drink since coming back up to his room. It was his fifth drink since they had met in the bar downstairs, played a little craps, and grabbed dinner at the famous Bacchanal.

Niko was down to a black mesh thong and matching bra. Her nipples were hard from the air conditioning. She was anxious for Rizzi to fall asleep. She could feel goose bumps up and down her arms.

She sat on the edge of the bed and leaned forward just enough for Rizzi to touch her breasts with his fingertips. She cooed for him softly.

"You make Niko feel nice," she said.

Rizzi sipped at his drink again. "You have beautiful tits," he said.

Niko pulled away as Rizzi leaned toward her. He extended his right arm and lost his balance. He fell forward on the bed.

"Shit," Niko said.

Rizzi had spilled his drink.

"Watch what you do," she said, scolding him. "Spill your drink like that."

She went to the table to pour another. This time she added twice the amount of codeine.

Rizzi was wiping sweat off his head. "How come it's so hot in here?"

Niko sat on the bed again. She took Rizzi's face with one hand, guiding his lips to hers. She darted her tongue inside his mouth for him to suck. She held the kiss a long time before slowly pulling back.

Then she guided the drink up to his lips and held it for him while he sipped. She tipped the glass up, forcing Rizzi to drink until he gagged on what he couldn't swallow.

He coughed loud and hard. She waited until he composed himself. She looked into his sleepy eyes and kissed Rizzi again. Then she held the glass up to his lips one more time.

Detectives Gold and Iandolli were close to the Bellagio when they received the emergency call from headquarters. An officer was down. He had been brought to Sunrise Hospital and Medical Center. Gold turned on the siren and maneuvered through traffic as he raced to the hospital.

When they met with the emergency room surgeon who had worked on Donald Gentry, they were told that the patient was stable.

Gold sweated profusely.

"He's either the luckiest man alive or the unluckiest," the surgeon said.

The detectives looked to each other.

"He shot a bullet clear through his throat," the surgeon continued. "He'll never talk again, but he'll live. He missed bone and artery by fractions of an inch. It's amazing there isn't more damage. His vocal cords were torn to shreds, though. There's nothing we can do for him there. He's also got a burn wound on both his lips that appears to be from the barrel of the gun. That might explain why he survived. He probably burned himself and altered the position of the gun just enough to miss killing himself."

The surgeon showed the two detectives the path of the bullet on his own throat. "The bullet went down and out just above his Adam's apple."

"Fuck," Iandolli said.

"I'm sure you already know about the wife," the surgeon continued. "DOA. Four shots in the chest."

Gold stared blankly at the emergency room doors.

"What happened?" the surgeon asked.

Iandolli motioned at the surgeon to leave.

"If you need me, I'll be around," the surgeon said. He apologized and headed back inside the emergency room.

"There was nothing anybody could do," Iandolli told Gold. "You have to know that."

"I could've told her to leave town," Gold said. "I could've told Wilkes to run off with her. I could've suggested the department put Gentry on leave."

"And Mrs. Gentry could've went home nights to her husband instead of screwing around with Michael Wilkes," Iandolli said. "It's not your fault, Abe. It doesn't work that way."

"Poor bastard will be on a suicide watch the rest of his life."

"Probably."

"They pick up Wilkes yet?"

"The highway patrol did. He was on his way out of town. At least he was heading that way. His car was packed with his stuff. He had more than ten grand on him."

"Who has him?" Gold asked.

"Us, right now," Iandolli said. "But the Feds'll put up a fight over him soon enough."

Gold shook his head. "What a joke. We can't get out of our own way, the good guys."

"It's a self-fulfilling nightmare."

Gold motioned toward the hospital exit. "Why don't you take off," he said. "I want to hang around here a while."

"You gonna be all right?"

"Nothing happened to me."

"You sure? I can stay, Abe. Talking with these clowns from New York can wait."

"Go," Gold said. "I'll catch up with you later."

Chapter 42

CHARLIE DECIDED TO TAKE the taxi drive to the hospital with John Denton before heading back to Samantha's apartment. He tried to call the apartment from a pay phone at the Bellagio but there was no answer.

Denton was quiet during the taxi ride back to the hospital. Charlie found himself feeling sorry for his wife's lover.

"I'll deny you were there if you want," he told Denton. "If you're worried about your law license."

"I'm on camera in the hallways same as you," Denton said. "Besides, I think that guy was right. I don't think they'll do anything while we have pictures."

"Why don't you two get the hell out of Las Vegas tonight?" Charlie asked.

"I don't know if she can yet," Denton said. "Besides, I think she'll want to know you're safe."

"What makes you think that?"

"She doesn't hate you, Charlie."

Charlie nodded, then glanced at his watch. "They must have hospitals in California," he said.

The taxi pulled into the Valley Hospital parking lot.

"You coming in?" Denton asked.

"She doesn't want to see me," Charlie said.

"You're wrong. She did want to see you. To apologize, I think."

Charlie rubbed his bruised knuckles. "This wasn't anybody's fault," he said. "Look, I know better. Shit happens."

Denton extended a hand to Charlie. Charlie looked at it a few seconds before taking it.

"Don't forget to get those developed," he told Denton. He was pointing at the plastic bag holding the disposable camera. "No matter what that other guy does, it's all we have."

Charlie gave the driver Samantha's address, then sat back in the seat to close his eyes. He pictured his wife upstairs in her hospital room and the smile she would greet her lover with. He felt a pang of jealousy for a smile that was no longer his.

Charlie thought about the new smile in his life and how grateful he would be to see Samantha again. He hoped she was home when the taxi dropped him off. He would hug and kiss her tight. He wouldn't let go.

Minh had delegated a second contract for the Italian mob to his wife back at the restaurant. He had stayed in touch with his men following Charlie Pellechia and immediately raced to the hospital after his sit-down with Lercasi.

Now Minh sat low behind a steering wheel as he observed a taxi from the edge of a hospital parking lot. A man got out of the cab and headed inside the hospital. Two of Minh's soldiers were in a car farther up the street. They called to confirm the man still sitting in the taxi to be Charlie Pellecchia.

Minh lit a cigarette as he waited for the taxi to turn up the street. He watched intently as the car passed. He could see the stocky man in the back clearly. Charlie Pellecchia seemed oblivious to his surroundings.

Minh took a few drags on the cigarette before shifting gears and following at a safe distance. When his men asked if they should cut the taxi off, Minh answered in French: "*Non. Revenez au restaurant. Aidez couper celui-là. Je me charge celui-ci.*"

"No," he had told them. "Get back to the restaurant. Help cut up that one. I'll take care of this one."

"*Tu sûr?*" one of his men asked.

"*Ne t'inquiéte pas de moi, huh,*" Minh said in French, then translated to English, "No worrey."

Chapter 43

ONCE BEAU REMOVED THE belt from Samantha's ankles, he pulled her pants down. Samantha knew she had to let him get closer.

He started to kiss her feet as she faked a moan for him.

"You do like that, don't you?" Beau whispered.

Samantha forced herself to open her legs a little.

"Yeah, baby, you do like it," he said. He kissed up the insides of her legs until he reached her knees. Then he flattened out on his stomach to kiss up the insides of her thighs.

She could kick him in the face right then, but she didn't think she could stun him long enough to escape the apartment. Samantha had to lie still and fake more moans of pleasure as the wife-beater crawled his way toward her crotch.

She still seemed groggy from the chloroform, but Beau guessed the anesthetic was making it easier. He licked and kissed the insides of her thighs as she continued to respond.

He could see some of her pubic hair underneath the navy blue underwear she was wearing. The sight of her pubic hair turned Beau on. He bit at his lower lip as he felt himself grow hard.

He looked to her face and saw her eyes slowly open. He paused a moment, then continued again as she closed her eyes and licked her lips.

"You are liking this, baby, ain't you?" Beau said.

He thought she said, "Yes" as he got up off his stomach and onto his knees to get closer to her crotch.

Samantha couldn't bear the thought of him touching her there. It looked as though he would use his mouth first. She forced herself to lick her lips when he saw she was awake. Then she arched her back just enough to bring her legs up and lay her feet flat on the floor.

He straddled her right leg as his head ducked down toward her crotch. She lowered her right leg just enough to create distance between his crotch and her right knee.

Beau's mouth touched Samantha through her panties a split second before he gagged hard as the wind was knocked from his lungs. His face turned to a grimace of pain. She tried to kick him again as he rolled off and smacked her foot against his knee. She winced from the bruise she gave herself.

Samantha was rolling away from Beau when she felt his hand weakly grab at one of her feet. She stood up and saw he was still trying to catch his breath in a half fetal position on the floor. She kicked at his face with her free foot and smashed his nose hard. Blood splattered across his face and T-shirt.

When she was free again, Samantha ran toward the front door. Her wrists were bound tightly but her hands were free enough to turn the doorknob. She heard Beau moaning in pain behind her as she struggled to open the door. She tried turning the knob a few times before she realized the dead bolt was locked. She reached up to turn the lock as Beau yelled, "You fuckin' bitch!"

The door was open, and she glanced back before stepping outside. Beau was leaning against the television, pointing something at her. Samantha was on the stoop when she heard the loud pop. She felt a burning pain in her left leg as she spun off balance.

She fell forward down the short flight of stairs. Her head struck something hard, and everything turned black.

• • •

A car raced in the opposite direction as the taxi turned up Samantha's street. The taxi driver jerked his wheel to the right to avoid the speeding car.

"Some people," he said.

Charlie turned in his seat to see the tail end of a small dark coupe heading around the corner behind them. The taxi driver pulled up in front of Samantha's house when Charlie noticed the front door was open. He was about to pay the driver when he saw someone lying at the foot of the stairs.

"Oh, God!" he yelled. "Oh, God!"

A minivan pulling out of a driveway blocked the street. As soon as Minh Quan started cursing at the woman driving the minivan, a small crowd of people on a nearby lawn started yelling at him.

"Fuck me," Minh said as he slammed his dashboard.

"Call the police!" he heard someone yell.

"Fuck you!" Minh yelled at them.

"Hey, you watch your mouth," Minh heard someone else say, but he was backing up on the street. He gave them the finger as he spun into a driveway to make a quick U-turn.

Chapter 44

AGENT THOMAS DIDN'T KNOW what to expect as he searched Cuccia's suite at the Bellagio. He was assuming he'd find Charlie Pellecchia's body in one of the closets or maybe inside the shower or the tub. Unless they had already cut Pellecchia up and were taking him out of the Bellagio a plastic bag at a time.

When he didn't find a body, Thomas scanned the floor from the doorway. The bloodstains were trailing exactly the way hotel security had described them. One trail headed toward the bathroom. The other trail led back to the door. Thomas stepped back out into the hallway and kneeled to check the rug for more blood.

"Fuck," he said when he spotted the stains. He stood up and started for the elevators.

"Where to now?" the hotel security supervisor asked.

"He has two friends on another floor," Thomas said. "Francone and Lano."

As he drove north on the Strip toward the desert, Vincent Lano thought about what might have been.

His remorse was palpable. Las Vegas had become Lano's final act of contrition. He had lived his entire life in the service of other men whose self-interest had always preceded his own. He had robbed, assaulted, killed, and spent seven years of his life in prison for those men.

He had been a good soldier in an army he was no longer proud to be associated with. He had come to Las Vegas on orders to do something he knew was wrong.

When he was far enough out in the desert, Lano pulled the car off the highway.

He lit a cigarette and set the grenade on the dashboard as he watched the traffic pass behind him in the rearview mirror. He wasn't sure whether the pictures he had left at the Bellagio would ever find their way back to his New York crew. He liked to believe they would. He liked to believe that Cuccia and Francone would be executed for the embarrassment they had brought on their crime family. He liked to believe something good would come from what had happened in Las Vegas.

Lano was nearly finished with his cigarette when he pulled the pin on the grenade. He dropped the explosive over his right shoulder into the back of the car and took his time inhaling a last drag on the cigarette. He coughed, and the grenade exploded.

When Anthony Rizzi finally awoke, he was cold and groggy. He shivered as he pushed himself off the bed and searched for signs of the woman he had brought up to his room. She was an Oriental woman, he remembered, a real looker.

He half-dressed in the bathroom as he tried to remember what had happened. He could see her face. He could still smell her. He checked his watch for the time and suddenly realized what had happened.

His Rolex was missing from his wrist. Rizzi slapped at his pants pockets for his wallet, but it was gone, too. He started going through drawers when he noticed his room had been tossed.

"Fuck!" he yelled.

He went through the room trying to take an inventory of what was stolen. He opened the closet door and found that his suitcase was already opened. He checked to see if the gold chains and gold Movado watch were in the zippered pocket inside the flap of the suitcase. He cursed again when he saw they also were missing.

He started to phone the front desk but stopped as he realized his predicament. How was he supposed to tell anyone about this? He had brought a hooker up to his room and was rolled for all his cash, credit cards, and jewelry. A quick estimate brought the figure to more than twenty thousand dollars.

Rizzi remembered why he was there, and it gave him an uneasy feeling. His relationship with Nicholas Cuccia had once offered the respect he had always assumed most men craved. The power over life and death was an ultimate power. Becoming a made man in a New York crime family would have reasserted his manhood in a way no one could ever deny or defy.

Except now his stomach was nervous from the thought of Nicholas Cuccia. Rizzi had been told that Las Vegas was where he would be tested as a man. He had been told that if he did what was expected of him, he would go home a made man.

Now the thought terrified him. Rizzi wanted out.

Chapter 45

DETECTIVE IANDOLLI STOPPED WHEN he saw the maids giggling in the hallway on the twenty-second floor. Two of the hotel security guards stood outside room 2232. Both of the guards smiled at Iandolli when he approached the door.

"What's so funny?" he asked.

"You'll see," one of the guards said as he opened the door. He let Iandolli pass into the room and quickly shut the door when the maids tried to peek inside.

Iandolli stopped dead in his tracks. Two men were tied together on a double bed. One man appeared to be unconscious. He lay on his back with his two legs wrapped and tied around the other man. Both men were dressed in Bellagio T-shirts and hats.

"Jesus Christ," Iandolli said as he shook his head.

The man who was still conscious was tied on his knees between the unconscious man's legs. A pair of white sweat socks had been jammed inside his mouth for a gag. A flesh-colored dildo jutted from his rectum.

Two emergency service workers waited while the hotel security guard untied the series of belts that seemed to hold the men in place.

"You two are mobsters?" Iandolli asked.

The conscious man spoke as soon as the pair of socks was pulled from his mouth. "Vincent Lano!" he yelled at Iandolli. "He did this! Lano! He's registered in this room with me. Vincent Lano, the motherfucker!"

"You really want to press charges?"

"Fuck!" the conscious man said.

Iandolli pulled out a notepad. "Well?"

The conscious man remained silent.

The security guard brought a paper bag to Iandolli. "This was left here," the guard said. He held it up so Iandolli could read the writing on the bag. "They wrote 'FBI' on it. See?" the guard said.

Iandolli took the bag and looked inside. When he saw the camera, he chuckled. "Right," he said.

"Should we secure the area?" the guard asked.

Iandolli winked at the guard. "That or sell tickets."

Minh Quan had circled around the neighborhood a few times before he spotted the commotion with the ambulance and police. Then he saw Charlie Pellecchia get inside the ambulance.

"Shit," Minh said.

He waited for the crowed to disperse before he drove by the address where the police were now investigating. Minh wrote the address on an extra delivery menu and turned his car around to follow Charlie Pellecchia yet again.

"What's going on?" Thomas asked Iandolli outside Francone's room. He had come off the elevator with a contingent of hotel security.

The detective smirked as he thumbed at the room. "In there? A lovefest."

Thomas pointed to the bag Iandolli was holding. "What's that?"

"Lunch."

Thomas saw the writing. "It says 'FBI.'"

"Yeah, it does. Not 'DEA,' though. Too bad."

Thomas motioned at Iandolli to hand over the bag. "I'll pass it on," he said.

Iandolli sneered. "Yeah, right. I don't think so."

Thomas stood his ground. "Then we both will."

"Not anytime soon," Iandolli said as he pointed to Francone's room. "I'm heading to the hospital. From the look of things in there, so's your boy." He held the bag up. "I'll have one of my guys bring this to Walsh, the FBI honcho in Vegas."

Thomas scowled. "And I'll go with him."

Iandolli shrugged. "That'd be up to you, but he isn't handing this bag to anyone but Walsh, so get used to the idea. It says 'FBI,' it goes to the FBI."

Thomas clenched his teeth and motioned at Francone's room. "Is Charlie Pellecchia in there?"

"Not exactly," Iandolli said

"Cuccia?" Thomas asked as he crossed the hall to the door.

"Bingo."

Chapter 46

"ARE YOU GUYS KIDDING me?" Charlie said. "I haven't even seen my girlfriend yet. She was shot in the leg, for Christ sakes."

"You can see her later," the detective named Gold said. "After you answer some questions."

Charlie shook his head. "I already told the cops in the emergency room," he said. "I found her on the walk outside her apartment. She was bleeding from the leg, and her head was all banged up. There's a guy did that to her driving around someplace. The police have a description. They know his fucking name."

The detective named Iandolli showed Charlie a set of pictures. "What about these?" he asked.

Charlie shrugged at the pictures. "What about them?"

"Fucking wiseass," Gold said.

"Fuck you," Charlie said.

Gold stepped chest to chest with Charlie. "Fuck me?" he said.

Iandolli pulled Gold back as he spoke to Charlie. "You and Mr. Denton and Mr. Lano are on Bellagio hotel cameras," he said. "We kind of know what happened. We want you to fill in the blanks. It might save your life."

"Save my life?" Charlie said as his face turned red. "That's what that asshole DEA agent told me, how he was going to make sure this punk stayed away from me. That was about an hour before some Asian kids tried to cut me in my hotel. I tell you what, I'll save my own life."

Iandolli looked to Gold. "What Asian kids?"

"Forget about it," Charlie said. "I'm not pressing charges against them either."

Gold pushed Iandolli out of his way. "Who the fuck do you think you are?" he asked Charlie.

Charlie glared from Gold to Iandolli. "He's close if he's trying to get me to take a swing," he said.

Gold reached for his handcuffs. Iandolli stopped him.

"What were you doing at the Bellagio?" Iandolli asked.

"I took a room at the Bellagio. I checked out of Harrah's, and I needed a room. I decided to stay in Las Vegas a few extra days. To be with my girlfriend."

"You trying to get her killed, too?" Gold asked.

"Enough," Iandolli told Gold. "What happened at Harrah's?" he asked Charlie.

Charlie was still glaring at Gold.

"Mr. Pellecchia?" Iandolli said.

"No way," Charlie said. "I'm not going there."

"Take him in," Gold said as he made another attempt at Charlie.

"Hold it!" Iandolli said, pulling Gold back a second time. "Damn it, Abe."

"Take me in for what?" Charlie asked Iandolli. "For getting beat up? For trying to protect myself?"

Gold tugged at Iandolli's arm. "I'm not in the mood for this bullshit," he said. "Not with what happened to Gentry. I'm not listening to this now."

"Look," Charlie said, pointing his finger toward the elevators, "my girlfriend is upstairs. They just removed a bullet from her leg. I haven't seen her yet."

"One minute," Iandolli said. He held on to Gold's left arm as he walked the senior detective across the hallway. "Let me handle this for now," he whispered. "You're too upset. Go get a soda. Talk to the other one, the boyfriend. Let me talk to this one alone."

Gold, clearly frustrated, pulled his arm from Iandolli's grip and walked away.

Iandolli returned to Charlie. "Go and visit your girlfriend," he said. "We'll talk again later."

Charlie nodded.

"Go ahead," Iandolli said.

Charlie watched as the detective took the stairs. As he waited for an elevator, Charlie felt uneasy about the pictures Vincent Lano had taken at the Bellagio. If the police already had pictures, the film he was holding on to would no longer serve as a deterrent to mobsters trying to cover their embarrassment.

He knew he couldn't beat the mob much longer. Once the men in the picture were on the street again, he knew they would come looking for him. The thought of the mob going after Samantha was even more terrifying.

He headed for the elevator but stopped a few feet from an open car. He felt himself sweating. He couldn't move.

Chapter 47

THE CHINESE RESTAURANT WAS Empty when Renato Freni walked inside. Except for the young woman working the counter and the two cooks in the kitchen, Freni was alone. He dropped his right hand inside his right pants pocket to touch the end of the Firestorm 10 Shot .22 Semi Automatic he was carrying.

The woman behind the counter had large oval eyes and thick lips. She smiled at Freni. "May I herp you, prease?" she asked in a heavy Asian accent.

Freni gave a quick glance over his shoulder. "I'm supposed to meet a friend," he said.

"Mr. Recasi?" she asked.

"Close enough," Freni said.

The woman pointed over her shoulder. "He in back," she said. "Waiting for dumpring."

Freni watched as the woman packaged a container of steamed dumplings and hot mustard. She handed it to Freni and pointed down the hall toward a door at the far end of the restaurant.

"Take prease," she said. "Mr. Recasi waiting for dumpring."

Freni did a double take at the woman before shrugging and taking the small package from her. He saw two doors in the rear, one leading outside. He was unsure of where to go.

"In back," she said, still pointing. "Through door outside. On patio."

"Oh," Freni said. "Sure, no problem."

• • •

Phuc Hanh was twenty-four years old, a part-time prostitute and killer, and Minh Quan's wife. Her name in Vietnamese meant blessing from above, as in good family. It also meant happiness.

Today she was executing a new contract the Italians had paid her husband thirty-five thousand dollars for. She had backup gang members in the basement and bathroom because she had never used a gun to kill before. A Walther P-22 had been hidden under loose menus under the front counter. She had briefly hefted the gun before it was hidden.

After the man she was to kill took the package and headed down the hallway toward the back of the restaurant, Phuc Hanh reached under the counter for the Walther. The man was about five feet from the counter when Phuc Hanh shot him in the back of the head. His body went into spasm on the floor, and she leaned over to fire a bullet into his right temple. She yelled something in French, and both cooks quickly dragged the body into the basement.

Phuc Hanh returned to the front counter, wiped sweat from her forehead, and used the telephone. When she hung up, she opened a can of Coke. She was perfectly calm a few minutes later when an Asian couple came in to order take-out.

After stalling his meeting with Renato Freni, Jerry Lercasi relaxed as he watched the highlights of a Dodgers-Giants game on satellite television. The next few days were going to be busy. He expected several more visits from the local authorities. He expected harassments from federal agents as well.

Then there would be the request for a meeting by the New York crew he would have to deal with. Without Allen Fein to run interference, Lercasi was thinking he might have to handle New York by himself.

He was waiting for a call. He stretched his arms out wide as he yawned. He heard his bones crack as he tightened his arm muscles.

When the telephone rang, Lercasi picked up the receiver but didn't speak.

"Your order is ready," a woman with an accent said.

"I think you have a wrong number," Lercasi said.

After taking care of all the business he could think of for one day, Lercasi thought about finishing the day off with some more Chinese. He dialed the reception desk and asked if Brenda was still around. When the girl working the desk told Lercasi that his girlfriend was gone for the day, he asked about the Asian woman who was giving Mr. Fein his massages the past few days.

Was she free? Lercasi wanted to know. And did she want a permanent job working at Vive la Body?

Joey Francone received five stitches in his rectum at the emergency room. He was given codeine for his pain and gauze bandaging for the bleeding. He was told the stitches would dissolve but that it would be a good idea to come back to the hospital in a few days to have the wound checked.

Francone was too embarrassed to care what the doctors in the emergency room had told him. He wanted out of there. He needed to find Nicholas Cuccia.

When he searched for his boss, Francone spotted two men he knew were federal agents outside the recovery room. He didn't bother to ask why they were there. Cuccia had either made a deal or was about to. Francone wasn't sticking around to find out.

Suddenly he saw himself for what he was in the bigger picture of the Vignieri crime family. He was a "nobody" in the mob world. Cuccia was a made man, a "somebody." Cuccia also was a skipper running his own crew, somebody directly linked to an underboss. Cuccia had clout. Francone had nothing.

This was one reason why he retraced his steps to the emergency room. He saw a pocketbook hanging from the back of a chair in the waiting area and snatched it. He found an exit and left the hospital. He knew he couldn't head back to the Bellagio yet, so he limped two blocks in pain to a taxi stand in front of a shopping mall instead. He waited ten minutes before a taxi could take him to a cheap motel off the Strip.

Francone was grateful for what was inside the small purse: $253. He paid for the taxi with a $10 bill and stashed the rest of the cash inside his pants pocket.

He took a room at a short-stay dump for one night. He left a $20 bill for local telephone calls at the front desk. Francone called Anthony Rizzi at Caesar's Palace to make sure the wannabe still was in Las Vegas. Rizzi was supposed to meet them with cash reinforcements. Rizzi was one way out of Las Vegas. Francone wasn't sure if there was another.

Chapter 48

ONCE HE WAS CHECKED out of his motel in Las Vegas, Beau Curitan drove south on Highway 95. Beau had never meant for things to get so carried away. He never intended to shoot the woman hiding his wife. He never intended to touch or to undress her.

Except Samantha Cole had seemed to respond to his teasing as she awoke from her chloroform sleep. It was just like the abducted women in the paperback books Beau had read. Samantha seemed to enjoy what he was doing to her. He swore she had responded verbally to his advances. He was positive he had heard her say "Yes."

Now Beau was fleeing the scene of what he guessed would be breaking and entering, assault, attempted rape, and attempted murder charges. He pulled off the highway when he spotted a cheap motel. He took a room for a short stay while he tried to retrace what had gone so wrong for him. Beau realized he had stolen money and credit cards from the wallet in Samantha's purse. Taking the money and credit cards would add robbery to the list of charges he was fleeing.

Then he realized he had left his gun behind, a Baretta .25 his father had given him on his eighteenth birthday.

He needed to get out of Nevada. He was sure the state police had a description of his car. They might even have his license plate numbers. Beau needed to either change cars or license plate numbers or have the car painted. He checked outside his window and saw he could steal license plates from another car parked in the lot.

He used the telephone book to locate used-car dealers and

mechanics. The nearest city Beau recognized on a map was Laughlin, less than an hour's drive. He unfolded his map of Nevada on the bed and plotted a route to the resort town in the mountains.

A drop of blood dripping from his nose landed on the map. Beau touched the tip of his nose and winced.

Charlie couldn't bring himself to see Samantha yet. He had started and stopped twice. He decided to see his wife first.

"It was kind of rushed," he said when he was standing alongside her bed. "I thought you were out shopping."

Lisa was trying to smile through her stitched mouth. "I felt horrible," she said. "I still do."

Charlie didn't say anything. There wasn't much to say. It was the first time he had spoken to his wife since she left him for another man. Each of them had since been assaulted. Each of them had suffered. Each of them had unknowingly dragged innocent victims into danger. Each of them was sorry for dragging out their own misery together.

"Are you all right?" Lisa asked.

Charlie managed a half smile. His wife didn't know about the new woman in his life.

"I'm fine," he said.

"What happens next?"

"Whatever you want. We sit down and file for divorce. I don't expect either of us will contest anything."

It was a half question. Lisa shook her head.

"It should go pretty fast," Charlie said.

Lisa pointed to her face. "What about this other mess?"

"I think it's over," Charlie said. "Your friend John was a big help." He wasn't sure if it was his place to go any farther. He had no idea of what his wife was aware of. "I think he cares for you very much," he added.

Lisa was silent. She began to cry as Charlie shifted from foot to foot alongside her bed.

"Do you hate me?" she asked.

It was an awkward question. He had felt anger and frustration but never hatred. "What makes you ask that?"

"Do you?"

"Of course not."

"The way it happened. I didn't plan it that way. I panicked, I think. I'm sorry."

"You don't have to apologize," Charlie said. "It's over."

Lisa wiped her eyes with a tissue.

"And think of the good stuff," he joked. "You don't have to listen to any more opera."

Lisa laughed through her tears. She reached for his hand. He accepted it but somehow felt funny holding his wife's hand. Somehow, he felt as if he were betraying Samantha. He let Lisa's hand go.

A few minutes later, Charlie stopped outside Samantha's room. He could hear her talking to another woman—a nurse, he assumed.

"This should teach me not to invite strange men into my house," he heard Samantha say.

"From the looks of it, you're a lucky lady," the woman said.

"He ruined a perfectly good gam there," Samantha said.

"Nothing a garter belt couldn't cover," the woman said.

Samantha laughed and said, "A garter belt? I have a friend thinks along the same lines as you."

Charlie leaned against the wall in the hallway. He couldn't bring himself any closer to Samantha. The detective's words haunted him.

"*You trying to get her killed, too?*" Gold had asked.

He pushed himself off the wall and turned away from the room. Detective Iandolli was waiting for him.

"She might be better off, you keep your distance," Iandolli said.

"I'm in love with her," Charlie said.

"Then at least until this is settled," Iandolli said.

"And when's that?"

Iandolli couldn't answer. "In the meantime, you're doing the right thing."

The elevator doors opened, and Gold was standing there. Iandolli and Charlie stepped onto the elevator to join him. They rode the car down to the lobby in silence. When they got off, Charlie spotted Denton and walked his way. The detectives headed for the vending machines.

Iandolli inserted a dollar bill into a soda machine and pushed a Diet Sprite button. The can of soda bounced its way down the chute to the open bin. Iandolli grabbed the soda and held the cold can against his forehead a few seconds before pulling the tab to open it.

"He's up against it," Iandolli said.

Gold made a face. "Pellecchia?"

"Big time," Iandolli said. "He won't tell us anything about anything. He's afraid for the girlfriend."

"Did you press him?"

"What's the point? How'd you make out with the other one?"

"The lawyer?" Gold asked. "Forget about it. I threatened to involve the Effa-Bee-Eye, but he's too well in tune with the law to bite."

"Lano left behind those pictures for his own reasons," Iandolli said. "I think we can assume they each have a set. They probably think the film is protection of some kind."

"These two clowns can't have delusions about getting away with this after another week or so," Gold said.

"That's the other kicker," Iandolli said. "I think Pellecchia intends to stay in Las Vegas. He's in love."

Gold's eyebrows furrowed. "Who does he think he is, this Pellecchia? Suppose we don't want him here? Who the fuck does he think he is?"

Iandolli laughed as he counted on his fingers. "A guy came to Vegas for a vacation with his wife, got dumped, got assaulted, found out his wife was assaulted, met some other broad who got shot by some nut chasing another broad all over the country. That's the point, I guess. Pellecchia thinks we look stupid for even asking."

"Yeah, well, I got one of ours over at another hospital who's staring at life for killing his wife. The doctors tell him he'll never be able to speak again for the bullet he tried to kill himself with. So excuse me for not feeling any sympathy for Mr. Pellecchia right now."

"Well, our two out-of-town mobsters aren't about to press charges," Iandolli said. "Right about now, I'd say they'd both like to leave the country."

"Hey, it's none of my fucking business anyway," Gold said. "What happens to wiseguys or this other wiseass from New York with his marital problems. Give him the key to the city, you want."

"I have another idea."

"I don't know that I want to hear it."

Iandolli nodded. "Maybe you shouldn't."

Chapter 49

MINH QUAN HAD HEARD from his wife immediately after the Italian was dead and cut up in the restaurant basement. She had told Minh they were waiting for a private sanitation truck to take his body parts away with the rest of the perishable garbage. One of Jerry Lercasi's men had already delivered the balance on the contract. It was good news.

When he called the hospital and learned that his brother had slipped into a coma, Minh's good mood instantly turned sour. He hung up on the nurse explaining the situation as he stared at the man responsible. Charlie Pellecchia was standing with a detective Minh recognized from the local newspapers, somebody with an Italian name.

Minh reached down under his seat and grabbed the .9 Baretta he had brought with him. He racked the slide and set the gun on the passenger seat. He covered the gun with a plastic bag. He lit a cigarette and noted the time.

If Minh had the opportunity, he would kill Pellecchia in a drive-by. He would wait until the detective was gone and pull up alongside the man who had clubbed his brother. Then he would beep his horn to get Pellecchia's attention. Then he would shoot until the Baretta's magazine was empty.

Agent Thomas looked at pictures of Cuccia and Francone tied together on a bed at the Bellagio Hotel. He dropped the pictures on a folding table in a small office in the Federal Building in downtown

Las Vegas. Federal agent Dale Walsh, the Special Agent In Charge with the FBI organized crime task force in Las Vegas, combed his reddish-gray hair back with both hands as Thomas rubbed his eyes.

"You get any sleep?" Walsh asked.

"No. Not a minute. Not for two days, I don't think. Maybe three."

"I've been apprised of your situation," Walsh said. "I spoke with your field supervisor back in New York. I spoke with our own people in New York as well. And I just spoke with a regional director in Washington."

Thomas took a seat across from Walsh and sipped at a cup of stale coffee. "So, what's the punch line?" he asked.

"I can have somebody freshen that for you," Walsh said.

"It's okay."

Walsh referred to a set of notes on a legal pad. "We think Vincent Lano killed himself early this morning. Out in the desert. We think he blew himself up. We don't know the device he used yet, but he was in a car when it went up."

"That's one less to account for."

"The other one, Joseph Francone, he skipped out of the hospital but he wasn't being held on anything. Apparently he was a victim."

Thomas chuckled. "Yeah, right."

Walsh ignored the sarcasm. "Our investigations here in Vegas revolve around Jerry Lercasi and his crew," he continued, "so we aren't as familiar with the New York crew that came into town last week."

"How public are the pictures? To save us both some time."

"The locals, our department and now you," Walsh said. "Nobody else. Certainly not the media."

"And what about the locals? That prick Iandolli gave me nothing but headaches from the get-go. What's the guarantee he doesn't talk about the pictures, if not show them around? What do you have, his word?"

"Detective Iandolli was first on the scene," Walsh said. "He's a pain in the ass, but I have a relationship with him here. I'm sure he won't do anything out of line without telling us first. Nobody else knows about the pictures."

"As far as you know," Thomas said.

"As far as we know."

Thomas picked up a few of the pictures: Francone with a dildo sticking out of his rectum, Francone with the dildo lying across his neck, Francone with the dildo in his mouth. Cuccia tied between Francone's legs.

"How the fuck did this happen?" Thomas asked. "Does anybody know?"

"No clue."

"Those pictures are a death sentence. You know that, right?"

"The Bureau wants to work something out."

"Cuccia's deal is with us," Thomas said. "It's a DEA case."

"We think we might be able to use those pictures here as well, to get at Jerry Lercasi," Walsh said. "Through Allen Fein, the man the New York crew contacted."

"Use the pictures? Are you crazy, use the pictures?"

"It's being discussed. You may as well get used to it."

"You show those pictures outside of this office and those two are dead men," Thomas said. "I can live with losing Francone, but Nicholas Cuccia is the key to a major drug operation back East, which you obviously already know about."

Walsh used his hands to comb his hair again. "Jerry Lercasi has been our version of the Teflon don for at least ten years now," he said. "We want him. If we can get him, we will. If those pictures can help us, we'll use them."

Thomas was incredulous. "Are you fucking kidding me?"

"We intend to go after Allen Fein, because this was obviously his deal with your friend from New York," Walsh said. "Fein is no tough guy. If we can tie him into this, he'll flip on Lercasi. He won't have a choice."

"And my people know about this back in New York?" Thomas asked. "They're putting up with this bullshit? Just say so. Because if they are, I'm taking the next fucking flight home alone."

The telephone rang. Walsh answered it.

"Walsh," he said. He listened as he looked up at Thomas. "Right," he said. "Okay."

Thomas opened both his hands when Walsh hung up. "Well?" Thomas asked. "What's it going to be?"

"Allen Fein is dead," Walsh said. "The pictures are yours."

Chapter 50

WHEN CHARLIE LEFT HIS first wife, their sons were twelve and fourteen years old. Leaving had been tough. He was absorbed with feelings of guilt and abandonment a long time afterward. Sometimes it still bothered him.

Leaving Samantha now was just as hard, maybe harder, but there was no way he would put her back into jeopardy after she had already been shot. The fact that it had been Carol's ex-husband who shot Sam didn't ease Charlie's concerns. After what the mob had done to Lisa and what he had redone to Nicholas Cuccia's jaw, Charlie was certain the vengeful gangster would do anything to get back at him.

He waited in the lobby until he learned she would be going home in a few hours. Then he searched for Detective Iandolli again and was anxious when he found him.

"Can we talk?" he asked.

"You thought it out, huh?"

"What do you need me to do?"

"I'm not sure yet," Iandolli said. "Maybe nothing. Maybe testify. Gold wants you to testify. The DEA sure doesn't."

"My friend Gold," Charlie said. "Where's he out crusading?"

"He's back at Harrah's trying to learn what happened with that Asian kid you mentioned."

"What can I do to protect Samantha?" Charlie asked.

"Like I said, you can testify, but I'm not sure yet. The Feds won't want you to, but it isn't their life. It could be dangerous once you get home, you testify out here."

"That's almost funny," Charlie said.

"Hey, it's the nature of the beast," Iandolli said. "The way these guys operate, they have a protocol. Mostly it doesn't make any sense whatsoever, but you're caught in the chaos of it right now. This guy you busted up again, he wants you dead, my friend, make no mistake."

"What can you do for me here, in Las Vegas?" Charlie asked.

"What do you mean, what can I do?"

"I'm worried about a woman upstairs."

"Which one?"

"Take your pick."

Iandolli scratched his forehead. "I get your point."

Gold sat in the control room above Harrah's casino floor and replayed the video of the assault outside an elevator bank from the day before. He watched in slow motion as Charlie Pellecchia avoided the knife and stepped into an overhead swing with a small baseball bat. He saw the bat make contact with the mugger's forehead. A shorter, second swing followed the first. The mugger fell into the elevator doors to his right.

When he called in for information on the assailant, Gold learned the mugger's name was Minh Nguyen, the younger brother of Minh Quan, the head of the Black Dragons, a local Vietnamese street gang who operated out of a section of Las Vegas recently nicknamed Little Saigon by the ethnic gang squad.

Gold knew that the connection between Minh Nguyen and Pellecchia wasn't a coincidental mugging. Ethnic gangs didn't stray that far from their turf without a reason. Little Saigon and Harrah's might as well be in different states.

Gold paged Iandolli to let him know there were more than a few mobsters trying to kill Charlie Pellecchia.

Reporters were pressing the police for information. A detective with a badge hanging from his neck took questions as Charlie made his way out of the hospital. When a reporter shoved a microphone at Charlie's face, he quickly veered away and jogged back inside the lobby. He found Iandolli, and they exited the hospital through a back door.

Charlie explained everything that had happened as they walked through a staff parking lot. He told the detective about the fight in the New York nightclub and the subsequent turn of events since he had come to Las Vegas on vacation. Iandolli listened carefully. He excused himself when his cell phone rang.

Charlie looked back at the hospital while the detective spoke on the cell phone. Charlie stared at the rooms on the third floor. One of them was Samantha's room.

Iandolli folded his cell phone and frowned at Charlie. "That was Gold," he said.

"My pal."

Iandolli waved a finger at Charlie. "He's having a rough couple days," he said. "A kid on the force he was close to killed his wife and tried to commit suicide in the middle of all this yesterday. Gold's under a lot of stress."

Charlie remained silent.

"He just reviewed the videotapes at Harrah's," Iandolli said. "The kid who tried to cut you is with a local Vietnamese gang here in Las Vegas."

"Great," Charlie said. "Everybody wants a piece of me."

"You mentioned the Asian kids with the cars stopping you and your girlfriend, right?"

Charlie nodded.

"That had to come from here," Iandolli explained. "From one of our wiseguys here in Las Vegas. Jerry Lercasi, specifically."

"This mean I'm moving to the Philippines?"

"I'm afraid they can probably get you there, too. But I'm pretty sure I can deal with Lercasi. Especially since yesterday."

Charlie looked confused as he opened the door. Iandolli waved at him to get in the car. "I'll explain later," he said. "Let's take a ride."

Chapter 51

BOUNCING BEDSPRINGS IN THE room next door woke Francone from a short nap. He called Caesar's Palace to make sure Anthony Rizzi was still checked in. After he left a phone message for Rizzi, Francone washed himself and left the dump of a motel.

He was still feeling pain from the stitches in his rectum as he sat in a taxi. He popped the last two painkillers while on his way to Caesar's Palace. As soon as he could find a water fountain inside the casino, Francone drank until his stomach hurt.

He used a house telephone to call Rizzi's room. The wannabe from Jersey City answered on the second ring.

"Anthony, it's Joey," Francone said.

"Ah-oh, hey, what's up?" Rizzi asked, sounding nervous. "I-ah, I've been trying to get you guys for two days already."

"I'm here now," Francone said. "I'm downstairs by the sports book, but I can't come up without a hotel card. Come down and bring me back up."

"The sports book?"

"Yeah, yeah. I'm watching the track screens and having a drink. Hurry up."

When he hung up with Rizzi, Francone wasn't sure if the stitches in his rectum would hold if he kept moving around. He found a chair with a desktop to sit at. He asked a cocktail waitress for an orange juice and a glass of water. There was no point drinking booze, he was thinking. Between the medication he was taking and the fact that it had been more than two full days since his last decent workout, how could he poison his body with booze?

Anthony Rizzi told the valet that he had changed his mind about checking out but would he please take the bags downstairs anyway. The valet looked confused until Rizzi palmed him a twenty-dollar bill.

"I got a friend's gonna stay in my place until the end of the week," Rizzi said.

"That's fine with me, sir," the valet said. "You want I should prepare these here bags for a taxi? I'll keep 'em close to the bell desk."

"That'll be fine, buddy," Rizzi said.

He waited until the valet left before stopping to examine himself in a mirror. Rizzi was minutes from leaving Las Vegas and his New York mobster friends for good. He had talked it over with his brother back in New Jersey and decided that a mob life wasn't for him after all. He would return to New Jersey and talk to somebody in law enforcement about the truck Nicholas Cuccia had asked him to keep in one of his warehouses. Rizzi wasn't exactly sure what was inside the truck, but he knew it was hot.

He stood up straight and nodded at himself in the mirror. Francone was waiting for him downstairs. It was time to get out of there.

He took the elevator down to the lobby, crossed the huge casino floor, and found the sports book. He spotted Francone sitting at one of the desks, but the young bodybuilder wasn't watching the screens. Francone seemed to be leaning forward as he touched himself in the crack of his ass.

"Joey?" Rizzi asked from behind.

Francone shifted fast on his chair. His face expressed pain when he looked up at Rizzi. "Hemorrhoids," he said. "Most painful fuckin' thing in the world."

Rizzi watched as Francone struggled out from the desk he was sitting at. "Everything all right?" Rizzi asked when he noticed his friend was limping.

"Not since I got these. But there are a few problems. You talk to Nicky yet?"

"Nicky? Ah, no, not yet. I've been trying to get you guys."

Francone grabbed onto one of Rizzi's arms for support. "Why don't we go upstairs and talk about it. It ain't good. Lano, that rat, did a flip on us while he's out here. He turned on Nicky."

Rizzi felt his stomach drop.

"Why don't you go up and I'll be right there," he said. "I was just going to get some money out of the deposit box."

Francone had looked upset that Rizzi was excusing himself. Then, at the mention of getting money, Francone seemed at ease again. "Money? Yeah, that's always a good idea. Gimme the room key and I'll use the bathroom while you're down here."

"Sure," Rizzi said. He handed Francone the flat electronic room key. "I'll be right up."

Francone stopped Rizzi. "Hey."

"What?"

"You didn't even kiss me hello."

Rizzi leaned forward to exchange the traditional cheek kisses. The two men exchanged phony smiles.

"Don't lose anything on the way back up," Francone joked.

Rizzi continued to smile until Francone wasn't looking. Then he walked away as fast as he could.

Chapter 52

"THIS UNOFFICIAL HARASSMENT OR the official kind?" Jerry Lercasi asked Detective Iandolli. The gangster ignored Charlie.

The three men stood behind the building model on the Palermo construction site. Charlie noticed that they were standing fewer than ten yards from where he had been assaulted. He looked back to the ditch where he had been left unconscious. The ditch was half-filled with gravel now.

"I wanted you to meet somebody," Iandolli told the Las Vegas gangster.

Lercasi nodded without looking at Charlie.

"His name is Charlie Pellecchia," Iandolli continued. "He's the poor bastard some wiseguy from New York is trying to kill."

Lercasi glanced at Charlie and turned back to the detective. "He looks alive to me," he said.

"He looks better than your accountant."

"My accountant? What happened to him now?"

Iandolli held both his hands up. "Let's not blow smoke at each other."

Lercasi looked in the direction of a bulldozer pushing dirt about a hundred yards from where the three men were standing. "I'm listening," he said.

"I want a trade-off," Iandolli said. "This guy gets a pass for information you can use when the shit hits the fan back East."

Lercasi shrugged. "What makes you think I can do anything for this guy?"

"Some Vietnamese kid in a hospital downtown," Iandolli said. "He got his head cracked trying to stab Mr. Pellecchia here. That one had to go through you, whether Nicholas Cuccia approached you or not."

"You give me way too much credit, pal."

"So let's make believe it went through you. For argument sake. The bottom line is you can get him a pass."

"Really? You think I'm that powerful, huh?"

"I know it. Which is why I don't want to go back and forth with you right now, just to waste time. I have something you can give to New York in exchange for that pass for Mr. Pellecchia here. So when he goes home, he doesn't have to hide under a couch."

"I'll ask you again," Lercasi said. "What makes you think I can do anything in New York?"

"Because Allen Fein arranged the assault at the Palermo," Iandolli said. "And he arranged the assault of a woman at a motel in town. Which you have to know by now or else Allen Fein wouldn't have a tag on his foot in the city morgue."

"That's very dramatic," Lercasi said.

"And true," Iandolli said. "Hey, nobody is complaining. The world is definitely a better place. Maybe the Feds care. Maybe not."

Lercasi checked his watch. "I'm running a little late," he said. "You want to tell me what I get out of all this?"

"Information. Except first I want your word that you'll help Mr. Pellecchia here. You call off the Viet Cong and talk to New York."

"What's the information?"

"Say the magic word."

Lercasi thought about it a few seconds, then said, "I'll do what I can."

"Nicholas Cuccia and the DEA," Iandolli said.

Lercasi was impressed. "The DEA?"

"The one and only. Which means you'll have clout dealing with New York."

"What about proof? I won't have anything but a headache without proof."

"Trust me," Iandolli said. "I have pictures."

Lercasi seemed impressed again. "They say those are worth a thousand words," he said. "Still, I can't make promises."

"I know how that is," Iandolli said. "It's the same way for me sometimes. I say I can do things, then find out later I can't deliver. You're going to get some federal flak from what's been going on here this week. If things don't happen the way we agreed, for Mr. Pellecchia here, there might be a few new things you can't avoid."

"Things like what? I'm just curious."

"Whatever our surveillance picked up," Iandolli said. "Where you ate yesterday. Who you ate with. A few back-and-forth telephone calls to the same restaurant. A surveillance tape with Mr. Fein and Nicholas Cuccia and another one of the New York crew. The Feds are much more meticulous than us local yokels, should they get the tape. They'd probably look into every detail, an indictment at a time. I don't have to turn that information over to the Feds. It could slip my mind."

Lercasi looked from Charlie to Iandolli. "Suppose they already have it, the Feds?"

"You'd be in cuffs by now," Iandolli said. "This place would be crawling with Feds. Your gym, your house, all your other fronts in this town. They'd be upside down from search warrants. This is a tourist town, Jerr. Nobody wants violence like this. Much less in the hotels themselves."

Lercasi nodded. "All right," he said. "I'll see what I can do."

"I'm not done yet," Iandolli said. "There's something else."

Lercasi looked to Charlie. "You his brother or something?"

Charlie didn't flinch.

"Beau Curitan," Iandolli said.

"Beau who?" Lercasi said.

Iandolli unfolded his notepad. He wrote the name out on a blank sheet of paper and handed it to Lercasi. He pointed at the name as he pronounced each letter. "C-U-R-I-T-A-N," he said. "Curitan. Pronounced just like it's spelled. He was last seen speeding toward the Strip after he tried to rape a woman. He did manage to shoot her in the leg."

Lercasi stared at the paper.

"You have friends across the good state of Nevada," Iandolli continued. "Some in the auto repair and used-car businesses. Maybe they'd like to help catch an abusive husband who tried to rape some poor woman, then shot her when he couldn't. In the event the guy tried to switch or sell a car, I mean."

"And this would be an unofficial request or an unofficial favor?" Lercasi asked.

Iandolli turned to Charlie. "Does it make a difference to you?"

Charlie glared at both men. He didn't think any of it was funny.

Chapter 53

WHEN AGENT THOMAS SAW Cuccia, the mobster was still groggy from painkillers. Cuccia's mouth was sore from a fresh fracture to his jawbone. Two of his teeth were missing. Both lips on the left side of his face were swollen.

Thomas was anxious to get Cuccia out of the hospital. He was working with a thin grace period the FBI had provided him because Allen Fein was dead. He hustled Cuccia to get dressed.

"I don't care your jaw hurts," he said. "We have a flight out of here in three hours. We're going to make it."

Cuccia was sitting on the bed. He wiped drool and blood from his mouth with a napkin.

"You can't say you didn't deserve it," Thomas continued. "This Pellecchia rebroke your jaw because you asked for it. Good for him. It'll give you something to think about on the flight back."

Thomas stood alongside Cuccia's bed. He set an envelope with copies of the embarrassing pictures on a table.

"Where's Francone?" Cuccia asked. He had to push the words from his mouth.

"Let's go," Thomas said. "Up and in the bathroom. Wash yourself and put your clothes on. We're out of here in ten minutes."

"Where's Francone?"

"I have no clue. Probably in Singapore somewhere."

Cuccia wasn't moving yet. "Where—"

"Get dressed," Thomas said. "I'm serious, we don't have time to play around here. Not if you don't want the FBI to take over."

Cuccia slid off the edge of his bed. He winced from the pain in his jaw when his feet touched the floor. He pointed to the envelope on the table. "What's that?"

"If you don't already know, you don't wanna know."

Cuccia took slow, deliberate steps to the bathroom. Thomas handed him his pants and shirt. "You have maybe a one-in-ten-million shot of keeping half your deal with us," Thomas said. "Maybe, if you can get your uncle to move that heroin from here, over the phone. If not, you're looking at life plus twenty or thirty years."

"What the fuck are you talkin' about?"

"Just get dressed."

On the drive to the Bellagio, Charlie wanted to know why the hell Detective Iandolli had introduced him to Jerry Lercasi and why the hell he had brought up Beau Curitan.

"What was the point?" Charlie asked. "I don't understand what you two were talking about back there. Except for Beau Curitan. And I didn't appreciate the game going on with that. The woman he tried to rape was my girlfriend."

"I took a shot," Iandolli said.

"Took a shot at what?"

"Finding Mr. Curitan. If he drove straight through the state, it won't make a difference, he's gone by now. Sometimes guys like that panic and think they have to maneuver. They assume we have the jump on them. They get nervous and make mistakes."

"What you said about the car dealers."

"That and the junkyards. If this clown didn't drive out of Nevada last night, he's probably waiting to change his transportation. Lercasi has a long reach inside this state. The guy tries to do something with the car, there's a chance he'll get caught."

"And why the fuck would Jerry Lercasi do that?"

"I offered him a carrot," Iandolli said. "The DEA and Cuccia."

"I don't get it," Charlie said.

"It has to do with mob protocol and leverage Lercasi might exert on his own behalf when the shit hits the fan," Iandolli said. "And it will, the shit will hit the fan, sooner or later. The kind of action this town has seen the past few nights is off-putting to the average Joe, but it's deadly to the casinos. If Lercasi can wave a deal Cuccia made with the DEA under New York's nose, it's a major coup for him. He'll be owed on a pretty grand scale."

Charlie shook his head. "I still don't trust the guy," he said. "What'll he do, turn Beau Curitan over if he finds him?"

Iandolli winked at Charlie. "Beau wishes," he said.

Charlie was still confused. "What?"

"Let's put it this way: Beau probably won't be going home for the holidays."

"That wouldn't upset me."

"Me either. Then hopefully Lercasi calls New York and gets you a pass while he's spilling his guts on Cuccia."

Charlie wasn't in the mood to hear about the virtues of wiseguys then. "A pass means I get to live?" he asked.

"Lercasi has the clout."

"And what would happen to Cuccia? Isn't that a little dangerous for your career, what you told this guy?"

"Only if I run for office."

Chapter 54

MINH WAS UPSET AT seeing the detective and Charlie Pellecchia visiting with Jerry Lercasi. He wondered what their conversation had been about at the construction site. He wondered if the Italians were giving him up.

He let off the gas pedal as he followed the cop and Pellecchia back to the Bellagio. He called one of his men and instructed him to drive another car to meet him. He would exchange cars and retreat to a hideout for the rest of the day. He would leave one of his men behind to follow Pellecchia.

When his cell phone rang, Minh was surprised to hear Jerry Lercasi's voice.

"Time to back down," the Italian gangster said. "I don't need—"

"Fuck you," Minh said.

"Hey!" Lercasi yelled, but Minh killed the connection.

Beau knew he was a fugitive. Now he had to think like one.

He brought his car to an auto body shop in Laughlin. He asked for the car to be painted bright yellow over the original navy blue. He paid an extra hundred dollars for the garage to forget about the paperwork.

The big man behind the counter joked with Beau. "You rob a bank or something?"

Beau shook his head. "I got a wife chasing me for back alimony," he said. "Crazy woman left me for another man and wants me to pay for it. Put a damn private dick on my ass. They chasin' me from Alabama, if you can believe it."

The man grunted. "How much you owe?"

"Six months," Beau said. "But it's not like she's a cripple or nothin'. Damn woman works. So does her boyfriend. I don't see why the hell I have to pay them."

"I feel your pain, buddy. I'm paying alimony, it has to be eight years now."

"Yeah, well, I'm hoping the new color will throw her off the chase."

The big man nodded. "I hear ya."

Beau counted the money in his wallet. After the paint job, he would be down to fewer than seven hundred dollars. The last few weeks had been expensive. Beau had a credit card with him, but he was afraid to use the card while he was in Nevada.

Beau guessed he had more than enough cash to make it out of the state. He figured Canada was the best place to hide for a while. At least they could speak English in Canada.

"I'll still need the registration," the big man said. "I'll leave it off the receipt, but I'll need it for our records."

"What, your boss against makin' cash or somethin'?"

"I gotta have it. It won't show on your paperwork, but I can lose my job, I don't take it down for our records."

Beau handed the big man his registration. "How long you think this'll take? The paint job, to dry and all?"

"End of day," the big man said. He copied the registration number onto an order form and handed the card back to Beau.

Cuccia examined his bruises in the mirror. He was a mess all over again. He touched his swollen lips with his fingertips. He touched his mouth where he felt the gap in his teeth. He sucked air from the pain.

He was obsessed with rage for Charlie Pellecchia. He remembered how Pellecchia had pushed his way into the hotel suite. He remembered how Pellecchia had spoken to him. He remembered how Pellecchia had kicked him in the face.

And now his jaw was broken again.

Cuccia splashed water on his face around his bruises. He combed his hair with his hands. He figured he had one last chance to kill Pellecchia, and he knew he would have to do it himself.

First he would have to escape the DEA agent on the other side of the bathroom door. Then he would have to find a gun. Then he would have to find Pellecchia.

He needed to move fast. He needed to get hold of some money. He needed to find Anthony Rizzi.

Samantha set the flowers on top of the television in the living room as she read the card.

"From work," she told Carol over the telephone. "Which may not be for much longer."

Carol said, "I don't think they would dare do anything about your job after what happened."

"It's policy," Samantha said. "We're not supposed to get involved with guests staying at the hotel. I know girls who were fired for it."

"Duh, you were shot," Carol said.

"How are you doing?" Samantha asked. She lowered herself onto the couch, felt something hard under her leg, and moved to one side. She started to reach between the couch pillows when she was distracted by Carol's sniffling.

"I'm so sorry, Sam," Carol said. "I should've known Beau would find me there sooner or later. I tried to get him to follow me. I found him online, I think."

"Forget it," Samantha said. "He's probably hiding in Canada someplace now. It wasn't your fault."

"I'm in California," Carol said. "I'm heading to San Diego tomorrow and then I'll decide whether to move farther north."

"I want you to stay in touch."

"Of course I will. Any word from Charlie?"

"Please, I feel like an ass about that."

"You shouldn't," Carol said. "He'll call as soon as he feels it's safe."

"Unless that was his excuse to blow me off."

"I'm sure he was just concerned about getting you more involved. He's trying to protect you."

"And maybe I moved too fast," Samantha said.

"You did what comes natural," Carol said. "You can't blame yourself for that."

"I'm not so sure," Samantha said.

"He would've run away before he got involved with you, baby."

"Maybe," Samantha said. "And maybe I'm what he's running from."

Chapter 55

BEAU GREW TIRED OF waiting for his car. He checked his watch and saw it was close to half an hour since he last saw anybody in the shop. He started his way around the garage when Beau spotted two men heading his way.

"Hey, either of you guys seen that big fella was working the counter before?" he yelled.

The two men didn't answer. They continued walking toward Beau.

"Fellas?" Beau said. "Either of you see—"

A large hand suddenly muffled Beau's mouth. He turned his head to the left as a kick knocked the air from his lungs. He rolled up on the ground as the two men tied his legs and hands with a rope.

"What the fuck?" Beau whispered just before a dirty cloth was jammed inside his mouth.

Jerry Lercasi was back with his girlfriend in the apartment above Vive la Body. He was getting head while he waited for an important telephone call. Things were getting out of control in Las Vegas. He was hoping something outside the city might help his upcoming situation with the law.

When the phone finally rang, Lercasi pushed Brenda away as he stood up to take the call. It was a message from associates in Laughlin about a package that had been delivered.

Brenda crawled to where Lercasi was standing and tried to keep him hard. He was distracted and lost his erection.

Brenda stood up in frustration. When he was finished with the call, she told Lercasi to blow himself.

"What's wrong with you?" he asked. "I had to take that call."

She was half naked. She grabbed a black Vive la Body T-shirt and pulled it over her head.

"It was important," Lercasi repeated. He was still holding the receiver in his right hand.

She lit a cigarette and pointed at the phone. "Why don't you call back whoever was so important and ask them to take care of it. Because I'm not starting over now. No way."

Lercasi remembered a call he had to make and started to dial. He paged the organized crime detective Iandolli as Brenda stormed out of the apartment.

Charlie checked out of the Bellagio as soon as the detective dropped him off. He read a map of Las Vegas in the back of a taxi as he headed south on the Strip. He stopped at a Hertz, where he rented a Buick Le Sabre for sixty-five dollars with unlimited mileage for two days.

He looked for a cheap motel in a tour book at the Hertz. He would stay in Las Vegas another few nights. He wasn't sure yet whether he could involve Samantha in his life. He wanted to. He missed her already.

He found a small place in the tour book and called the South of Vegas Motel to book the room for two days. It would cost him twenty-five dollars per night, he learned. Cable was extra. So were the pay-per-view movies the motel offered.

Twenty-five minutes later, he signed the register. He grabbed a Diet Coke from a soda machine in the office and hurried out to his car. He drove the Buick to the far end of the lot, closer to his room. He grabbed his suitcase from the backseat and hustled up the stairs. When he was inside the tiny room, he felt the heat of the afternoon desert sun.

Charlie looked at himself in the small cracked mirror across from the bed. He had lost weight the past few days. He looked tired and disheveled. He looked crazy, he thought.

• • •

At sunset, Lercasi discussed helping his friends back East with his attorney at a law office in Spring Valley. The two men sat across a coffee table in the office with a ceiling-to-floor view of the mountains. Lercasi's lawyer was well tanned. He wore an expensive Italian suit and lots of gold. Lercasi was dressed in a red-and-white workout suit.

"I don't know that I should be having this conversation with you," Lercasi's lawyer said.

"The fuck does that mean? You're my lawyer."

"Because I can be disqualified from any future representation of you. The same as what happened in New York. The government had somebody they couldn't beat, they found reasons to disqualify him from litigation. They can call it conflict of interest or whatever they want. They're the government."

"They can disqualify you for having a vowel in your name," Lercasi said. "It ever comes to that, they don't need a reason."

Lercasi's lawyer was fidgety in his chair. "Well, there is something else," he said. "About me representing you in that way. What happened to Mr. Fein, specifically?"

Lercasi nodded. "I can respect that," he said.

"Well?"

"Mr. Fein was involved in my day-to-day business. Accounting, real estate. Business parties. He represented my business, some of it. You represent me. Therein is the difference."

His lawyer thought about it a moment. "What is it you want?"

"I need a courier to go see another lawyer back East. It doesn't have to be you, but it should be somebody from this office, to give it some weight."

"What is it that needs weight?"

Lercasi leaned forward to speak. "One of Angelo Vignieri's captains has a deal with the DEA," he said. "Put it however diplomatically you want, but that's the message has to get to this other lawyer back East. For his client's best interest, of course."

"Of course," his lawyer said.

Chapter 56

CUCCIA CONSIDERED RUNNING. AGENT Thomas was busy arguing with two other agents in the hospital parking lot. He would have about an eighty-yard head start before Thomas and the other agents would give chase. Two busy intersections at the corner might provide him with enough cover to escape, but there wasn't much he could do from the hospital without a car and some money.

He waited for Thomas while he searched for escape routes. The sun was setting. He guessed it would be another half hour before dark.

"I'm out of here in two hours," Marshall Thomas told FBI Special Agent In Charge Dale Walsh.

Walsh combed a wave of hair from his forehead. "And what if we need to see him?"

"Uh-uh, no way. You're not pulling this bullshit now. No fucking way. What possible reason could you have to detain Cuccia? This is a DEA case from New York. You already said the guy you needed to lean on Lercasi is dead."

"For questioning," a tall man said. He was standing alongside Walsh. He adjusted his sunglasses with both hands.

"Bullshit," Thomas told the tall man. He turned to Walsh again. "No way. This is horseshit. Nickel-and-dime horseshit."

Walsh held up his cellular telephone. "I can call Washington if you really need to hear this from somebody higher than myself."

"I'm wasting time I don't have to waste," Thomas said. "I'm taking him back to the Bellagio to try and salvage an operation. Then I'm taking him back to New York, in or out of handcuffs. Unless you intend to shoot me in the back, I'm going to wish you two guys good luck."

"Thomas!" Walsh yelled. "Goddamn it!"

Thomas flipped Walsh the finger as he crossed the parking lot.

"He's never going to do this over a telephone," Cuccia told Thomas.

They were pulling into the Bellagio driveway. Thomas drove the white Ford Taurus around the valet parking line to the front entrance. He checked in his rearview mirror for Walsh and the other FBI agents. He spotted the light blue sedan as it pulled to the side of the driveway.

"Let's go," Thomas told Cuccia. He grabbed the mobster by an arm and half-dragged him through the lobby. Cuccia tried to pull back, but his jaw hurt from the jostling.

"You're fuckin' killin' me over here," he moaned through his rewired jaw.

"Don't give me any ideas," Thomas said.

"I'm tellin' you my uncle will never go for it over the phone."

"That's not what you said when we left New York."

"Because I didn't want to hear you then."

"Right," Thomas said. He pulled Cuccia's arm as he stepped onto an elevator.

"Ouch, motherfucker!"

A woman holding a plastic bucket full of coins gasped at the language.

"Fuck you, too," Cuccia told the woman.

Thomas smacked the back of Cuccia's head. The mobster froze from the pain he felt in his jaw.

When they were inside the hotel room, Thomas walked straight to the windows and handed Cuccia his cell phone.

"Make the call," he said. "Now."

Cuccia had picked up the binoculars he had used to watch the women around the pool. He set them on a chair and dialed a number in Brooklyn.

"Anthony, it's Nicky," he said into the phone.

"Nicky who?" the voice on the other end said. "This is Frank's Pizza."

"I know, I know. That thing is ready to go."

"What thing?" the voice said. "This is Frank's Pizza. Who do you want? What number?"

"Jersey City. Right. Tonight. Yes."

"Ba-fongool," the voice said.

Cuccia turned the phone off and handed it back to Thomas. He picked up the binoculars and feigned scanning the pool area. Thomas turned the phone back on and punched in a few numbers. He held the receiver against his ear and shook his head at Cuccia.

"Nice try," he said. "Frank's Pizza. They any good?"

Cuccia was desperate. He swung the binoculars as hard as he could at the side of Thomas's head. He was shocked when he cracked the DEA agent's skull. He was stunned to see tiny pieces of bone on the edge of the binocular lens.

Chapter 57

DETECTIVES GOLD AND IANDOLLI sat in the back of a white surveillance van disguised as a floral delivery service. A third man, dressed in a bright green uniform, drove the van. He wore a microphone transmitter in his left ear.

They were parked across the street from the South of Vegas Motel. Pellecchia had taken a room there. Iandolli was scanning the area for Asian men. So far he hadn't seen any.

When Joey Francone realized that Anthony Rizzi had skipped out on him, the wannabe mobster threw a fit in the Caesar's Palace hotel room. He punched at the mattress on the king-size bed over and over. He threw the ice bucket across the room. He forgot about the stitching in his rectum and kicked at the suitcase stand. He flinched from the pain.

He counted his money one more time as he sat on the bed in Rizzi's hotel room. He had barely enough cash to make an escape and nowhere to go.

Francone was ready to give up.

He stared at the telephone as he tried to compile a list of things he could trade with the FBI about Nicholas Cuccia and the Vignieri crime family. He cried to himself as he realized he didn't have much to deal for the protection he would need.

• • •

Charlie wasn't sure if it was a short dream or a long one. He had tried to wake himself several times, but the lure of the nightmare was too great. He was sweating when he awoke. He was paralyzed on the bed, straining to remember the dream and concerned about what it had meant.

The villain in *Tosca*, Baron Scarpia, was caught in a giant spider's web. Samantha, wearing a hooded shawl, was pacing back and forth across a small room. The spider's web holding Scarpia hung in one corner of the room. Samantha didn't see it. Each time she paced, she drew closer to the web, and Scarpia reached out to grab her.

Charlie was somewhere outside the room and couldn't find a way in. Lisa was suddenly outside the room with him. Charlie did his best to ignore his wife. He heard a chorus from his favorite aria over and over: *"Ma, nel ritrar costei. Il mio solo pensiero. Ah! Il mio sol pensier sei tu, Tosca, sei tu!"*

It meant, "But in portraying this woman my only thought, ah, my only thought is you. Tosca, it's you!"

He bolted off the bed and splashed cold water on his face. He called Samantha, but she hung up on him. He immediately called back, and she hung up again. When he tried a third time, Samantha finally answered.

"I'm sorry," he said.

Samantha remained silent on her end of the line.

"Sam?"

"I feel like you ran out on me," she finally said.

"I didn't run out on you," Charlie said.

"That's what it feels like," Samantha said and hung up.

"Fuck," Charlie said.

He hung up the receiver and grabbed the Taurus P-22 off the night table. He held the gun in his right hand and stared at it. Except for target practice at a range on Long Island in New York, he had never fired a gun. It had made him nervous having one in the house. He gave up the sport a few months after buying his first handgun, a Smith & Wesson .38 revolver, because he'd left it out one night after drinking with friends from the pistol range. A handgun accident was something that haunted him for the next few days until he finally sold the revolver to a friend.

Now he realized that he might need one to stay alive. He pocketed the handgun until he was inside the rental. He pulled the handgun out and shoved it under the front seat. When he spotted an Asian kid standing near a pay phone alongside the motel office, Charlie slid off the front seat without thinking about the gun.

Chapter 58

WALSH DIRECTED HIS MEN from the suite of Nicholas Cuccia in the Bellagio Hotel. He watched as a team of emergency medical staff tried to stabilize the DEA agent on a stretcher. Thomas was bleeding from an open wound in the side of his head. Walsh recognized bone chips around the wound.

"Have hotel security block every exit in the hotel and casino," Walsh told one of his men. "Get through to the office for every available man in the area. I want an all-points on Nicholas Cuccia right now. I want an all-points on Joseph Francone as well. I want both of those men taken pronto. Contact the locals. Have them take over security downstairs as soon as they arrive."

Walsh handed his cellular telephone to another one of his men. "Get DEA on the line right now and explain the situation. We have one of their men down with a possible skull fracture. Give it back to me when you have a supervisor."

Walsh knew his chances of finding Cuccia were small. His team had waited outside the Bellagio for more than half an hour before he and one of his men decided to check up on the DEA agent. Thomas and Cuccia were scheduled to leave Las Vegas on a nine-o'clock flight. He had tried to page Thomas twice before he suspected something was wrong.

Now the New York wiseguy was missing. Walsh guessed Cuccia had a fifteen-minute head start on them. He wasn't sure where Cuccia would try to run, but the New York mobster had the cash, a credit card, and the agent's handgun.

Walsh figured both the airport and the train station would be a waste of time. Cuccia had to know he couldn't show his face at either place, although most times desperate men did desperate things.

"Get Iandolli on the phone!" Walsh yelled. "Have him call me back pronto. Get a fax of Cuccia to the airport and train station security. Get one to every hotel registration desk in Las Vegas. Get one to the car rental agencies, the tour buses, and the tour helicopters."

Walsh ordered one of his men to stay behind. He watched one of the medical team insert an intravenous needle in Thomas's arm. He looked at Thomas's eyes, but the agent was unconscious. Walsh tapped his Smith & Wesson .9 strapped in a shoulder holster. He glanced back at Thomas one last time and headed for the door.

"What the fuck?" Gold said.

They were watching the fistfight from the street alongside the motel parking lot. Charlie Pellecchia had approached a man using a pay telephone. When the man turned, Iandolli saw he was Asian.

"Let's go," Iandolli instructed his driver.

As the van turned into the motel parking lot, the Asian gave Pellecchia the finger. Pellecchia smacked his hand away, and the fight started.

Iandolli scanned the surrounding area for members of the Black Dragons. When he didn't see any, he glanced at Gold. Gold was watching the fight.

The Asian kicked at Pellecchia karate-style. The kick missed, and Pellecchia threw a left hook from a crouch and slammed the Asian man across a nearby bench.

"He's pretty good," Iandolli said.

The two squared off again, the Asian using martial arts and Pellecchia in a classic boxer's crouch.

• • •

"I fucking kill you, white boy," the Asian said.

Charlie remembered the same taunt from the day before. He glared at the Asian and realized it was the same kid from the car.

Charlie motioned him in closer. "Go for it," he said.

The Asian was rotating his open hands in a slow, even motion. Charlie didn't know if the guy knew what he was doing, but the Asian had exposed a weak spot earlier. Charlie intended to go for it again.

The Asian raised his right hand and quickly kicked Charlie in the left shin.

"Fuck," Charlie said as he winced from the sharp pain.

"What you do now, white boy?" the Asian said just before he rushed Charlie with a feigned kick and a straight punch that missed.

Charlie's left hand was still stinging from his first punch. His bruised fingers were throbbing. He stepped to his right and noticed a white van pulling into the lot as he feigned a punch of his own. The Asian glanced at the van and landed a few knuckles on Charlie's forehead.

Charlie went down low and came up with a hard left to the ribs. The Asian grunted as both his hands dropped. Charlie threw another short, hard hook and this time nailed the Asian in the right temple. The Asian was staggered from the blow. He backpedaled until he went down.

Iandolli returned an emergency page. When someone answered the call, Gold could see Iandolli's expression change.

"Right away," Iandolli said into the cell phone.

"What's that about?" Gold asked.

"That DEA agent, Thomas. Nicholas Cuccia just cracked his head open. Cuccia is on the run. He has a gun. Nobody knows where he is."

"Give me two guesses," Gold said.

"He doesn't know where Pellecchia is," Iandolli said.

"That was my second guess. We never checked on the one flew in the other day. The one you mentioned with the trucking business. The rich one."

"Rizzi. Shit."

"We never checked up on him. At least you didn't mention it."

"You're right," Iandolli said.

"The Feds know about him?"

"Not from me."

"I can go," Gold said.

"You sure?"

"I'm not supposed to be here with you anyway. I might as well sit in traffic."

"Be careful," Iandolli said.

Gold motioned toward the scene in the parking lot. He said, "Lucky punch."

Chapter 59

CUCCIA USED A TAXI to take him to a hotel off the Strip. He saw the driver looking at him funny in the rearview mirror, and Cuccia explained how he had been robbed and mugged the day before. He pointed to his jaw. He explained how two black kids had broken his jaw with a baseball bat. His wife, Cuccia told the driver, was still recovering in the hospital.

The driver sympathized. He told Cuccia he should have a gun. "For protection," the driver said with a Russian accent.

It was an unexpected bonus. Two guns were better than one. Cuccia asked the driver if he knew where a guy could get one. He said, "I'm scared shit, tell you the truth."

"How much you are to pay?" the driver asked. He tried to examine Cuccia again in the rearview mirror.

Cuccia was contemplating the second weapon and extra ammunition. He would need transportation as well.

"How much?" the driver repeated.

"Huh?" Cuccia said. He leaned forward, an overanxious, desperate, but grateful tourist. "Anything," he said. "Can you get me one?"

"Not me, no," the driver said. "But I have friend can get. For two hundred, maybe three hundred dollar, I think."

"Really?"

"Yes, I think. Where you are staying? Here, this place?"

They were parked off Boulder Highway, alongside a Super 8 Motel. Cuccia shook his head. "At the MGM. But I thought it was better if I did this from here."

The driver shrugged. "Is fine here, too. You want to wait, I come back. Anything you are want? Magnum, automatic?"

"A nine," Cuccia said. "And an extra clip."

The driver nodded. "I am right back," he said. "Half an hour."

"So much for your friend Lercasi," Charlie told Iandolli.

They were standing in the motel parking lot. Three police cruisers had pulled in behind the van. The Asian was in handcuffs. The right side of his face was swollen.

"I got a call from him before," Iandolli said. "About Beau Curitan, I think."

"That's pretty funny," Charlie said. He was still catching his breath from the fight. He cradled his left hand in his right hand. He could barely move his fingers.

"The message said the package was delivered," Iandolli said. "I asked for proof but he hung up."

Charlie squinted at Iandolli. "Is that supposed to mean anything to me? Jesus Christ, give it a break."

Charlie opened the door to his rental.

"Where you going?" Iandolli asked.

"Why?"

"Because Nicholas Cuccia is still out there. He almost killed that DEA agent. Gold just went to look for him."

"And now you're gonna follow me?"

Iandolli was adamant. "Where are you going?"

"A pet store, if I can find one is still open."

"A pet store?"

"I owe a woman an apology."

Minh Quan snorted two lines of cocaine after receiving the phone call from his man following Charlie Pellecchia. When he arrived at the small motel south of the Strip, Minh was just in time to see one of his men handcuffed and shoved into a police van. Another member of his gang arrived on a motorcycle a few minutes later. Minh instructed him to follow Pellecchia.

When a group of police cruisers pulled into the motel parking lot, Minh decided to get out of the area before he was spotted. He drove out toward the desert, where he would wait until he knew where Pellecchia settled for the night.

Then he would kill him.

The Russian was back in fewer than twenty minutes. He handed Cuccia a Glock .9 handgun with a fully loaded eight-bullet clip. The Russian produced a second fully loaded clip and dropped it on the bed.

"Was little expensive," he said.

Of course it was, Cuccia was thinking. "How much?" he asked.

"Four hundred for gun and single clip. Another fifty for extra clip."

"Fifty for the clip?"

"Is very fast business. No time to bargain. I take back you don't want clip."

Cuccia liked the feel of the Glock in his right hand. He aimed it at the pillows as he turned the gun sideways in his hand.

"Can you take me back to my hotel?" Cuccia asked.

"Sure. No charge, we have deal."

"You have your car keys?"

The Russian held them up.

"Thanks," Cuccia said. He turned the gun on the Russian and squeezed off three rounds.

Chapter 60

GOLD WAS LESS THAN a mile from Caesar's when a dump truck crossing the boulevard slammed into a jitney and blocked the northbound traffic. He was stuck in the middle lane and couldn't escape. He leaned on his horn a few times until he realized it was pointless.

Gold flashed his badge at the cars on his left and crept across the lane until a UPS truck blocked his path.

When Francone heard the lock in the hotel door open, he sat up on the bed with the hope that it was Anthony Rizzi. Maybe Rizzi had changed his mind. Maybe he was coming back to give Francone some money after all.

Or maybe it was the federal agents Francone had spotted at the hospital. At that point, he no longer cared which law enforcement agency found him. At least he wouldn't have to go look for them.

Francone looked puzzled when the Hispanic woman in the maid's uniform stumbled into the room. He leaned forward when he saw Nicholas Cuccia standing in the doorway holding a handgun. Francone drew back on the bed.

Cuccia pushed the maid inside the room. He checked the hallway before letting the door close behind him. He stood to one side of the door as he spotted Francone moving back on the bed.

"Joey-boy!" Cuccia yelled.

The Hispanic woman backstepped toward the window behind her. Her eyes were focused on the gun in Cuccia's right hand. Her face was full of terror.

"Na-Nick," Francone stuttered. "What's up? How, uh, how'd you get out?"

Cuccia was enjoying watching his protégé stutter. "Same way as you, I guess. Except I had to kill somebody first."

The maid gasped.

"Easy does it, signora. I no kill you."

"Rizzi took off on us," Francone said. "I was downstairs with him a while ago. He gave me this bullshit story about getting some money and split."

Cuccia smiled.

"I swear it," Francone said. "I was downstairs with him."

"I guess I'm too late then."

"Maybe we can still catch him at the airport. At least there's two of us can look for him now."

Cuccia looked from Francone to the maid. "Tie her up," he said. "Fast. Let's go."

"Tropicana Avenue off I-Fifteen," Walsh told the agent driving the car. "There's a Super Eight there."

Walsh set down the radio as the car jerked to the left and sped south on Paradise Road. Walsh called a set of backup agents over his radio. "Las Vegas police have a report of shots fired at a Super Eight Motel on Boulder Highway. Converge at that location."

"You want to back off the locals?" the agent driving the car asked.

"What's the point? Let's just hope this isn't some estranged husband taking out his old lady and her boyfriend. This guy Cuccia gets out of Las Vegas it'll be all our asses."

"Jurisdiction?"

"That's the least of it. That DEA agent, Thomas. I never should have let him take Cuccia. This is nothing but a Chinese fire drill right now. That kid dies . . . I don't even want to think about it."

"Hold on," the agent doing the driving said. He whipped the car around a milk truck making a left turn. A taxi attempting the same left turn from the middle lane blocked them from crossing the intersection. The car screeched to a stop inches from the bumper of the taxi.

"Let's go!" Walsh screamed at the taxi. "Let's go!"

Chapter 61

CHARLIE DIDN'T RECOGNIZE THE voice that answered the phone.

"Can I speak to Sam?" he asked.

"Who's calling?" a woman asked.

"Charlie. Charlie Pellechia."

"Hold a second."

Charlie could hear the woman talking with Samantha. She told Charlie, "One second."

"I thought you might've lost this number," Samantha said.

Charlie was relieved when he heard her voice. "Never," he said. "How's your leg?"

"All right."

"Can you walk?"

"I can get around. I have a home attendant for the day. Part of my coverage, thank God."

An awkward moment of silence passed. Charlie swallowed hard. "Can I see you?" he asked.

"Only if you want to."

"I want to."

"Would this be a quick visit on your way to the airport?" Samantha asked. "If it is, don't bother."

"How about I cook you dinner?"

"Eat and run?"

"Why don't you give me a break here?" Charlie said. Another moment of silence frustrated him. "I'm on my way."

He took a deep breath as he hung up the receiver. He was anxious all over again about seeing the woman he knew he was in love with. He looked inside the pet store window for dog cages. When he spotted them along a wall, Charlie went inside.

When the maid was tied and gagged, Cuccia had Francone help her into the bathtub face down.

"You have any money?" he asked Francone.

The look on Francone's face was pure shock. He saw Cuccia holding a pillow in one hand and the gun in his other.

"Na-na-no," he stuttered. "I'm ba-broke. I have a few dollars. Somebody—"

Francone started to explain why he was broke when Cuccia shot him in the chest twice through the pillow. Francone's body slammed into the wall behind the bathtub. He was dead before he stopped sliding down the wall. His body listed to one side on top of the maid.

Cuccia fished Francone's pockets for money. He stashed it inside his own front pants pocket. He pushed Francone onto his side and turned the hot water in the bathtub on. He could hear the maid trying to scream through her gag.

"Quit moanin'," he told her. "I ain't had a bath in three days."

It had taken Gold more than twenty minutes to free himself from the traffic snarl on Las Vegas Boulevard. When he drove into the long driveway in front of Caesar's Palace, Gold spotted Iandolli pulling in behind him.

"There was a shooting at a Super Eight Motel," Gold told him. "The one on Boulder Highway. The Feds are already there. Some Russian taxi driver except there's no taxi in the lot."

"Cuccia?" Iandolli asked.

"On his way here?" Gold said.

"Unless he's already been," Iandolli said.

Both detectives pushed their way through the revolving doors into the Caesar's Palace lobby.

• • •

Nicholas Cuccia made his way through the casino to the Caesar's Palace shopping mall. He followed the flow of the crowd heading out of the mall and rode the moving walkway to the street, where he turned left and headed into the Mirage. Cuccia used two twenty-dollar bills to move up to the front of the taxi line at the Mirage. He jumped into the next car and told the driver to take him to the MGM Grand. As the taxi headed south on Las Vegas Boulevard, Cuccia could see the flashing lights of police cars headed in the opposite direction.

He walked through the main casino of the MGM to one of the novelty stores off the front lobby. He bought himself a "Classic Films" MGM T-shirt and a baseball cap, then exited the MGM on Tropicana Boulevard. He crossed the footbridge over the busy road and entered the Tropicana Casino. He found his way to a bathroom to change into the T-shirt and wash up.

When he felt safe enough, Cuccia sat at a bar with several television screens above it. He ordered vodka rocks. His jaw was hurting, and he didn't have painkillers. He used a straw to sip the booze. It wasn't as strong as a painkiller, but it was better than nothing.

As both detectives ran through the casino lobby, Iandolli looked for the federal agents he thought might already be there. When he didn't spot any, he told Gold.

"I think we're alone, *amigo*."

Iandolli drew his weapon from an ankle holster as they entered a tower elevator. A young couple gasped at the sight of the gun. Gold flashed his badge to relieve them.

"Go call security," he told the couple. "Tell them to block this elevator bank off."

When the elevator doors closed, Iandolli winked at Gold. "Nice try. But I don't think the Feds will listen to six-dollar-an-hour security guards."

"Six?" Gold joked. "Remind me to apply on our way out."

When they reached Anthony Rizzi's floor, Iandolli tapped Gold on the shoulder. "I got lead," he said.

Gold pulled Iandolli back to step in front of him. "Bullshit," he said. "You have a family."

Chapter 62

CHARLIE MANAGED TO FIND a three-month-old male bichon frise at the pet store. After paying for a leash, a bowl, a bed, a carrying case, a bag of puppy food, grooming tools, a few teething toys, and vitamins, he asked the heavy-set black woman if she had a bow or a ribbon of some kind.

"This puppy a present?" the woman asked. She had a deep throaty voice. It surprised Charlie.

"Huh? Oh, yeah, he is," he said. "For my wife." Charlie didn't know why he said "wife," but he had.

The woman handed him a folder with the dog's papers. She asked him to fill in the information. The pedigree was listed on one of the papers in the folder.

"What you gonna call him?" the woman asked just before Charlie filled the dog's name in.

"Rigoletto," he said.

"That's a funny name. Where'd you get it?"

"An opera," Charlie said. "It's an opera."

"Who?"

"It's an Italian name. From an opera I like."

"I hope your wife likes the same opera."

"My wife hates opera."

"Maybe you want to give her a call and run it by her once."

Telling the woman that his wife hated opera was a reflex response from being married to Lisa. Charlie thought about correcting himself, but the dog was crying inside the carrying case on the floor.

"She'll get used to it," Charlie said.

"The dog or its name?"

From his seat at the bar, Cuccia quickly learned that an all-points-bulletin had been issued for him throughout the state of Nevada. He tugged down on the cap he was wearing and crouched low on his stool.

His swollen facial wounds somewhat disguised the picture on the television. The bar wasn't crowded yet, but the few people who were seated there glanced up at the television every so often. Cuccia hoped the television was nothing more than a distraction. Since they couldn't really hear the audio over the sounds of the casino behind them, Cuccia figured the real danger had passed once his face was off the screen.

When he looked up at the television again, he recognized Charlie Pellecchia turning his head away from a microphone. The camera followed Pellecchia a few steps before it turned toward a Las Vegas detective. Cuccia tried to hear what the reporter was saying, but the noise inside the casino was too loud. He asked the bartender to turn up the volume. When the bartender said he really wasn't supposed to, Cuccia pushed a twenty-dollar bill across the bar and pleaded.

"For two minutes," he said. "I think that's my cousin on the news there."

The bartender turned up the volume as he stuffed the twenty into his tip cup. Cuccia listened attentively as the news aired a previously recorded clip from earlier in the day describing a shooting that had occurred "in the quiet valley neighborhood the day before."

When the recorded clip finished, the newscaster said, "According to police, Mr. Pellecchia is not a suspect. He was dating Ms. Samantha Cole, a local bartender. Mr. Pellecchia brought Ms. Cole to the hospital. She's expected to recover fully and was released earlier in the day. The police had no further comment but said . . ."

Cuccia didn't bother to wait for the rest of the story. He headed straight for a side exit to Tropicana Boulevard. He made his way across the footbridge to the Excalibur, where he found a bank of pay telephones. He used the phone books to try to find the name he heard on the local news program.

Cole. Samantha Cole.

As they entered the hotel room, Gold and Iandolli both heard the sound of running water. When Iandolli pushed the door open for Gold to enter with his weapon drawn, both men saw the steam coming from the bathroom.

Gold was first inside the bathroom. "Jesus Christ!" he yelled as he pulled Joey Francone's dead body off the woman lying facedown in the hot water.

Iandolli helped Gold pull the maid from the tub. Her face was scalded from the steaming water, but they couldn't tell if she was alive or dead. Gold removed the gag to administer mouth-to-mouth. He pinched the woman's burned nose, opened her mouth, and pressed his own against hers. He blew air into her lungs in strong, steady breaths.

The Russian taxi driver they found dead in the hotel had been robbed of all his cash and his taxi. Agent Walsh called the Las Vegas organized crime unit to locate Iandolli. When Walsh finally reached him, the detective filled him in.

"He was just here," Iandolli said. "At Caesar's Palace. He came for Rizzi. Another one of his crew that flew up here the other day. He killed Francone. Maybe a housemaid, too."

"Who the hell is Rizzi?" Walsh asked. "And why didn't you come to the hotel when we called earlier?"

"Because I was busy. Are you coming here or not? Because I'm not staying. Cuccia is out there somewhere."

Until today, Agent Walsh had maintained a fairly good relationship with the local police. Detective Iandolli sometimes liked to do things a little off the beaten track, but Walsh always had managed to work with the local organized crime unit.

Now the Nicholas Cuccia dilemma was a sideshow. Walsh had had enough of Detective Iandolli for one day. He instructed the organized crime detective to stay where he was. "I'm ordering you to wait there for me," he said. "I'm ordering you to stay right there at the crime scene. Don't move. Don't dare move."

When the connection was broken, Agent Walsh punched the roof of the sedan he was standing alongside. It was bad enough that the detective had cut him off and was disobeying orders. It was another, more important, issue that Walsh had no idea where Iandolli was going.

Iandolli left Gold in the hotel room with the maid as he searched the pool area just outside the tower elevator bank. He tried the shopping arcade and some of the stores along the Appian Way. When he spotted the entrance to the big shopping mall, Iandolli knew it was where Nicholas Cuccia had escaped. Still, he had no idea how long ago or in which direction the New York mobster-killer had gone.

Iandolli returned to Anthony Rizzi's room to see how the maid was doing. When he got there, Iandolli saw Gold sobbing on the edge of the bed. The maid lay at Gold's feet. Her eyes were opened wide in an all-too-familiar death stare.

Chapter 63

"IF YOU LET ME, when he shows, I'll shoot the son of a bitch right in the face," Gold told Iandolli.

They were watching Charlie Pellecchia from the surveillance van parked across the street from Samantha Cole's residence. Pellecchia was walking up the block from the corner. A taxi had dropped him off. He walked a small white dog on a leash. He carried a small cage with his free hand. They could see a large plastic bag inside the cage.

"It's not your way," Iandolli said, "whacking somebody in cold blood. It's not my way, either."

Gold was holding his weapon on his lap. He wiped sweat from his forehead with the back of his free hand.

"I just hope he shows," he said. "I hope he didn't make it out of Vegas."

Iandolli was checking his rearview and sideview mirrors. "Don't worry," he said. "Cuccia isn't leaving Las Vegas without taking a last shot at this poor slob walking that dog. Not after what Pellecchia did to his life."

Gold watched as Pellecchia stopped to let the dog urinate on a small patch of grass. "He thinks he's back in New York," he said.

Iandolli said, "You want to write him up?"

Samantha decided to wait on the porch for Charlie. It was early evening. She sat on the top step and nodded at the officer sitting behind the wheel of the cruiser parked in front of her apartment. She noticed the white van parked across the street and wondered if Charlie had sent flowers ahead of his arrival.

When she heard a snippy bark to her left, Samantha craned her neck to look over the bushes. She spotted Charlie's head and used her crutches to stand up. When she saw the small white dog on the leash, Samantha waved.

"What's her name?" she asked from the top of the porch. Samantha held her hands out for the dog to come to her.

Charlie scooped up the bichon frise and brought it to her. He talked at the dog as he carried it. "Okay," he said. "Now you really have to perform or she'll kick us both out."

"Did you name her?" Samantha asked again. She held the dog up to her face to kiss. The puppy was in the middle of a licking frenzy. Samantha had to turn her head away.

"Rigoletto," Charlie said. "And she's a he."

Samantha checked the dog's sex. "Oh," she said. "That's a weird name, Rigo-what?"

"Rigoletto."

Samantha set her crutches to the side and sat again. "That's a real name?" she asked. "Rigo-something?"

"Rigoletto," Charlie repeated. "Rigoletto is an opera."

"Opera?" Samantha said, as she rolled her eyes. "You poor baby," she told the dog in a high-pitched voice. "Yes, yes, yes. You poor baby."

"Oh, boy," Charlie said.

The tiny bulb above the mirror in the bathroom provided just enough light to read the local street map. Cuccia had been sitting quietly in the women's bathroom of a Texaco station for the past forty minutes. His legs were numb. He stood up and down over and over to pump blood through his legs.

He knew he had to stay off the streets. His face was too bruised not to attract attention. Every cop and federal agent in the area was looking for him.

His jaw hurt. He could taste blood around the stitches inside his mouth. The tiny mirror above the small sink in the bathroom reflected Cuccia's badly bruised face. He parted his lips as much as he could to see the gap where two teeth were missing. He saw gauze and blood instead. He wiped at blood that trickled out of his mouth.

According to the street map, Samantha Cole lived less than half a mile from the gas station. Cuccia opened the bathroom door a crack to peek outside. It was dark and time to move.

They had moved the van after Charlie Pellecchia and the woman went inside the apartment. Iandolli drove the van around the corner, out of sight of the apartment. He took a pair of night vision binoculars from the equipment box in the console, and the two detectives headed around the back of the complex.

"What do you think?" he asked Gold.

"I think he'll come this way, but we're too far from the door."

"Me, too."

"We may be here all night," Gold said. "We don't communicate with anybody, we won't know if he's been found or not. Cuccia could be dead for all we know."

"I can have Gina monitor the radio at home," Iandolli said. "Just in case."

"Don't involve your wife," Gold said. "Trust me."

Iandolli smiled. "Where do you think we should post?"

"Close as possible. But you're the surveillance expert."

"I agree. He'll be looking for an address, but he'll come this way when he spots the cruiser."

"You really think Cuccia will find his way here?"

"It was our first thought, both of us," Iandolli said.

"Great minds," Gold said.

Chapter 64

SPECIAL AGENT WALSH FLASHED his badge to stop John Denton and Lisa Pellecchia. The couple was leaving the hospital for the airport. "Sorry, sir. Ma'am. You can't leave Las Vegas just yet."

Lisa looked up at Denton from her wheelchair. "Why not?" Denton asked.

"Because Nicholas Cuccia has escaped custody, for one thing. And I say so is the other reason."

"You say so?" Denton asked.

"This is serious, Mr. Denton. A federal drug enforcement agent is in a coma right now because of Nicholas Cuccia. We have reason to believe Cuccia may be looking for Mr. Pellecchia. Until we can locate the suspect, we don't think you or Mrs. Pellecchia should be left unprotected."

"Then take us to the airport," Lisa said.

"She has a point," Denton said. "If this is really about protection."

"We don't have the manpower," Walsh said. "Sorry."

"So we're detained until this guy is caught?" Denton asked. "Are you serious?"

"I'm afraid so."

"For what? Unless you're going to arrest us. Are we being arrested?"

Walsh wasn't in the mood for a lawyer. "I can do that. If you'd like. I can arrest you."

"For what?" Denton repeated.

"For what?" Lisa added.

"Assault," Walsh said. He turned to Denton. "Back at the Bellagio. I think you know what I'm talking about."

"This is bullshit," Denton said.

"We need to find Mr. Pellecchia," Walsh said. "Ma'am, do you know where he is? You might save his life. Nicholas Cuccia has killed at least three people today."

Lisa spoke without thinking. "His girlfriend," she said. She looked to Denton. "Right?"

Denton frowned. Walsh waited. "Mr. Denton?" he said. "You could save the man's life."

Denton looked down at Lisa. She looked up at him with a gentle smile. "I lived with the man for five years," she said. "I figured it out."

Denton nodded at Walsh. "All right," Denton said. "All right."

The puppy lay asleep on Samantha's lap as Charlie set a cover on the pot of sauce he was cooking. She smiled at him when he took a seat on the couch beside her.

"Smells pretty good," she said.

Charlie leaned across her lap to pet the dog. He kissed Samantha on the cheek. "So do you."

"About how long will that sauce take?" Samantha asked.

"Forty minutes."

"Can you make it take forty-five?"

They kissed.

"I missed that," he told her.

"Me, too," she said.

They kissed again. Samantha held Charlie tight. It was good holding him again. She missed him. She was glad he was there.

He moved closer as they embraced around the dog. He leaned into a kiss when he felt something hard under his leg. "What's this?"

He pulled a .25 from between the couch pillows.

"Oh, shit," Samantha said. "That's what he shot me with. Beau, Carol's husband. I just assumed he took it with him."

"Yeah, and so did the cops," Charlie said as he set the gun on an end table. "Which reminds me," he added as he removed the .22 he had bought from the hookers from his pants pocket and set it alongside Beau's gun.

"Where did you get that?" Samantha asked.

"You wouldn't believe me if I told you," Charlie said.

The puppy was climbing on Samantha's chest. It licked at both their faces as its tail wagged excitedly.

"Ooooh, the pretty baby!" Samantha said in a high-pitched voice. "Oooh, the pretty baby!"

She picked the dog up to hold against her face. Charlie shook his head as he backed away from them on the couch. He said, "I knew I should've bought flowers."

Chapter 65

WHEN MINH LEARNED WHERE Charlie Pellecchia was, he grinned. It was the same address Minh had copied on the street where all the police activity had been the day before.

"Police cruiser park in front," his man told Minh in broken English. "One cop in car."

Minh told his man to make sure he was waiting behind the apartment complex and that his gas tank was full. Then he screwed a silencer onto the end of his weapon's barrel and picked up an order of Chinese food from a local restaurant.

Minh planned to make a delivery to the address where the police cruiser was parked. Then, as soon as Minh was inside the apartment, he would shoot Charlie Pellecchia.

Gold was crouched behind the bushes alongside the narrow gap between buildings where Samantha Cole lived. On the other side of the gap, Iandolli used night vision binoculars to scan the area behind the complex.

"How long before you figure the Feds roll up?" Gold whispered.

"They may already be here. Up the block somewhere we can't see, or on a roof. Who knows? They're anxious to get Cuccia after what happened."

"They're probably still tripping over their own feet."

"Maybe," Iandolli said. He could tell Gold was nervous. Neither detective had ever been in this type of situation before, laying in wait for a killer.

Iandolli scanned the area to his left. He held the binoculars steady as he moved slowly from left to right across the tops of the hedges around the pool. When he reached the last hedge to his right, Iandolli noticed somebody walking alongside it. He whispered to Gold to remain quiet.

The Glock was stuffed inside Cuccia's pants against his lower back. The agent's weapon was jammed in the front of his pants. He pulled down the baggy Hard Rock Café sweatshirt he had bought from a souvenir shop to cover both guns.

It was too dark to spot a surveillance team, but the police cruiser parked up the block couldn't be more obvious. Cuccia had walked the half mile from the gas station without a problem.

Samantha Cole lived at number 6325. Cuccia stopped to read one of the addresses on a building to his right. "Sixty-three thirteen," he whispered to himself. He walked around the corner to the back of the apartment complex.

As Cuccia passed the building on his left now, he counted to himself. He did the same with the next building and the one after that. When he came to a stop again, Cuccia was standing directly behind 6325. He reached for the gun in his waistband when he heard the sound of a motorbike nearby.

Minh Quan parked two spots behind the police cruiser and crossed the front lawn diagonally to the front door. He carried the bag of Chinese food to cover the Baretta tucked in his pants. When he reached the short stairway, the policeman was out of the car and called to him.

"Food delivery," Minh said, affecting a more pronounced accent.

The policeman eyed him a few seconds until Minh held up the bag of food. Then the cop waved him on and sat back inside the cruiser.

Minh rang the doorbell two times as he grabbed the gun.

Chapter 66

GOLD HADN'T PRAYED FOR anything in a long time. The veteran detective didn't have much faith in religion. He believed that mankind made its own bed. He believed in the justice his police work was supposed to provide. He believed in the law.

But the law had failed miserably for a forty-six-year-old maid going about the business of earning a living, and Gold couldn't get over her death. Ever since he had tried and failed to revive the poor woman, Gold prayed for the chance to kill the man who had killed her.

Now that man was standing about ten feet away.

Iandolli saw the motorcycle make a sharp U-turn in the background. He watched it until he saw Nicholas Cuccia reaching for and holding the gun. Iandolli set the night vision glasses on the grass and stood up in a firing stance.

"Hold it!" he yelled. "Drop your weapon!"

"Fuck me," Cuccia said. He had half-turned toward the sound of the motorcycle. When he looked back, Iandolli sighted his weapon on Cuccia's chest.

"Drop it!" Iandolli repeated. "Drop your weapon!"

Iandolli waited for Cuccia to drop his gun before half-stepping across the back lawn toward the gangster. "Don't fucking breathe," Iandolli said.

Cuccia raised his hands slowly as the sound of screeching tires filled the night air. "Take it easy, big man," he said. "You could hurt some-body with that thing."

"Shut the fuck up," Iandolli said.

Cuccia saw another cop coming out from behind the bushes. He was short and bald. The cop held his weapon loosely in his right hand. He was close to a foot shorter than the big cop standing to his left.

Cuccia wondered if he could position himself between the two cops somehow and maybe make a move that would cause one of them to shoot the other. He grinned at the image.

"What's so funny?" the short cop asked.

Cuccia shook his head. He noticed that the big cop was almost in line with a potential crossfire. The sound of the screeching tires grew louder.

"You got me," he said.

"Yes, we do," the short cop said.

The big cop stopped short of a crossfire line. Cuccia frowned. He turned toward the motorcycle and saw it was stopped about a block away. The rider was holding a cell phone. The sound of the car making time caught Cuccia's attention. If both cops blinked, he might be able to get to the gun against his back.

"I surrender," he told the short cop. "Let's make a deal."

"Fuck," Charlie said when he saw the gun pointed at him.

He had answered the doorbell without looking through the peephole. He had assumed the police cruiser parked out front would deter trouble.

"Back inside or I shoot you right now, white boy," the Asian man holding the gun said.

Charlie's jaw tightened as he stepped back inside the apartment.

The Asian man closed the door behind him and set the bag of food on the floor.

"Hungry?" he asked.

• • •

Samantha could see both guns on the end table from where she sat on the couch, but they were too far to reach. When the Asian man hit Charlie across the face with his gun, Samantha jumped on the couch and moved a few inches closer to Beau's gun.

"Please don't!" she pleaded.

The Asian man pointed the gun at her. "Shut up, lady, or I kill you, too."

Samantha gasped. The gun was pointed at her chest. She was helpless on the couch. She looked to Charlie and felt her heart race. He had something in his hand.

Samantha gasped again, but the Asian man wasn't watching her anymore.

"See?" Cuccia told Gold. "Everybody's happy now."

Iandolli was about to frisk the killer when he heard a loud crash.

"The fuck was that?" Gold said.

Both detectives turned toward the apartment.

When the Asian hit him across the face with the gun, Charlie saw the gun was muffled with a silencer. He figured he had one shot at saving Samantha, and that was to break the front window to alert the cop sitting in the cruiser outside.

He could feel blood flowing over his left eye. He heard Samantha plead before the Asian threatened her.

Charlie grabbed a crystal ashtray on a shelf above the television and threw it as hard as he could at the front bay window. The Asian flinched as the glass shattered. Charlie saw the Asian come out of his crouch, aiming the gun. Charlie leaned to one side and could feel the television explode next to him. He started to turn into the Asian when he heard Samantha scream.

Gold and Iandolli ducked when they heard the shot fired inside the house. Cuccia reached behind him and grabbed the Glock. Iandolli had turned toward the apartment. Gold crouched low and turned his weapon on Cuccia.

"Freeze!" he yelled.

Cuccia dropped to one knee and tried to draw on the detective. He was fumbling for the trigger when he saw the flash from Gold's gun. Cuccia felt a jolt against his right shoulder as his arm flung back from the force of the bullet. He lost his grip on the Glock, and it bounced off the grass a few yards away. Cuccia looked up at Gold with a blank stare before seeing a second flash at the end of the gun barrel. There were two more flashes Cuccia never saw.

Minh saw the ashtray coming and ducked. It shattered the front window of the apartment. Pellecchia was off-balance from the throw. Minh shot at his torso but missed. The television screen exploded instead.

As he took a step closer, Minh flinched from the sound of his cell phone ringing. Then he was flying backward into a wall from a pain in his chest that had caught him off guard.

His face revealed shock as another piercing pain sent him bouncing off the wall a second time. Minh hit the floor and rolled onto his side. He pointed his gun straight up and unsteadily squeezed off two shots before a third bullet struck him in the chest. He dropped the gun as a fourth shot missed his head by inches.

"Open your eyes," Charlie said.

Samantha was rigid on the couch. Her arms were extended as she continued to aim Beau's gun at the Asian man on the floor.

"Sam?" Charlie said. "It's okay now."

She opened her eyes and immediately started to shake. Charlie stepped toward her as he guided the gun down before taking it from her.

"It's okay," he said. "It's over."

He took her hands and pulled her from the couch. Samantha was sobbing quietly as she collapsed into Charlie's arms.

Chapter 67

"I FEEL LIKE A wife-beater," Denton whispered.

Lisa leaned against his shoulder as the jet taxied slowly on the runway. She held a paper napkin up to cover her facial bruises as a stewardess passed in the aisle.

"I feel like a bandit," she said.

"You look like one."

The federal agents had let them go a few hours after news of Nicholas Cuccia's death was public. They planned to spend a week relaxing in California. Then Lisa would have to call Charlie and start the process of getting a divorce. Denton was anxious to start their lives together. When the jet left the ground, he turned to kiss Lisa on the forehead.

"Finally," he said.

"Don't jinx it."

Denton took her right hand and set it on his lap. "Jinx this," he said.

Lisa turned to him with a surprised smile on her face. "Why, counselor," she said.

"Shut up and give me a kiss."

"Shut up and give you a kiss?"

He winked at her. "I've been hanging around gangsters the past few days."

"Me, too," she said. She kissed Denton from one side of her mouth.

"That was weird," he said.

"Tell me about it," she said.

They held each other's hand as the jet climbed. They closed their eyes from exhaustion. They were both asleep when the jet finally leveled.

The first person Agent Marshall Thomas saw when he awoke from his coma was his wife. Her image was blurred. He heard her say that she loved him. He heard her crying.

He was out of the coma just under forty minutes. He tried but couldn't move his arms. He wanted to sit up. He wanted to see without the blurring.

Thomas wasn't sure what had happened to him. He couldn't remember.

He watched as a nurse adjusted one of the intravenous tubes hanging from a stand. He felt sleepy again as the blur of a white uniform passed in front of him. He looked for his wife again. He saw that she was holding his hand. He closed his eyes as the touch of her hand registered somewhere in his brain.

When Beau Curitan's body was found, it was by a pair of coyotes on the Arizona side of the Black Mountains. The coyotes had sniffed the flesh through the hastily made grave covered with dried sticks and branches. The blood from Beau's fresh bullet wounds filled the air with his smell for the predators.

Beau had been shot twice in the back of the head. The coyotes licked at the blood from the bullet wounds first, but Beau's skull impeded their feast. They pulled at his arms and legs until his body turned to one side. The coyotes found the softer flesh of Beau's stomach and ate through it until they tasted his intestines. Then the coyotes growled at one another over pecking order.

Chapter 68

TWO DAYS LATER, WHEN the police were finished with their investigation and they were finally alone, Charlie dressed Samantha's leg wound with fresh gauze. They were in the living room. The new window had already been installed, but they were still missing a television.

They were listening to the intermezzo of Mascagni's *Cavalleria Rusticana*. Samantha sat with the dog asleep in her lap. Charlie finished with the bandages and stood in the sliding glass doorway to the patio. He used the remote to adjust the volume on Samantha's stereo.

"The dog likes it," Samantha said.

"It's therapeutic," Charlie said. "It's used to show the passage of time during the opera."

"How do they wake the audience up?" Samantha asked.

"Gently," Charlie said. "The ushers come and shake them gently."

Samantha laughed.

Charlie moved to a chair in front of Samantha. He set her wounded leg across one of his knees.

"This is looking better," he said.

"It's going to be hot again tomorrow. One-twenty."

"We'll stay inside."

Samantha petted the dog. "Carol is in California. I hope she's okay."

"I'm sure she is. Iandolli, one of the detectives, claims Beau won't be a problem anymore."

"Huh?" Samantha said.

"It's nothing to bank on," Charlie said. "But I'm sure Carol is safe now anyway. The guy can't show his face anywhere after what he did."

Samantha peeled some of the gauze back to air her wound. "Do you really think it's over now?" she asked. "For you, I mean. For both of us?"

"According to Iandolli," Charlie said. "You decapitated that particular gang, my dear. They're officially headless. The one I nailed had outstanding warrants besides the new charges."

Samantha frowned. "I wish I could believe it's that easy."

Charlie kissed her. "Maybe this time it is."

They sat quietly for a while. When the music stopped, Charlie stood up to stretch. Samantha used the empty chair to rest her leg again.

"We're missing something," Charlie said.

"What's that?"

"A nice, light aria."

Samantha made a face.

"Trust me," he said, "it's better than Aerosmith."

Charlie was at the stereo searching for a CD from the collection he had brought to Las Vegas. He held one up. "'*Una furtiva làgrima*,'" he said. "Down her soft cheek, a furtive tear."

He set the disc in the CD player and pressed PLAY. He adjusted the volume as the first few strings of a harp were plucked. He sat on the couch alongside Samantha and kissed her cheek.

"What happens now?" she whispered in his ear.

Charlie pointed to the dog. "We need a bigger place," he said.

"He can sleep with me," Samantha said.

"What about me?"

"We'll see."

"You still holding a grudge?"

"I should."

"I was—"

"Shhh," she said. "I think I love you."

Charlie could feel the dog moving on her lap. "You talking to me or the dog?"

Samantha reached for him. Charlie picked the dog up from her lap and set it on the couch. "There," he said. "My turn."

Epilogue

DONNA BELLA WAS ANCHORED in the shade of the Marine Park Bridge. Anthony Cuccia argued into a cell phone with an associate about a truck seized in a Jersey City warehouse.

"Hey, that's my nephew's guy, break his balls," Cuccia said. "It's almost a week now I haven't heard from that one."

He downed half a glass of white wine as he dropped into a chair. He watched a woman racing on Jet Skis make a third pass by the boat. The woman removed her bikini top this time. She held it in one hand as she passed alongside *Donna Bella*.

"I don't care there was DEA there," Cuccia said into the cell phone. "That's got nothing to do with me, my friend. I'm on this boat all week. Now you tell me this, I'm not getting off."

The jet skier had turned around and was on her way back. She slowed alongside *Donna Bella*, and Cuccia stood up to get a better look at her breasts.

"Can I use bathroom?" she asked with a Russian accent.

Cuccia heard the accent and immediately hesitated. He noticed that a wallet belt was tied to a steering handle and that the woman was wearing sandals. He glanced at her bare breasts and shook his head.

"Can I use?" the woman asked. "Please."

"I'll call you back," Cuccia said into the cell phone. He turned it off and waved at the woman to come aboard.

The woman smiled as her top fell from her neck. She grabbed it off her leg and held it up for Cuccia.

"Nice," he said and dropped a rope ladder over the back of the boat.

The woman brought her Jet Ski up against the back of *Donna Bella* as Cuccia leaned over the transom. She revved the Jet Ski engine hard as it touched the back of the boat, and Cuccia lost his balance. He grabbed at the transom to keep from falling.

"What the hell . . ." he said just before a bullet tore through his neck.

He fell backward onto the floor of the boat and clutched his throat. As he rolled on the deck, he saw the woman level the gun against the top of the transom. He tried to roll away as the next bullet entered his stomach. He coughed up blood before the next bullet pierced his heart.

Acknowledgments

APPLES DON'T FALL FAR from their trees . . . and such is the case with Dave and Ross Gresham. Since Dave retired from teaching, I've been trying to give him a break (he's put up with my writing attempts for twenty-five-plus years now—it may well be what sent him and his wonderful wife, Linda, packing to live on a boat). Enter Ross . . . who was an innocent kid when I first met him (he wasn't a Dallas Cowboys fan yet) and has since graduated from Harvard and earned an M.A. at the University of Southern Mississippi, married Jess Randall, a Columbia graduate, has taken a teaching position at the Air Force Academy at Colorado Springs, and has proved every bit as valuable as his dad to this writer. Luckily, Ross and Jess have a son of their own now (young William), so the Gresham-Randall line of genius continues. I sincerely thank Ross for his careful and insightful eye with *Charlie Opera*.

Others I need to acknowledge here are my editor (and maestro), Peter Skutches; my heartbeat, Ann Marie (I fall more in love with you every day); my mother, Speranza (Hope) (for *always, always, always* being there); The Palm Too (the best steak joint in the world); my beloved New York State Buffalo Bills; the wonderful city of Las Vegas (heaven on earth); and, of course, our fierce (and never groomed like some puffy show dog) Bichon frise, Rigoletto.